Father Brown
and the
Ten Commandments

G. K. Chesterton

Father Brown
and the
Ten Commandments

Selected Mystery Stories

*Edited and with an introduction
by John Peterson*

IGNATIUS PRESS   SAN FRANCISCO

Cover art and design by
Enrique Javier Aguilar Pinto/Roxanne Mei Lum

© 2017 by Ignatius Press, San Francisco
ISBN 978-1-62164-035-6
Library of Congress Control Number 2015948576
Printed in the United States of America ∞

CONTENTS

INTRODUCTION

Some readers may be uncomfortable with the mixture of detective stories—which are read for recreation—and the scriptural prohibitions of the Hebrew Bible—which are supposed to be taken solemnly and with the purpose of guiding our lives. And furthermore, at least until Chesterton entered the scene, the detective story was limited to crimes of murder and theft and to these two felonies only. The stories were decidedly not concerned with such character flaws as impiety or covetousness.

However, when Chesterton introduced his priest-detective Father Brown to the world of detective fiction, he brought a new dimension to that world. This was the dimension of sin, as distinct from crime.

The key to Chesterton's radical approach is that the criminal is not necessarily the worst sinner in the story, nor is his crime its guiltiest offense. The priest is most interested in God's Commandments, not in the legal code of the State. Thus Chesterton opened up the wider possibilities of the Decalogue with crimes against the Sabbath, for example, or outrages of covetousness, dishonor to one's parents, or idolatry.

There are but two who regularly keep the Sabbath in "The Salad of Colonel Cray". Fortunately for the Colonel, Father Brown is one of them. That the other is the Colonel's fiancée is equally fortunate. She is worried about getting herself to the Sunday musical service:

[The major said,] "I know you want to hear the music."

"I want to go to church," she said, with rather severe eyes.

Idolatry? Remember "The Arrow of Heaven", the tale of Brandon Merton, the millionaire sitting in his heavily guarded fortress in evil solitude for a quarter of an hour each day to worship his "Coptic Cup". Then there is Kalon, the pagan high priest in "The Eye of Apollo", who does a lucrative business in the worship of strange gods.

Readers with progressive moral sensibilities will feel some discomfort (or more probably contempt) when confronted by Father Brown's frequent sermons on the Decalogue. However, everyone else should find interesting new twists and turns in his moral preachments.

In 1948, the poet and critic W. H. Auden published an influential essay on detective fiction in *Harper's Magazine*. In the essay, titled "The Guilty Vicarage", Auden claimed that the reason Father Brown does not hand his criminals over to the police is that he is a priest and feels obligated to work instead for the criminal's repentance. The priest sees a felon, in Auden's view, not primarily as a fugitive from the human legal system but, rather, as a sinner "who can save his soul if he will confess and repent". Auden's is a plausible answer, and many respected critics have embraced it. In the stories, however, the number of criminals whom Father Brown asked to confess and repent is quite small. (There are fifty-one Father Brown stories, and Father Brown counsels with the criminal in but ten of them at the very most.)

A plainer answer is that Father Brown did not see himself as a member of the law enforcement community. It was not his responsibility to bring criminals before the bar of justice. Such matters were quite simply none of his business. He makes this clear in "The Ghost of Gideon Wise":

> "It's a strange case," said Byrne.
> "It's no business of ours," said Father Brown.

We might look at those occasions when Father Brown does play an active role. He will intervene to stop a crime if he can, as in "The God of the Gongs" or "The Perishing of the Pendragons" or "The Insoluble Problem"—but that is quite a different thing from exposing a lawbreaker to the police after the fact.

If we attend to the stories, we find that Father Brown will expose the criminal if (and only if) he must act to prevent the innocent from being blamed. You will note that he keeps the killer's identity to himself in "The Mirror of the Magistrate" until it becomes obvious that the wrong person will be convicted.

Father Brown stated the principle precisely in "The Sign of the Broken Sword":

> There is so much good and evil in breaking secrets, that I put my conduct to a test.... I told myself that if anywhere, by name, ... any innocent man was wrongly blamed, then I would speak. If it were only that [General] St. Clare was wrongly praised, I would be silent. And I will.

Was Father Brown justified in keeping his secrets? Before we answer, we are reminded that Chesterton's priest did not think that criminals were the worst people walking about. "You must remember," he once told the Reverend John Cope, "in a murder case, the guiltiest person is not always the murderer." To miss that point is to miss the meaning of the Father Brown stories.

It is my sincere hope that this volume will appeal to members of two audiences: first, Chesterton fans who are not thoroughly familiar with the Father Brown stories and, second, readers of detective fiction who have, for one reason or another, thus far not given Father Brown a serious look. These stories are a treasure chest of fun and surprises, but also they reveal surprising depths of meaning, and all of Chesterton's followers and all detective-story enthusiasts owe it to themselves to take a new look at these easily overlooked masterpieces.

A final note of explanation is perhaps required to explain why there are eleven stories in a volume dedicated to the *Ten* Commandments. The simple answer is that there is disagreement among the experts as to how the Commandments should be numbered. Some count "You shall have no other gods before me" and "You shall not make for yourself a graven image" as two separate commandments, while others count these prohibitions as a single decree against idolatry. Similarly, some count "You shall not covet your neighbor's wife" and "You shall not covet ... anything that is your neighbor's" as a single rule against covetousness, while others find two separate rules, the one against lust and the other against jealousy.

Rather than take sides in this dispute of long standing, I have accepted both interpretations. That provides the excuse for eleven stories.

And now I conclude this introduction with the oft-told yarn about a young bishop who heard that one of his older pastors was wearying his congregation with fiery sermons on the Commandments. Accordingly, the bishop ordered this pastor henceforth to preach on love and on no other topic. Thus, with admirable humility and obedience, the story goes, the old pastor gave his very next homily the title, "The Ten Ways We Fall Short of the Virtue of Love."

"You shall have no other gods before me."

The Eye of Apollo

That singular smoky sparkle, at once a confusion and a transparency, which is the strange secret of the Thames, was changing more and more from its grey to its glittering extreme as the sun climbed to the zenith over Westminster, and two men crossed Westminster Bridge. One man was very tall and the other very short; they might even have been fantastically compared to the arrogant clock-tower of Parliament and the humbler humped shoulders of the Abbey, for the short man was in clerical dress. The official description of the tall man was M. Hercule Flambeau, private detective, and he was going to his new offices in a new pile of flats facing the Abbey entrance. The official description of the short man was the Reverend J. Brown, attached to St. Francis Xavier's Church, Camberwell, and he was coming from a Camberwell deathbed to see the new offices of his friend.

The building was American in its sky-scraping altitude, and American also in the oiled elaboration of its machinery of telephones and lifts. But it was barely finished and still understaffed; only three tenants had moved in; the office just above Flambeau was occupied, as also was the office just below him; the two floors above that and the three

"The Eye of Apollo" first appeared in the United States in the February 25, 1911, issue of *The Saturday Evening Post.*

floors below were entirely bare. But the first glance at the new tower of flats caught something much more arresting. Save for a few relics of scaffolding, the one glaring object was erected outside the office just above Flambeau's. It was an enormous gilt effigy of the human eye, surrounded with rays of gold, and taking up as much room as two or three of the office windows.

"What on earth is that?" asked Father Brown, and stood still.

"Oh, a new religion," said Flambeau, laughing; "one of those new religions that forgive your sins by saying you never had any. Rather like Christian Science, I should think. The fact is that a fellow calling himself Kalon (I don't know what his name is, except that it can't be that) has taken the flat just above me. I have two lady typewriters underneath me, and this enthusiastic old humbug on top. He calls himself the New Priest of Apollo, and he worships the sun."

"Let him look out," said Father Brown. "The sun was the cruellest of all the gods. But what does that monstrous eye mean?"

"As I understand it, it is a theory of theirs," answered Flambeau, "that a man can endure anything if his mind is quite steady. Their two great symbols are the sun and the open eye; for they say that if a man were really healthy he could stare at the sun."

"If a man were really healthy," said Father Brown, "he would not bother to stare at it."

"Well, that's all I can tell you about the new religion," went on Flambeau carelessly. "It claims, of course, that it can cure all physical diseases."

"Can it cure the one spiritual disease?" asked Father Brown, with a serious curiosity.

"And what is the one spiritual disease?" asked Flambeau, smiling.

"Oh, thinking one is quite well," said his friend.

Flambeau was more interested in the quiet little office below him than in the flamboyant temple above. He was a lucid Southerner, incapable of conceiving himself as anything but a Catholic or an atheist; and new religions of a bright and pallid sort were not much in his line. But humanity was always in his line, especially when it was good-looking; moreover, the ladies downstairs were characters in their way. The office was kept by two sisters, both slight and dark, one of them tall and striking. She had a dark, eager and aquiline profile, and was one of those women whom one always thinks of in profile, as of the clean-cut edge of some weapon. She seemed to cleave her way through life. She had eyes of startling brilliancy, but it was the brilliancy of steel rather than of diamonds; and her straight, slim figure was a shade too stiff for its grace. Her younger sister was like her shortened shadow, a little greyer, paler, and more insignificant. They both wore a business-like black, with little masculine cuffs and collars. There are thousands of such curt, strenuous ladies in the offices of London, but the interest of these lay rather in their real than their apparent position.

For Pauline Stacey, the elder, was actually the heiress of a crest and half a county, as well as great wealth; she had been brought up in castles and gardens, before a frigid fierceness (peculiar to the modern woman) had driven her to what she considered a harsher and a higher existence. She had not, indeed, surrendered her money; in that there would have been a romantic or monkish abandon quite alien to her masterful utilitarianism. She held her wealth, she would say, for use upon practical social objects. Part of it she had put into her business, the nucleus of a model typewriting emporium; part of it was distributed in various leagues and causes for the advancement of such work among women. How far Joan, her sister and partner, shared this slightly prosaic idealism no one could be very sure. But she followed her leader with a dog-like affection which was somehow more attractive, with its touch of tragedy, than the hard, high spirits of the elder. For Pauline Stacey had nothing to say to tragedy; she was understood to deny its existence.

Her rigid rapidity and cold impatience had amused Flambeau very much on the first occasion of his entering the flats. He had lingered outside the lift in the entrance hall waiting for the lift-boy, who generally conducts strangers to the various floors. But this bright-eyed falcon of a girl had openly refused to endure such official delay. She said sharply that she knew all about the lift, and was not dependent on boys—or men either. Though her flat was only three floors above, she managed in the few seconds of ascent to give Flambeau a great many of her fundamental views in an off-hand manner; they were to the general effect that she was a modern working woman and loved modern working machinery. Her bright black eyes blazed with abstract anger against those who rebuke mechanic science and ask for the return of romance. Everyone, she said, ought to be able to manage machines, just as she could manage the lift. She seemed almost to resent the fact of Flambeau opening the lift-door for her; and that gentleman went up to his own apartments smiling with somewhat mingled feelings at the memory of such spit-fire self-dependence.

She certainly had a temper, of a snappy, practical sort; the gestures of her thin, elegant hands were abrupt or even destructive. Once Flambeau entered her office on some typewriting business, and found she had just flung a pair of spectacles belonging to her sister into the middle of the floor and stamped on them. She was already in the rapids of an ethical tirade about the "sickly medical notions" and the morbid admission of weakness implied in such an apparatus. She dared her sister to bring such artificial, unhealthy rubbish into the place again. She asked if she was expected to wear wooden legs or false hair or glass eyes; and as she spoke her eyes sparkled like the terrible crystal.

Flambeau, quite bewildered with this fanaticism, could not refrain from asking Miss Pauline (with direct French logic) why a pair of spectacles was a more morbid sign of weakness than a lift, and why, if science might help us in the one effort, it might not help us in the other.

"That is *so* different," said Pauline Stacey, loftily. "Batteries and motors and all those things are marks of the force of man—yes, Mr. Flambeau, and the force of woman, too! We shall take our turn at these great engines that devour distance and defy time. That is high and splendid—that is really science. But these nasty props and plasters the doctors sell—why, they are just badges of poltroonery. Doctors stick on legs and arms as if we were born cripples and sick slaves. But I was free-born, Mr. Flambeau! People only think they need these things because they have been trained in fear instead of being trained in power and courage, just as the silly nurses tell children not to stare at the sun, and so they can't do it without blinking. But why among the stars should there be one star I may not see? The sun is not my master, and I will open my eyes and stare at him whenever I choose."

"Your eyes," said Flambeau, with a foreign bow, "will dazzle the sun." He took pleasure in complimenting this strange stiff beauty, partly because it threw her a little off her balance. But as he went upstairs to his floor he drew a deep breath and whistled, saying to himself: "So she has got into the hands of that conjurer upstairs with his golden eye." For, little as he knew or cared about the new religion of Kalon, he had heard of his special notion about sun-gazing.

He soon discovered that the spiritual bond between the floors above and below him was close and increasing. The man who called himself Kalon was a magnificent creature, worthy, in a physical sense, to be the pontiff of Apollo. He was nearly as tall even as Flambeau, and very much better looking, with a golden beard, strong blue eyes, and a mane flung back like a lion's. In structure he was the blonde beast of Nietzsche,[1] but all this animal beauty was heightened, brightened and softened by genuine intellect and spirituality. If he looked like one of the great Saxon kings, he looked like one of the kings that were also saints. And this despite the cockney incongruity of his surroundings; the fact that he had an office half-way up a building in Victoria Street; that the clerk (a commonplace youth in cuffs and collars) sat in the outer room, between him and the corridor; that his name was on a brass plate, and the gilt emblem of his creed hung above his street, like the advertisement of an oculist. All this vulgarity could not take away from the man called Kalon the vivid oppression and inspiration that came from his soul and body. When all was said, a man in the presence of this quack did feel in the presence of a great man. Even in the loose jacket-suit of linen that he wore as a workshop dress in his office he was a fascinating and formidable figure; and when robed in the white vestments and crowned with the golden circlet, in which he daily saluted the sun, he really looked so splendid that the laughter of the street people sometimes died suddenly on their lips. For three times in the day the new sun-worshipper went out on his little balcony, in the face of all Westminster, to say some litany to his shining lord:

[1] The blond beast referred to is the African lion.

once at daybreak, once at sunset, and once at the shock of noon. And it was while the shock of noon still shook faintly from the towers of Parliament and parish church that Father Brown, the friend of Flambeau, first looked up and saw the white priest of Apollo.

Flambeau had seen quite enough of these daily salutations of Phoebus, and plunged into the porch of the tall building without even looking for his clerical friend to follow. But Father Brown, whether from a professional interest in ritual or a strong individual interest in tomfoolery, stopped and stared up at the balcony of the sunworshipper, just as he might have stopped and stared up at a Punch and Judy.[2] Kalon the Prophet was already erect, with argent garments and uplifted hands, and the sound of his strangely penetrating voice could be heard all the way down the busy street uttering his solar litany. He was already in the middle of it; his eyes were fixed upon the flaming disc. It is doubtful if he saw anything or anyone on this earth; it is substantially certain that he did not see a stunted, round-faced priest who, in the crowd below, looked up at him with blinking eyes. That was perhaps the most startling difference between even these two far divided men. Father Brown could not look at anything without blinking; but the priest of Apollo could look on the blaze at noon without a quiver of the eyelid.

"O sun," cried the prophet, "O star that art too great to be allowed among the stars! O fountain that flowest quietly in that secret spot that is called space. White Father of all white unwearied things, white flames and white flowers and white peaks. Father, who art more innocent than all thy most innocent and quiet children; primal purity, into the peace of which——"

[2] Punch and Judy is a traditional English puppet show.

A rush and crash like the reversed rush of a rocket was cloven with a strident and incessant yelling. Five people rushed into the gate of the mansions as three people rushed out, and for an instant they all deafened each other. The sense of some utterly abrupt horror seemed for a moment to fill half the street with bad news—bad news that was all the worse because no one knew what it was. Two figures remained still after the crash of commotion: the fair priest of Apollo on the balcony above, and the ugly priest of Christ below him.

At last the tall figure and titanic energy of Flambeau appeared in the doorway of the mansions and dominated the little mob. Talking at the top of his voice like a foghorn, he told somebody or anybody to go for a surgeon; and as he turned back into the dark and thronged entrance his friend Father Brown dipped in insignificantly after him. Even as he ducked and dived through the crowd he could still hear the magnificent melody and monotony of the solar priest still calling on the happy god who is the friend of fountains and flowers.

Father Brown found Flambeau and some six other people standing round the enclosed space into which the lift commonly descended. But the lift had not descended. Something else had descended; something that ought to have come by a lift.

For the last four minutes Flambeau had looked down on it; had seen the brained and bleeding figure of that beautiful woman who denied the existence of tragedy. He had never had the slightest doubt that it was Pauline Stacey; and, though he had sent for a doctor, he had not the slightest doubt that she was dead.

He could not remember for certain whether he had liked her or disliked her; there was so much both to like and dislike. But she had been a person to him, and the unbearable pathos of details and habit stabbed him with all the small daggers of bereavement. He remembered her pretty face and priggish speeches with a sudden secret vividness which is all the bitterness of death. In an instant like a bolt from the blue, like a thunderbolt from nowhere, that beautiful and defiant body had been dashed down the open well of the lift to death at the bottom. Was it suicide? With so insolent an optimist it seemed impossible. Was it murder? But who was there in those hardly inhabited flats to murder anybody? In a rush of raucous words, which he meant to be strong and suddenly found weak, he asked where was that fellow Kalon. A voice, habitually heavy, quiet and full, assured him that Kalon for the last fifteen minutes had been away up on his balcony worshipping his god. When Flambeau heard the voice, and felt the hand of Father Brown, he turned his swarthy face and said abruptly:

"Then, if he has been up there all the time, who can have done it?"

"Perhaps," said the other, "we might go upstairs and find out. We have half an hour before the police will move."

Leaving the body of the slain heiress in charge of the surgeons, Flambeau dashed up the stairs to the typewriting office, found it utterly empty, and then dashed up to his own. Having entered that, he abruptly returned with a new and white face to his friend.

"Her sister," he said, with an unpleasant seriousness, "her sister seems to have gone out for a walk."

Father Brown nodded. "Or, she may have gone up to the office of that sun man," he said. "If I were you I should just verify that, and then let us all talk it over in your office. No," he added suddenly, as if remembering something, "shall I ever get over that stupidity of mine? Of course, in their office downstairs."

Flambeau stared; but he followed the little father downstairs to the empty flat of the Staceys, where that impenetrable pastor took a large red-leather chair in the very entrance, from which he could see the stairs and landings, and waited. He did not wait very long. In about four minutes three figures descended the stairs, alike only in their solemnity. The first was Joan Stacey, the sister of the dead woman—evidently she *had* been upstairs in the temporary temple of Apollo; the second was the priest of Apollo himself, his litany finished, sweeping down the empty stairs in utter magnificence—something in his white robes, beard and parted hair had the look of Doré's Christ leaving the Pretorium;[3] the third was Flambeau, black browed and somewhat bewildered.

Miss Joan Stacey, dark, with a drawn face and hair prematurely touched with grey, walked straight to her own desk and set out her papers with a practical flap. The mere action rallied everyone else to sanity. If Miss Joan Stacey was a criminal, she was a cool one. Father Brown regarded her for some time with an odd little smile, and then, without taking his eyes off her, addressed himself to somebody else.

"Prophet," he said, presumably addressing Kalon, "I wish you would tell me a lot about your religion."

"I shall be proud to do it," said Kalon, inclining his still crowned head, "but I am not sure that I understand."

"Why, it's like this," said Father Brown, in his frankly doubtful way: "We are taught that if a man has really bad first principles, that must be partly his fault. But, for all that, we can make some difference between a man who insults his quite clear conscience and a man with a conscience

---

[3] *Christ Leaving the Pretorium* is a painting by the French illustrator Gustave Doré (1832–1883).

more or less clouded with sophistries. Now, do you really think that murder is wrong at all?"

"Is this an accusation?" asked Kalon very quietly.

"No," answered Brown, equally gently, "it is the speech for the defence."

In the long and startled stillness of the room the prophet of Apollo slowly rose; and really it was like the rising of the sun. He filled that room with his light and life in such a manner that a man felt he could as easily have filled Salisbury Plain. His robed form seemed to hang the whole room with classic draperies; his epic gesture seemed to extend it into grander perspectives, till the little black figure of the modern cleric seemed to be a fault and an intrusion, a round, black blot upon some splendour of Hellas.

"We meet at last, Caiaphas," said the prophet. "Your church and mine are the only realities on this earth. I adore the sun, and you the darkening of the sun; you are the priest of the dying and I of the living God. Your present work of suspicion and slander is worthy of your coat and creed. All your church is but a black police; you are only spies and detectives seeking to tear from men confessions of guilt, whether by treachery or torture. You would convict men of crime, I would convict them of innocence. You would convince them of sin, I would convince them of virtue.

"Reader of the books of evil, one more word before I blow away your baseless nightmares for ever. Not even faintly could you understand how little I care whether you can convict me or no. The things you call disgrace and horrible hanging are to me no more than an ogre in a child's toy-book to a man once grown up. You said you were offering the speech for the defence. I care so little for the cloudland of this life that I will offer you the speech for the prosecution. There is but one thing that can be said against me in this matter, and I will say it myself. The woman that is dead was my love and my bride; not after such manner as your tin chapels call lawful, but by a law purer and sterner than you will ever understand. She and I walked another world from yours, and trod palaces of crystal while you were plodding through tunnels and corridors of brick. Well, I know that policemen, theological and otherwise, always fancy that where there has been love there must soon be hatred; so there you have the first point made for the prosecution. But the second point is stronger; I do not grudge it you. Not only is it true that Pauline loved me, but it is also true that this very morning, before she died, she wrote at that table a will leaving me and my new church half a million. Come, where are the handcuffs? Do you suppose I care what foolish things you do with me? Penal servitude will only be like waiting for her at a wayside station. The gallows will only be going to her in a headlong car."

He spoke with the brain-shaking authority of an orator, and Flambeau and Joan Stacey stared at him in amazed admiration. Father Brown's face seemed to express nothing but extreme distress; he looked at the ground with one wrinkle of pain across his forehead. The prophet of the sun leaned easily against the mantelpiece and resumed:

"In a few words I have put before you the whole case against me—the only possible case against me. In fewer words still I will blow it to pieces, so that not a trace of it remains. As to whether I have committed this crime, the truth is in one sentence: I could not have committed this crime. Pauline Stacey fell from this floor to the ground at five minutes past twelve. A hundred people will go into the witness-box and say that I was standing out upon the balcony of my own rooms above from just before the stroke of noon to a quarter-past—the usual period of my public prayers. My clerk (a respectable youth from Clapham, with no sort of connection with me) will swear that he sat in my outer office all the morning, and that no communication passed through. He will swear that I arrived a full ten minutes before the hour, fifteen minutes before any whisper of the accident, and that I did not leave the office or the balcony all that time. No one ever had so complete an alibi; I could subpoena half Westminster. I think you had better put the handcuffs away again. The case is at an end.

"But last of all, that no breath of this idiotic suspicion remain in the air, I will tell you all you want to know. I believe I do know how my unhappy friend came by her death. You can, if you choose, blame me for it, or my faith and philosophy at least; but you certainly cannot lock me up. It is well known to all students of the higher truths that certain adepts and illuminati have in history attained the power of levitation—that is, of being self-sustained upon the empty air. It is but a part of that general conquest of matter which is the main element in our occult wisdom. Poor Pauline was of an impulsive and ambitious temper. I think, to tell the truth, she thought herself somewhat deeper in the mysteries than she was; and she has often said to me, as we went down in the lift together, that if one's will were strong enough, one could float down as harmlessly as a feather. I solemnly believe that in some ecstasy of noble thoughts she attempted the miracle. Her will, or faith, must have failed her at the crucial instant, and the lower law of matter had its horrible revenge. There is the whole story, gentlemen, very sad and, as you think, very presumptuous and wicked, but certainly not criminal or in any way connected with me. In the short-hand of the police-courts, you had better call it suicide. I shall always call it heroic failure for the advance of science and the slow scaling of heaven."

It was the first time Flambeau had ever seen Father Brown vanquished. He still sat looking at the ground, with a painful and corrugated brow, as if in shame. It was impossible to avoid the feeling which the prophet's winged words had fanned, that here was a sullen, professional suspecter of men overwhelmed by a prouder and purer spirit of natural liberty and health. At last he said, blinking as if in bodily distress: "Well, if that is so, sir, you need do no more than take the testamentary paper you spoke of and go. I wonder where the poor lady left it."

"It will be over there on her desk by the door, I think," said Kalon, with that massive innocence of manner that seemed to acquit him wholly. "She told me specially she would write it this morning, and I actually saw her writing as I went up in the lift to my own room."

"Was her door open then?" asked the priest, with his eye on the corner of the matting.

"Yes," said Kalon calmly.

"Ah! it has been open ever since," said the other, and resumed his silent study of the mat.

"There is a paper over here," said the grim Miss Joan, in a somewhat singular voice. She had passed over to her sister's desk by the doorway, and was holding a sheet of blue foolscap in her hand. There was a sour smile on her face that seemed unfit for such a scene or occasion, and Flambeau looked at her with a darkening brow.

Kalon the prophet stood away from the paper with that loyal unconsciousness that had carried him through. But Flambeau took it out of the lady's hand, and read it with the utmost amazement. It did, indeed, begin in the formal manner of a will, but after the words "I give and bequeath all of which I die possessed" the writing abruptly stopped with a set of scratches, and there was no trace of the name of any legatee. Flambeau, in wonder, handed this truncated testament to his clerical friend, who glanced at it and silently gave it to the priest of the sun.

An instant afterwards that pontiff, in his splendid sweeping draperies, had crossed the room in two great strides, and was towering over Joan Stacey, his blue eyes standing from his head.

"What monkey tricks have you been playing here?" he cried. "That's not all Pauline wrote."

They were startled to hear him speak in quite a new voice, with a Yankee shrillness in it; all his grandeur and good English had fallen from him like a cloak.

"That is the only thing on her desk," said Joan, and confronted him steadily with the same smile of evil favour.

Of a sudden the man broke out into blasphemies and cataracts of incredulous words. There was something shocking about the dropping of his mask; it was like a man's real face falling off.

"See here!" he cried in broad American, when he was breathless with cursing, "I may be an adventurer, but I guess you're a murderess. Yes, gentlemen, here's your death explained, and without any levitation. The poor girl is writing a will in my favour; her cursed sister comes in, struggles for the pen, drags her to the well, and throws her down before she can finish it. Sakes! I reckon we want the handcuffs after all."

"As you have truly remarked," replied Joan, with ugly calm, "your clerk is a very respectable young man, who knows the nature of an oath; and he will swear in any court that I was up in your office arranging some typewriting work for five minutes before and five minutes after my sister fell. Mr. Flambeau will tell you that he found me there."

There was a silence.

"Why, then," cried Flambeau, "Pauline was alone when she fell, and it was suicide!"

"She was alone when she fell," said Father Brown, "but it was not suicide."

"Then how did she die?" asked Flambeau impatiently.

"She was murdered."

"But she was alone," objected the detective.

"She was murdered when she was all alone," answered the priest.

All the rest stared at him, but he remained sitting in the same old dejected attitude, with a wrinkle in his round forehead and an appearance of impersonal shame and sorrow; his voice was colourless and sad.

"What I want to know," cried Kalon, with an oath, "is when the police are coming for this bloody and wicked sister. She's killed her flesh and blood; she's robbed me of half a million that was just as sacredly mine as—"

"Come, come, prophet," interrupted Flambeau, with a kind of sneer; "remember that all this world is a cloudland."

The hierophant of the sun-god made an effort to climb back on his pedestal. "It is not the mere money," he cried, "though that would equip the cause throughout the world. It is also my beloved one's wishes. To Pauline all this was holy. In Pauline's eyes—"

Father Brown suddenly sprang erect, so that his chair fell over flat behind him. He was deathly pale, yet he seemed fired with a hope; his eyes shone.

"That's it!" he cried in a clear voice. "That's the way to begin. In Pauline's eyes—"

The tall prophet retreated before the tiny priest in an almost mad disorder. "What do you mean? How dare you?" he cried repeatedly.

"In Pauline's eyes," repeated the priest, his own shining more and more. "Go on—in God's name, go on. The foulest crime the fiends ever prompted feels lighter after confession; and I implore you to confess. Go on, go on—in Pauline's eyes—"

"Let me go, you devil!" thundered Kalon, struggling like a giant in bonds. "Who are you, you cursed spy, to weave your spiders' webs round me, and peep and peer? Let me go."

"Shall I stop him?" asked Flambeau, bounding towards the exit, for Kalon had already thrown the door wide open.

"No; let him pass," said Father Brown, with a strange deep sigh that seemed to come from the depths of the universe. "Let Cain pass by, for he belongs to God."

There was a long-drawn silence in the room when he had left it, which was to Flambeau's fierce wits one long agony of interrogation. Miss Joan Stacey very coolly tidied up the papers on her desk.

"Father," said Flambeau at last, "it is my duty, not my curiosity only—it is my duty to find out, if I can, who committed the crime."

"Which crime?" asked Father Brown.

"The one we are dealing with, of course," replied his impatient friend.

"We are dealing with two crimes," said Brown, "crimes of very different weight—and by very different criminals."

Miss Joan Stacey, having collected and put away her papers, proceeded to lock up her drawer. Father Brown went on, noticing her as little as she noticed him.

"The two crimes," he observed, "were committed against the same weakness of the same person, in a struggle for her money. The author of the larger crime found himself thwarted by the smaller crime; the author of the smaller crime got the money."

"Oh, don't go on like a lecturer," groaned Flambeau; "put it in a few words."

"I can put it in one word," answered his friend.

Miss Joan Stacey skewered her business-like black hat on to her head with a business-like black frown before a little mirror, and, as the conversation proceeded, took her handbag and umbrella in an unhurried style, and left the room.

"The truth is one word, and a short one," said Father Brown. "Pauline Stacey was blind."

"Blind!" repeated Flambeau, and rose slowly to his whole huge stature.

"She was subject to it by blood," Brown proceeded. "Her sister would have started eyeglasses if Pauline would have let her; but it was her special philosophy or fad that one must not encourage such diseases by yielding to them. She would not admit the cloud; or she tried to dispel it by will. So her eyes got worse and worse with straining; but the worst strain was to come. It came with this precious prophet, or whatever he calls himself, who taught her to stare at the hot sun with the naked eye. It was called accepting Apollo. Oh, if these new pagans would only be old pagans, they would be a little wiser! The old pagans knew that mere naked Nature-worship must have a cruel side. They knew that the eye of Apollo can blast and blind."

There was a pause, and the priest went on in a gentle and even broken voice. "Whether or no that devil deliberately made her blind, there is no doubt that he deliberately killed her through her blindness. The very simplicity of the crime is sickening. You know he and she went up and down in those lifts without official help; you know also how smoothly and silently the lifts slide. Kalon brought the lift to the girl's landing, and saw her, through the open door, writing in her slow, sightless way the will she had promised him. He called out to her cheerily that he had the lift ready for her, and she was to come out when she was ready. Then he pressed a button and shot soundlessly up to his own floor, walked through his own office, out on to his own balcony, and was safely praying before the crowded street when the poor girl, having finished her work, ran gaily out to where lover and lift were to receive her, and stepped——"

"Don't!" cried Flambeau.

"He ought to have got half a million by pressing that button," continued the little father, in the colourless voice in which he talked of such horrors. "But that went smash. It went smash because there happened to be another person who also wanted the money, and who also knew the secret about poor Pauline's sight. There was one thing about that will that I think nobody noticed: although it was unfinished and without signature, the other Miss Stacey and some servant of hers had already signed it as witnesses. Joan had signed first, saying Pauline could finish it later, with a typical feminine contempt for legal forms. Therefore, Joan wanted her sister to sign the will without real witnesses. Why? I thought of the blindness, and felt sure she had wanted Pauline to sign in solitude because she had wanted her not to sign at all.

"People like the Staceys always use fountain pens; but this was specially natural to Pauline. By habit and her strong will and memory she could still write almost as well as if she saw; but she could not tell when her pen needed dipping. Therefore, her fountain pens were carefully filled by her sister—all except this fountain pen. This was carefully *not* filled by her sister; the remains of the ink held out for a few lines and then failed altogether. And the prophet lost five hundred thousand pounds and committed one of the most brutal and brilliant murders in human history for nothing."

Flambeau went to the open door and heard the official police ascending the stairs. He turned and said: "You must have followed everything devilish close to have traced the crime to Kalon in ten minutes."

Father Brown gave a sort of start.

"Oh! to him," he said. "No; I had to follow rather close to find out about Miss Joan and the fountain pen. But I knew Kalon was the criminal before I came into the front door."

"You must be joking!" cried Flambeau.

"I'm quite serious," answered the priest. "I tell you I knew he had done it, even before I knew what he had done."

"But why?"

"These pagan stoics," said Brown reflectively, "always fail by their strength. There came a crash and a scream down the street, and the priest of Apollo did not start or look round. I did not know what it was. But I knew that he was expecting it."

"You shall not make for yourself a graven image."

The Arrow of Heaven

It is to be feared that about a hundred detective stories have begun with the discovery that an American millionaire has been murdered; an event which is, for some reason, treated as a sort of calamity. This story, I am happy to say, has to begin with a murdered millionaire; in one sense, indeed, it has to begin with three murdered millionaires, which some may regard as an *embarras de richesse*.[1] But it was chiefly this coincidence or continuity of criminal policy that took the whole affair out of the ordinary run of criminal cases and made it the extraordinary problem that it was.

It was very generally said that they had all fallen victims to some vendetta or curse attaching to the possession of a relic of great value both intrinsically and historically: a sort of chalice inlaid with precious stones and commonly called the Coptic Cup. Its origin was obscure, but its use was conjectured to be religious; and some attributed the fate that followed its possessors to the fanaticism of some Oriental Christian horrified at its passing through such materialistic hands. But the mysterious slayer, whether or no he was such a fanatic, was already a figure of lurid and sensational

---

"The Arrow of Heaven" first appeared in the July 1925 issue of *Nash's and Pall Mall Magazine.*

[1] Too much of a good thing (literally, "an embarrassment of riches").

interest in the world of journalism and gossip. The nameless
being was provided with a name, or a nickname. But it is
only with the story of the third victim that we are now
concerned; for it was only in this case that a certain Father
Brown, who is the subject of these sketches, had an opportunity of making his presence felt.

When Father Brown first stepped off an Atlantic liner
on to American soil, he discovered as many another
Englishman has done, that he was a much more important
person than he had ever supposed. His short figure, his
short-sighted and undistinguished countenance, his rather
rusty-black clerical clothes, could pass through any crowd
in his own country without being noticed as anything
unusual, except perhaps unusually insignificant. But
America has a genius for the encouragement of fame; and
his appearance in one or two curious criminal problems,
together with his long association with Flambeau, the ex-
criminal and detective, had consolidated a reputation in
America out of what was little more than a rumour
in England. His round face was blank with surprise when
he found himself held up on the quay by a group of journalists, as by a gang of brigands, who asked him questions
about all the subjects on which he was least likely to
regard himself as an authority, such as the details of female
dress and the criminal statistics of the country that he had
only that moment clapped his eyes on. Perhaps it was the
contrast with the black embattled solidarity of this group
that made more vivid another figure that stood apart from
it, equally black against the burning white daylight of
that brilliant place and season, but entirely solitary; a tall,
rather yellow-faced man in great goggles, who arrested
him with a gesture when the journalists had finished and
said: "Excuse me, but maybe you are looking for Captain Wain."

Some apology may be made for Father Brown; for he himself would have been sincerely apologetic. It must be remembered that he had never seen America before, and more especially that he had never seen that sort of tortoise-shell spectacles before; for the fashion at this time had not spread to England. His first sensation was that of gazing at some goggling sea-monster with a faint suggestion of a diver's helmet. Otherwise the man was exquisitely dressed; and to Brown, in his innocence, the spectacles seemed the queerest disfigurement for a dandy. It was as if a dandy had adorned himself with a wooden leg as an extra touch of elegance. The question also embarrassed him. An American aviator of the name of Wain, a friend of some friends of his own in France, was indeed one of a long list of people he had some hope of seeing during his American visit; but he had never expected to hear of him so soon.

"I beg your pardon," he said doubtfully, "are you Captain Wain? Do you—do you know him?"

"Well, I'm pretty confident I'm not Captain Wain," said the man in goggles, with a face of wood. "I was pretty clear about that when I saw him waiting for you over there in the car. But the other question's a bit more problematical. I reckon I know Wain and his uncle, and old man Merton, too. I know old man Merton, but old man Merton don't know me. And he thinks he has the advantage, and I think I have the advantage. See?"

Father Brown did not quite see. He blinked at the glittering seascape and the pinnacles of the city, and then at the man in goggles. It was not only the masking of the man's eyes that produced the impression of something impenetrable. Something in his yellow face was almost Asiatic, even Chinese; and his conversation seemed to consist of stratified layers of irony. He was a type to be found here and there in that hearty and sociable population; he was the inscrutable American.

"My name's Drage," he said, "Norman Drage, and I'm an American citizen, which explains everything. At least I imagine your friend Wain would like to explain the rest; so we'll postpone The Fourth of July till another date."

Father Brown was dragged in a somewhat dazed condition towards a car at some little distance, in which a young man with tufts of untidy yellow hair and a rather harassed and haggard expression, hailed him from afar, and presented himself as Peter Wain. Before he knew where he was he was stowed in the car and travelling with considerable speed through and beyond the city. He was unused to the impetuous practicality of such American action, and felt about as bewildered as if a chariot drawn by dragons had carried him away into fairyland. It was under these disconcerting conditions that he heard for the first time, in long monologues from Wain, and short sentences from Drage, the story of the Coptic Cup and the two crimes already connected with it.

It seemed that Wain had an uncle named Crake who had a partner named Merton, who was number three in the series of rich business men to whom the cup had belonged. The first of them, Titus P. Trant, the Copper King, had received threatening letters from somebody signing himself Daniel Doom. The name was presumably a pseudonym, but it had come to stand for a very public if not a very popular character; for somebody as well known as Robin Hood and Jack the Ripper combined. For it soon became clear that the writer of the threatening letter did not confine himself to threatening. Anyhow, the upshot was that old Trant was found one morning with his head in his own lily-pond, and there was not the shadow of a clue. The cup was, fortunately, safe in the bank; and it passed with the rest of Trant's property to his cousin, Brian Horder, who was also a man of great wealth and who was also threatened by the nameless enemy. Brian Horder was picked up dead at the foot of a cliff outside his seaside residence, at which there was a burglary, this time on a large scale. For though the cup apparently again escaped, enough bonds and securities were stolen to leave Horder's financial affairs in confusion.

"Brian Horder's widow," explained Wain, "had to sell most of his valuables, I believe, and Brander Merton must have purchased the cup at that time, for he had it when I first knew him. But you can guess for yourself that it's not a very comfortable thing to have."

"Has Mr. Merton ever had any of the threatening letters?" asked Father Brown, after a pause.

"I imagine he has," said Mr. Drage; and something in his voice made the priest look at him curiously, until he realised that the man in goggles was laughing silently, in a fashion that gave the newcomer something of a chill.

"I'm pretty sure he has," said Peter Wain, frowning. "I've not seen the letters, only his secretary sees any of his letters, for he is pretty reticent about business matters, as big business men have to be. But I've seen him real upset and annoyed with letters; and letters that he tore up, too, before even his secretary saw them. The secretary himself is getting nervous and says he is sure somebody is laying for the old man; and the long and the short of it is, that we'd be very grateful for a little advice in the matter. Everybody knows your great reputation, Father Brown, and the secretary asked me to see if you'd mind coming straight out to the Merton house at once."

"Oh, I see," said Father Brown, on whom the meaning of this apparent kidnapping began to dawn at last. "But, really, I don't see that I can do any more than you can.

You're on the spot, and must have a hundred times more data for a scientific conclusion than a chance visitor."

"Yes," said Mr. Drage dryly; "our conclusions are much too scientific to be true. I reckon if anything hit a man like Titus P. Trant, it just came out of the sky without waiting for any scientific explanation. What they call a bolt from the blue."

"You can't possibly mean," cried Wain, "that it was supernatural!"

But it was by no means easy at any time to discover what Mr. Drage could possibly mean; except that if he said somebody was a real smart man, he very probably meant he was a fool. Mr. Drage maintained an Oriental immobility until the car stopped, a little while after, at what was obviously their destination. It was rather a singular place. They had been driving through a thinly-wooded country that opened into a wide plain, and just in front of them was a building consisting of a single wall or very high fence, round, like a Roman camp, and having rather the appearance of an aerodrome. The barrier did not look like wood or stone, and closer inspection proved it to be of metal.

They all alighted from the car, and one small door in the wall was slid open with considerable caution, after manipulations resembling the opening of a safe. But, much to Father Brown's surprise, the man called Norman Drage showed no disposition to enter, but took leave of them with sinister gaiety.

"I won't come in," he said. "It 'ud be too much pleasurable excitement for old man Merton, I reckon. He loves the sight of me so much that he'd die of joy."

And he strode away, while Father Brown, with increasing wonder, was admitted through the steel door which instantly clicked behind him. Inside was a large and elaborate garden of gay and varied colours, but entirely without any trees or tall shrubs or flowers. In the centre of it rose a house of handsome and even striking architecture, but so high and narrow as rather to resemble a tower. The burning sunlight gleamed on glass roofing here and there at the top, but there seemed to be no windows at all in the lower part of it. Over everything was that spotless and sparkling cleanliness that seemed so native to the clear American air. When they came inside the portal, they stood amid resplendent marble and metals and enamels of brilliant colours, but there was no staircase. Nothing but a single shaft for a lift went up the centre between the solid walls, and the approach to it was guarded by heavy, powerful men like plain-clothes policemen.

"Pretty elaborate protection, I know," said Wain. "Maybe it makes you smile a little, Father Brown, to find Merton has to live in a fortress like this without even a tree in the garden for anyone to hide behind. But you don't know what sort of proposition we're up against in this country. And perhaps you don't know just what the name of Brander Merton means. He's a quiet-looking man enough, and anybody might pass him in the street; not that they get much chance nowadays, for he can only go out now and then in a closed car. But if anything happened to Brander Merton there'd be earthquakes from Alaska to the Cannibal Islands. I fancy there was never a king or emperor who had such power over the nations as he has. After all, I suppose if you'd been asked to visit the tsar, or the king of England, you'd have had the curiosity to go. You mayn't care much for tsars or millionaires; but it just means that power like that is always interesting. And I hope it's not against your principles to visit a modern sort of emperor like Merton."

"Not at all," said Father Brown, quietly. "It is my duty to visit prisoners and all miserable men in captivity."

There was a silence, and the young man frowned with a strange and almost shifty look on his lean face. Then he said, abruptly:

"Well, you've got to remember it isn't only common crooks or the Black Hand[2] that's against him. This Daniel Doom is pretty much like the devil. Look how he dropped Trant in his own gardens and Horder outside his house, and got away with it."

The top floor of the mansion, inside the enormously thick walls, consisted of two rooms; an outer room which they entered, and an inner room that was the great millionaire's sanctum. They entered the outer room just as two other visitors were coming out of the inner one. One was hailed by Peter Wain as his uncle—a small but very stalwart and active man with a shaven head that looked bald, and a brown face that looked almost too brown to have ever been white. This was old Crake, commonly called Hickory Crake in reminiscence of the more famous Old Hickory, because of his fame in the last Red Indian wars. His companion was a singular contrast—a very dapper gentleman with dark hair like a black varnish and a broad, black ribbon to his monocle: Barnard Blake, who was old Merton's lawyer and had been discussing with the partners the business of the firm. The four men met in the middle of the outer room and paused for a little polite conversation, in the act of respectively going and coming. And through all goings and comings another figure sat at the back of the room near the inner door, massive and motionless in the half-light from the inner window; a man with a Negro face and enormous shoulders. This was what the humorous self-criticism of America playfully calls the

---

[2] The Black Hand was an early-twentieth-century New York blackmailing and extortion organization.

Bad Man; whom his friends might call a bodyguard and his enemies a bravo.

This man never moved or stirred to greet anybody; but the sight of him in the outer room seemed to move Peter Wain to his first nervous query.

"Is anybody with the chief?" he asked.

"Don't get rattled, Peter," chuckled his uncle. "Wilton the secretary is with him, and I hope that's enough for anybody. I don't believe Wilton ever sleeps for watching Merton. He is better than twenty bodyguards. And he's quick and quiet as an Indian."

"Well, you ought to know," said his nephew, laughing. "I remember the Red Indian tricks you used to teach me when I was a boy and liked to read Red Indian stories. But in my Red Indian stories Red Indians seemed always to have the worst of it."

"They didn't in real life," said the old frontiersman grimly.

"Indeed?" inquired the bland Mr. Blake. "I should have thought they could do very little against our firearms."

"I've seen an Indian stand under a hundred guns with nothing but a little scalping-knife and kill a white man standing on the top of a fort," said Crake.

"Why, what did he do with it?" asked the other.

"Threw it," replied Crake, "threw it in a flash before a shot could be fired. I don't know where he learnt the trick."

"Well, I hope you didn't learn it," said his nephew, laughing.

"It seems to me," said Father Brown, thoughtfully, "that the story might have a moral."

While they were speaking Mr. Wilton, the secretary, had come out of the inner room and stood waiting; a pale, fair-haired man with a square chin and steady eyes with a look like a dog's; it was not difficult to believe that he had the single-eye of a watchdog.

He only said, "Mr. Merton can see you in about ten minutes," but it served for a signal to break up the gossiping group. Old Crake said he must be off, and his nephew went out with him and his legal companion, leaving Father Brown for the moment alone with his secretary; for the negroid giant at the other end of the room could hardly be felt as if he were human or alive; he sat so motionless with his broad back to them, staring towards the inner room.

"Arrangements rather elaborate here, I'm afraid," said the secretary. "You've probably heard all about this Daniel Doom, and why it isn't safe to leave the boss very much alone."

"But he is alone just now, isn't he?" said Father Brown.

The secretary looked at him with grave, grey eyes. "For fifteen minutes," he said. "For fifteen minutes out of the twenty-four hours. That is all the real solitude he has; and that he insists on, for a pretty remarkable reason."

"And what is the reason?" inquired the visitor. Wilton, the secretary, continued his steady gaze, but his mouth, that had been merely grave, became grim.

"The Coptic Cup," he said. "Perhaps you've forgotten the Coptic Cup; but he hasn't forgotten that or anything else. He doesn't trust any of us about the Coptic Cup. It's locked up somewhere and somehow in that room so that only he can find it; and he won't take it out till we're all out of the way. So we have to risk that quarter of an hour while he sits and worships it; I reckon it's the only worshipping he does. Not that there's any risk really; for I've turned all this place into a trap I don't believe the devil himself could get into—or at any rate, get out of. If this infernal Daniel Doom pays us a visit, he'll stay to dinner and a good bit later, by God! I sit here on hot bricks for the fifteen minutes, and the instant I heard a shot or a sound of struggle I'd press this button and an electrocuting current would run in a ring round that garden wall, so that it 'ud be death to cross or climb it. Of course, there couldn't be a shot, for this is the only way in; and the only window he sits at is away up on the top of a tower as smooth as a greasy pole. But, anyhow, we're all armed here, of course; and if Doom did get into that room he'd be dead before he got out."

Father Brown was blinking at the carpet in a brown study. Then he said suddenly, with something like a jerk: "I hope you won't mind my mentioning it, but a kind of a notion came into my head just this minute. It's about you."

"Indeed," remarked Wilton, "and what about me?"

"I think you are a man of one idea," said Father Brown, "and you will forgive me for saying that it seems to be even more the idea of catching Daniel Doom than of defending Brander Merton."

Wilton started a little and continued to stare at his companion; then very slowly his grim mouth took on a rather curious smile. "How did you—what makes you think that?" he asked.

"You said that if you heard a shot you could instantly electrocute the escaping enemy," remarked the priest. "I suppose it occurred to you that the shot might be fatal to your employer before the shock was fatal to his foe. I don't mean that you wouldn't protect Mr. Merton if you could, but it seems to come rather second in your thoughts. The arrangements are very elaborate, as you say, and you seem to have elaborated them. But they seem even more designed to catch a murderer than to save a man."

"Father Brown," said the secretary, who had recovered his quiet tone, "you're very smart, but there's something more to you than smartness. Somehow you're the sort of man to whom one wants to tell the truth; and besides, you'll probably hear it, anyhow, for in one way it's a joke against me already. They all say I'm a monomaniac about running down this big crook, and perhaps I am. But I'll tell you one thing that none of them know. My full name is John Wilton Horder." Father Brown nodded as if he were completely enlightened, but the other went on.

"This fellow who calls himself Doom killed my father and uncle and ruined my mother. When Merton wanted a secretary I took the job, because I thought that where the cup was the criminal might sooner or later be. But I didn't know who the criminal was and could only wait for him; and I meant to serve Merton faithfully."

"I understand," said Father Brown gently; "and, by the way, isn't it time that we attended on him?"

"Why, yes," answered Wilton, again starting a little out of his brooding, so that the priest concluded that his vindictive mania had again absorbed him for a moment. "Go in now by all means."

Father Brown walked straight into the inner room. No sound of greetings followed, but only a dead silence; and a moment after the priest reappeared in the doorway.

At the same moment the silent bodyguard sitting near the door moved suddenly; and it was as if a huge piece of furniture had come to life. It seemed as though something in the very attitude of the priest had been a signal; for his head was against the light from the inner window and his face was in shadow.

"I suppose you will press that button," he said with a sort of sigh.

Wilton seemed to awake from his savage brooding with a bound and leapt up with a catch in his voice.

"There was no shot," he cried.

"Well," said Father Brown, "it depends what you mean by a shot."

Wilton rushed forward, and they plunged into the inner room together. It was a comparatively small room and simply though elegantly furnished. Opposite to them one wide window stood open, over-looking the garden and the wooded plain. Close up against the window stood a chair and a small table, as if the captive desired as much air and light as was allowed him during his brief luxury of loneliness.

On the little table under the window stood the Coptic Cup; its owner had evidently been looking at it in the best light. It was well worth looking at, for that white and brilliant daylight turned its precious stones to many-coloured flames so that it might have been a model of the Holy Grail. It was well worth looking at; but Brander Merton was not looking at it. For his head had fallen back over his chair, his mane of white hair hanging towards the floor, and his spike of grizzled beard thrust up towards the ceiling, and out of his throat stood a long, brown painted arrow with red feathers at the other end.

"A silent shot," said Father Brown, in a low voice; "I was just wondering about those new inventions for silencing firearms. But this is a very old invention, and quite as silent."

Then, after a moment, he added: "I'm afraid he is dead. What are you going to do?"

The pale secretary roused himself with abrupt resolution. "I'm going to press that button, of course," he said, "and if that doesn't do for Daniel Doom, I'm going to hunt him through the world till I find him."

"Take care it doesn't do for any of our friends," observed Father Brown; "they can hardly be far off; we'd better call them."

"That lot know all about the wall," answered Wilton. "None of them will try to climb it, unless one of them ... is in a great hurry."

Father Brown went to the window by which the arrow had evidently entered and looked out. The garden, with its flat flower-beds, lay far below like a delicately coloured map of the world. The whole vista seemed so vast and empty, the tower seemed set so far up in the sky that as he stared out a strange phrase came back to his memory.

"A bolt from the blue," he said. "What was that somebody said about a bolt from the blue and death coming out of the sky? Look how far away everything looks; it seems extraordinary that an arrow could come so far, unless it were an arrow from heaven."

Wilton had returned, but did not reply, and the priest went on as in soliloquy. "One thinks of aviation. We must ask young Wain ... about aviation."

"There's a lot of it round here," said the secretary.

"Case of very old or very new weapons," observed Father Brown. "Some would be quite familiar to his old uncle, I suppose; we must ask him about arrows. This looks rather like a Red Indian arrow. I don't know where the Red Indian shot it from; but you remember the story the old man told. I said it had a moral."

"If it had a moral," said Wilton warmly, "it was only that a real Red Indian might shoot a thing farther than you'd fancy. It's nonsense your suggesting a parallel."

"I don't think you've got the moral quite right," said Father Brown.

Although the little priest appeared to melt into the millions of New York next day, without any apparent attempt to be anything but a number in a numbered street, he was, in fact, unobtrusively busy for the next fortnight with the commission that had been given him, for he was filled with profound fear about a possible miscarriage of justice. Without having any particular air of singling them out from his other new acquaintances, he found it easy to fall into talk with the two or three men recently involved in the mystery; and with old Hickory Crake especially he had a curious and interesting conversation. It took place on a seat in Central Park, where the veteran sat with his bony hands and hatchet face resting on the oddly-shaped head of a walking-stick of dark red wood, possibly modelled on a tomahawk.

"Well, it may be a long shot," he said, wagging his head, "but I wouldn't advise you to be too positive about how far an Indian arrow could go. I've known some bow-shots that seemed to go straighter than any bullets, and hit the mark to amazement, considering how long they had been travelling. Of course, you practically never hear now of a Red Indian with a bow and arrows, still less of a Red Indian hanging about here. But if by any chance there were one of the old Indian marksmen, with one of the old Indian bows, hiding in those trees hundreds of yards beyond the Merton outer wall—why, then I wouldn't put it past the noble savage to be able to send an arrow over the wall and into the top window of Merton's house; no, nor into Merton, either. I've seen things quite as wonderful as that done in the old days."

"No doubt," said the priest, "you have done things quite as wonderful, as well as seen them."

Old Crake chuckled, and then said gruffly: "Oh, that's all ancient history."

"Some people have a way of studying ancient history," the priest said. "I suppose we may take it there is nothing in your old record to make people talk unpleasantly about this affair."

"What do you mean?" demanded Crake, his eyes shifting sharply for the first time, in his red, wooden face, that was rather like the head of a tomahawk.

"Well, since you were so well acquainted with all the arts and crafts of the Redskin—" began Father Brown slowly.

Crake had had a hunched and almost shrunken appearance as he sat with his chin propped on its queer-shaped crutch. But the next instant he stood erect in the path like a fighting bravo with the crutch clutched like a cudgel.

"What?" he cried—in something like a raucous screech—"What the hell! Are you standing up to me to tell me I might happen to have murdered my own brother-in-law?"

From a dozen seats dotted about the path people looked towards the disputants, as they stood facing each other in the middle of the path, the bald-headed energetic little man brandishing his outlandish stick like a club, and the black, dumpy figure of the little cleric looking at him without moving a muscle, save for his blinking eyelids. For a moment it looked as if the black, dumpy figure would be knocked on the head, and laid out with true Red Indian promptitude and dispatch; and the large form of an Irish policeman could be seen heaving up in the distance and bearing down on the group. But the priest only said, quite placidly, like one answering an ordinary query:

"I have formed certain conclusions about it, but I do not think I will mention them till I make my report."

Whether under the influence of the footsteps of the policeman or of the eyes of the priest, old Hickory tucked his stick under his arm and put his hat on again, grunting. The priest bade him a placid good morning, and passed in an unhurried fashion out of the park, making his way to the lounge of the hotel where he knew that young Wain was to be found. The young man sprang up with a greeting; he looked even more haggard and harassed than before, as if some worry were eating him away; and the priest had a suspicion that his young friend had recently been engaged, with only too conspicuous success, in evading the last Amendment to the American Constitution.[3] But at the first word about his hobby or favourite science he was vigilant and concentrated enough. For Father Brown had asked, in an idle and conversational fashion, whether much flying was done in that district, and had told how he had at first mistaken Mr. Merton's circular wall for an aerodrome.

"It's a wonder you didn't see any while we were there," answered Captain Wain. "Sometimes they're as thick as flies; that open plain is a great place for them, and I shouldn't wonder if it were the chief breeding-ground, so to speak, for my sort of birds in the future. I've flown a good deal there myself, of course, and I know most of the fellows about here who flew in the war; but there are a whole lot of people taking to it out there now whom I never heard of in my life. I suppose it will be like motoring soon, and every man in the States will have one."

"Being endowed by his Creator," said Father Brown with a smile, "with the right to life, liberty, and the pursuit of motoring—not to mention aviation. So I suppose we may take it that one strange aeroplane passing over that house, at certain times, wouldn't be noticed much."

"No," replied the young man; "I don't suppose it would."

"Or even if the man were known," went on the other, "I suppose he might get hold of a machine that wouldn't be recognised as his. If you, for instance, flew in the ordinary way, Mr. Merton and his friends might recognise the rig-out, perhaps; but you might pass pretty near that

[3] The amendment, adopted in 1919, prohibited the sale of intoxicating liquors.

window on a different pattern of plane, or whatever you call it; near enough for practical purposes."

"Well, yes," began the young man, almost automatically, and then ceased, and remained staring at the cleric with an open mouth and eyes standing out of his head.

"My God!" he said, in a low voice, "my God!"

Then he rose from the lounge seat, pale and shaking from head to foot and still staring at the priest.

"Are you mad?" he said; "are you raving mad?"

There was a silence and then he spoke again in a swift hissing fashion. "You positively come here to suggest—"

"No; only to collect suggestions," said Father Brown, rising. "I may have formed some conclusions provisionally, but I had better reserve them for the present."

And then saluting the other with the same stiff civility, he passed out of the hotel to continue his curious peregrinations.

By the dusk of that day they had led him down the dingy streets and steps that straggled and tumbled towards the river in the oldest and most irregular part of the city. Immediately under the coloured lantern that marked the entrance to a rather low Chinese restaurant he encountered a figure he had seen before, though by no means presenting itself to the eye as he had seen it.

Mr. Norman Drage still confronted the world grimly behind his great goggles, which seemed somehow to cover his face like a dark musk of glass. But except for the goggles, his appearance had undergone a strange transformation in the month that had elapsed since the murder. He had then, as Father Brown had noted, been dressed up to the nines—up to that point, indeed, where there begins to be too fine a distinction between the dandy and the dummy outside a tailor's shop. But now all those externals were mysteriously altered for the worse;

as if the tailor's dummy had been turned into a scarecrow. His top hat still existed, but it was battered and shabby; his clothes were dilapidated; his watch-chain and minor ornaments were gone. Father Brown, however, addressed him as if they had met yesterday, and made no demur to sitting down with him on a bench in the cheap eating-house whither he was bound. It was not he, however, who began the conversation.

"Well?" growled Drage, "and have you succeeded in avenging your holy and sainted millionaire? We know all millionaires are holy and sainted; you can find it all in the papers next day, about how they lived by the light of the Family Bible they read at their mother's knee. Gee! if they'd only read out some of the things there are in the Family Bible, the mother might have been startled some. And the millionaire, too, I reckon. The old Book's full of a lot of grand fierce old notions they don't grow nowadays; sort of wisdom of the Stone Age and buried under the Pyramids. Suppose somebody had flung old man Merton from the top of that tower of his, and let him be eaten by dogs at the bottom, it would be no worse than what happened to Jezebel. Wasn't Agag hacked into little pieces, for all he went walking delicately? Merton walked delicately all his life, damn him—until he got too delicate to walk at all. But the shaft of the Lord found him out, as it might have done in the old Book, and struck him dead on the top of his tower to be a spectacle to the people."

"The shaft was material, at least," said his companion.

"The Pyramids are mighty material, and they hold down the dead kings all right," grinned the man in the goggles. "I think there's a lot to be said for these old material religions. There's old carvings that have lasted for thousands of years, showing their gods and emperors with bended bows; with hands that look as if they could really bend bows of stone. Material, perhaps—but what materials! Don't you sometimes stand staring at those old Eastern patterns and things, till you have a hunch that old Lord God is still driving like a dark Apollo, and shooting black rays of death?"

"If he is," replied Father Brown, "I might call him by another name. But I doubt whether Merton died by a dark ray or even a stone arrow."

"I guess you think he's St. Sebastian," sneered Drage, "killed with an arrow. A millionaire must be a martyr. How do you know he didn't deserve it? You don't know much about your millionaire, I fancy. Well, let me tell you he deserved it a hundred times over."

"Well," asked Father Brown gently, "why didn't you murder him?"

"You want to know why I didn't?" said the other, staring. "Well, you're a nice sort of clergyman."

"Not at all," said the other, as if waving away a compliment.

"I suppose it's your way of saying I did," snarled Drage. "Well, prove it, that's all. As for him, I reckon he was no loss."

"Yes, he was," said Father Brown, sharply. "He was a loss to you. That's why you didn't kill him."

And he walked out of the room, leaving the man in goggles gaping after him.

It was nearly a month later that Father Brown revisited the house where the third millionaire had suffered from the vendetta of Daniel Doom. A sort of council was held of the persons most interested. Old Crake sat at the head of the table with his nephew at his right hand, the lawyer on his left; the big man with the African features, whose name appeared to be Harris, was ponderously present, if only as a material witness; a red-haired, sharp-nosed

individual addressed as Dixon seemed to be the representative of Pinkerton's or some such private agency; and
Father Brown slipped unobtrusively into an empty seat
beside him.

Every newspaper in the world was full of the catastrophe of the colossus of finance, of the great organiser of the
Big Business that bestrides the modern world; but from
the tiny group that had been nearest to him at the very
instant of his death very little could be learned. The uncle,
nephew, and attendant solicitor declared they were well
outside the outer wall before the alarm was raised; and
inquiries of the official guardians at both barriers brought
answers that were rather confused, but on the whole con-
firmatory. Only one other complication seemed to call for
consideration. It seemed that round about the time of the
death, before or after, a stranger had been found hanging
mysteriously round the entrance and asking to see Mr.
Merton. The servants had some difficulty in understanding what he meant, for his language was very obscure;
but it was afterwards considered to be also very suspicious,
since he had said something about a wicked man being
destroyed by a word out of the sky.

Peter Wain leaned forward, the eyes bright in his
haggard face, and said:

"I'll bet on that, anyhow. Norman Drage."

"And who in the world is Norman Drage?" asked his
uncle.

"That's what I want to know," replied the young
man. "I practically asked him, but he has got a wonderful
trick of twisting every straight question crooked; it's
like lunging at a fencer. He hooked on to me with hints
about the flying-ship of the future; but I never trusted
him much."

"But what sort of a man is he?" asked Crake.

"He's a mystagogue," said Father Brown, with innocent promptitude. "There are quite a lot of them about; the sort of men about town who hint to you in Paris cafés and cabarets that they've lifted the veil of Isis or know the secret of Stonehenge. In a case like this they're sure to have some sort of mystical explanations."

The smooth, dark head of Mr. Barnard Blake, the lawyer, was inclined politely towards the speaker, but his smile was faintly hostile.

"I should hardly have thought, sir," he said, "that you had any quarrel with mystical explanations."

"On the contrary," replied Father Brown, blinking amiably at him. "That's just why I can quarrel with 'em. Any sham lawyer could bamboozle me, but he couldn't bamboozle you; because you're a lawyer yourself. Any fool could dress up as a Red Indian and I'd swallow him whole as the only original Hiawatha; but Mr. Crake would see through him at once. A swindler could pretend to me that he knew all about aeroplanes, but not to Captain Wain. And it's just the same with the other, don't you see? It's just because I have picked up a little about mystics that I have no use for mystagogues. Real mystics don't hide mysteries, they reveal them. They set a thing up in broad daylight, and when you've seen it it's still a mystery. But the mystagogues hide a thing in darkness and secrecy, and when you find it, it's a platitude. But in the case of Drage, I admit he had also another and more practical notion in talking about fire from heaven or bolts from the blue."

"And what was his notion?" asked Wain. "I think it wants watching, whatever it is."

"Well," replied the priest, slowly, "he wanted us to think the murders were miracles because ... well, because he knew they weren't."

"Ah," said Wain, with a sort of hiss, "I was waiting for that. In plain words, he is the criminal."

"In plain words, he is the criminal who didn't commit the crime," answered Father Brown calmly.

"Is that your conception of plain words?" inquired Blake politely.

"You'll be saying I'm the mystagogue now," said Father Brown somewhat abashed, but with a broad smile, "but it was really quite accidental. Drage didn't commit the crime—I mean this crime. His only crime was black-mailing somebody, and he hung about here to do it; but he wasn't likely to want the secret to be public property or the whole business to be cut short by death. We can talk about him afterwards. Just at the moment, I only want him cleared out of the way."

"Out of the way of what?" asked the other.

"Out of the way of the truth," replied the priest, looking at him tranquilly, with level eyelids.

"Do you mean," faltered the other, "that you know the truth?"

"I rather think so," said Father Brown modestly.

There was an abrupt silence, after which Crake cried out suddenly and irrelevantly in a rasping voice:

"Why, where is that secretary fellow? Wilton! He ought to be here."

"I am in communication with Mr. Wilton," said Father Brown gravely; "in fact, I asked him to ring me up here in a few minutes from now. I may say that we've worked the thing out together, in a manner of speaking."

"If you're working together, I suppose it's all right," grumbled Crake. "I know he was always a sort of blood-hound on the trail of his vanishing crook, so perhaps it was well to hunt in couples with him. But if you know the truth about this, where the devil did you get it from?"

"I got it from you," answered the priest, quietly, and continued to gaze mildly at the glaring veteran. "I mean I made the first guess from a hint in a story of yours about an Indian who threw a knife and hit a man on the top of a fortress."

"You've said that several times," said Wain, with a puzzled air; "but I can't see any inference, except that this murderer threw an arrow and hit a man on the top of a house very like a fortress. But of course the arrow wasn't thrown but shot, and would go much further. Certainly it went uncommonly far; but I don't see how it brings us any farther."

"I'm afraid you missed the point of the story," said Father Brown. "It isn't that if one thing can go far another can go farther. It is that the wrong use of a tool can cut both ways. The men on Crake's fort thought of a knife as a thing for a hand-to-hand fight and forgot that it could be a missile like a javelin. Some other people I know thought of a thing as a missile like a javelin and forgot that, after all, it could be used hand-to-hand as a spear. In short, the moral of the story is that since a dagger can be turned into an arrow, so can an arrow be turned into a dagger."

They were all looking at him now; but he continued in the same casual and unconscious tone: "Naturally we wondered and worried a good deal about who shot that arrow through the window and whether it came from far away, and so on. But the truth is that nobody shot the arrow at all. It never came in at the window at all."

"Then how did it come there?" asked the swarthy lawyer, with a rather lowering face.

"Somebody brought it with him, I suppose," said Father Brown; "it wouldn't be hard to carry or conceal. Somebody had it in his hand as he stood with Merton in Merton's own room. Somebody thrust it into Merton's throat like a poignard, and then had the highly intelligent idea of placing the whole thing at such a place and angle that we all assumed in a flash that it had flown in at the window like a bird."

"Somebody," said old Crake, in a voice as heavy as stone.

The telephone bell rang with a strident and horrible clamour of insistence. It was in the adjoining room, and Father Brown had darted there before anybody else could move.

"What the devil is it all about?" cried Peter Wain, who seemed all shaken and distracted.

"He said he expected to be rung up by Wilton, the secretary," replied his uncle in the same dead voice.

"I suppose it is Wilton?" observed the lawyer, like one speaking to fill up a silence. But nobody answered the question until Father Brown reappeared suddenly and silently in the room, bringing the answer.

"Gentlemen," he said, when he had resumed his seat, "it was you who asked me to look into the truth about this puzzle; and having found the truth, I must tell it, without any pretence of softening the shock. I'm afraid anybody who pokes his nose into things like this can't afford to be a respecter of persons."

"I suppose," said Crake, breaking the silence that followed, "that means that some of us are accused, or suspected."

"All of us are suspected," answered Father Brown. "I may be suspected myself, for I found the body."

"Of course we're suspected," snapped Wain. "Father Brown kindly explained to me how I could have besieged the tower in a flying-machine."

"No," replied the priest, with a smile; "you described to me how you could have done it. That was just the interesting part of it."

"He seemed to think it likely," growled Crake, "that I killed him myself with a Red Indian arrow."

"I thought it most unlikely," said Father Brown, making rather a wry face. "I'm sorry if I did wrong, but I couldn't think of any other way of testing the matter. I can hardly think of anything more improbable than the notion that Captain Wain went careering in a huge machine past the window, at the very moment of the murder, and nobody noticed it; unless, perhaps, it were the notion that a respectable old gentleman should play at Red Indians with a bow and arrow behind the bushes, to kill somebody he could have killed in twenty much simpler ways. But I had to find out if they had had anything to do with it; and so I had to accuse them in order to prove their innocence."

"And how have you proved their innocence?" asked Blake the lawyer, leaning forward eagerly.

"Only by the agitation they showed when they were accused," answered the other.

"What do you mean, exactly?"

"If you will permit me to say so," remarked Father Brown, composedly enough, "I did undoubtedly think it my duty to suspect them and everybody else. I did suspect Mr. Crake and I did suspect Captain Wain, in the sense that I considered the possibility or probability of their guilt. I told them I had formed conclusions about it; and I will now tell them what those conclusions were. I was sure they were innocent, because of the manner and the moment in which they passed from unconsciousness to indignation. So long as they never thought they were accused, they went on giving me materials to support the accusation. They practically explained to me how they might have committed the crime. Then they suddenly realised with a shock and a shout of rage that they were accused; they realised it long after they might well have expected to be

accused, but long before I had accused them. Now no
guilty person could possibly do that. He might be snappy
and suspicious from the first; or he might simulate unconsciousness and innocence up to the end. But he wouldn't
begin by making things worse for himself and then give
a great jump and begin furiously denying the notion he
had himself helped to suggest. That could only come by
his having really failed to realise what he was suggesting.
The self-consciousness of a murderer would always be at
least morbidly vivid enough to prevent him first forget-
ting his relation with the thing and then remembering
to deny it. So I ruled you both out and others for other
reasons I needn't discuss now. For instance, there was
the secretary—

"But I'm not talking about that just now. Look here,
I've just heard from Wilton on the phone, and he's given
me permission to tell you some rather serious news. Now
I suppose you all know by this time who Wilton was, and
what he was after."

"I know he was after Daniel Doom and wouldn't be
happy till he got him," answered Peter Wain; "and I've
heard the story that he's the son of old Horder, and that's
why he's the avenger of blood. Anyhow, he's certainly
looking for the man called Doom."

"Well," said Father Brown, "he has found him."

Peter Wain sprang to his feet in excitement.

"The murderer!" he cried. "Is the murderer in the
lock-up already?"

"No," said Father Brown, gravely; "I said the news was
serious, and it's more serious than that. I'm afraid poor
Wilton has taken a terrible responsibility. I'm afraid he's
going to put a terrible responsibility on us. He hunted
the criminal down, and just when he had him cornered at
last—well, he has taken the law into his own hands."

"You mean that Daniel Doom—" began the lawyer.

"I mean that Daniel Doom is dead," said the priest. "There was some sort of wild struggle, and Wilton killed him."

"Serve him right," growled Mr. Hickory Crake.

"Can't blame Wilton for downing a crook like that, especially considering the feud," assented Wain; "it was like stepping on a viper."

"I don't agree with you," said Father Brown. "I suppose we all talk romantic stuff at random in defence of lynching and lawlessness; but I have a suspicion that if we lose our laws and liberties we shall regret it. Besides, it seems to me illogical to say there is something to be said for Wilton committing murder, without even inquiring whether there was anything to be said for Doom committing it. I rather doubt whether Doom was merely a vulgar assassin; he may have been a sort of outlaw with a mania about the cup, demanding it with threats and only killing after a struggle; both victims were thrown down just outside their houses. The objection to Wilton's way of doing it is that we shall never hear Doom's side of the case."

"Oh, I've no patience with all this sentimental white-washing of worthless, murderous blackguards," cried Wain, heatedly. "If Wilton croaked the criminal he did a jolly good day's work, and there's an end of it."

"Quite so, quite so," said his uncle, nodding vigorously.

Father Brown's face had a yet heavier gravity as he looked slowly round the semicircle of faces. "Is that really what you all think?" he asked. Even as he did so he realised that he was an Englishman and an exile. He realised that he was among foreigners, even if he was among friends. Around that ring of foreigners ran a restless fire that was not native to his own breed; the fiercer spirit of the western nation that can rebel and lynch, and above all, combine. He knew that they had already combined.

"Well," said Father Brown, with a sigh, "I am to understand, then, that you do definitely condone this unfortunate man's crime, or act of private justice, or whatever you call it. In that case it will not hurt him if I tell you a little more about it."

He rose suddenly to his feet; and though they saw no meaning in his movement, it seemed in some way to change or chill the very air in the room.

"Wilton killed Doom in a rather curious way," he began.

"How did Wilton kill him?" asked Crake, abruptly.

"With an arrow," said Father Brown.

Twilight was gathering in the long room, and daylight dwindling to a gleam from the great window in the inner room, where the great millionaire had died. Almost automatically the eyes of the group turned slowly towards it, but as yet there was no sound. Then the voice of Crake came cracked and high and senile in a sort of crowing gabble.

"What you mean? What you mean? Brander Merton killed by an arrow. This crook killed by an arrow—"

"By the same arrow," said the priest, "and at the same moment."

Again there was a sort of strangled and yet swollen and bursting silence, and young Wain began: "You mean—"

"I mean that your friend Merton was Daniel Doom," said Father Brown firmly; "and the only Daniel Doom you'll ever find. Your friend Merton was always crazy after that Coptic Cup that he used to worship like an idol every day; and in his wild youth he had really killed two men to get it, though I still think the deaths may have been in a sense accidents of the robbery. Anyhow, he had it; and that man Drage knew the story and was blackmailing him. But Wilton was after him for a very different purpose; I fancy he only discovered the truth when he'd got into this house. But anyhow, it was in this house, and in that room, that this hunt ended, and he slew the slayer of his father."

For a long time nobody answered. Then old Crake could be heard drumming with his fingers on the table and muttering:

"Brander must have been mad. He must have been mad."

"But, good Lord!" burst out Peter Wain; "what are we to do? What are we to say? Oh, it's all quite different! What about the papers and the big business people? Brander Merton is a thing like the President or the Pope of Rome."

"I certainly think it is rather different," began Barnard Blake, the lawyer, in a low voice. "The difference involves a whole—"

Father Brown struck the table so that the glasses on it rang; and they could almost fancy a ghostly echo from the mysterious chalice that still stood in the room beyond.

"No!" he cried, in a voice like a pistol-shot. "There shall be no difference. I gave you your chance of pitying the poor devil when you thought he was a common criminal. You wouldn't listen then; you were all for private vengeance then. You were all for letting him be butchered like a wild beast without a hearing or a public trial, and said he had only got his deserts. Very well then, if Daniel Doom has got his deserts, Brander Merton has got his deserts. If that was good enough for Doom, by all that is holy it is good enough for Merton. Take your wild justice or our dull legality; but in the name of Almighty God, let there be an equal lawlessness or an equal law."

Nobody answered except the lawyer, and he answered with something like a snarl: "What will the police say if we tell them we mean to condone a crime?"

"What will they say if I tell them you did condone it?" replied Father Brown. "Your respect for the law comes rather late, Mr. Barnard Blake."

After a pause he resumed in a milder tone: "I, for one, am ready to tell the truth if the proper authorities ask me; and the rest of you can do as you like. But as a fact, it will make very little difference. Wilton only rang me up to tell me that I was now free to lay his confession before you; for when you heard it, he would be beyond pursuit."

He walked slowly into the inner room and stood there by the little table beside which the millionaire had died. The Coptic Cup still stood in the same place, and he remained there for a space staring at its cluster of all the colours of the rainbow, and beyond it into a blue abyss of sky.

"You shall not take the name of the
LORD your God in vain."

The Resurrection of Father Brown

There was a brief period during which Father Brown enjoyed, or rather did not enjoy, something like fame. He was a nine days' wonder in the newspapers; he was even a common topic of controversy in the weekly reviews; his exploits were narrated eagerly and inaccurately in any number of clubs and drawing-rooms, especially in America. Incongruous and indeed incredible as it may seem to anyone who knew him, his adventures as a detective were even made the subject of short stories appearing in magazines.

Strangely enough, this wandering limelight struck him in the most obscure, or at least the most remote, of his many places of residence. He had been sent out to officiate, as something between a missionary and a parish priest, in one of those sections of the northern coast of South America, where strips of country still cling insecurely to European powers, or are continually threatening to become independent republics, under the gigantic shadow of President Monroe.[1] The population was

"The Resurrection of Father Brown" first appeared as the lead story in *The Incredulity of Father Brown*, published in June 1926.

[1] The Monroe Doctrine, promulgated in 1823 by the fifth United States president, James Monroe, barred from the Western Hemisphere "further colonization by any European powers".

red and brown with pink spots; that is, it was Spanish-American, and largely Spanish-American-Indian, but there was a considerable and increasing infiltration of Americans of the northern sort—Englishmen, Germans, and the rest. And the trouble seems to have begun when one of these visitors, very recently landed and very much annoyed at having lost one of his bags, approached the first building of which he came in sight—which happened to be the mission-house and chapel attached to it, in front of which ran a long veranda and a long row of stakes, up which were trained the black twisted vines, their square leaves red with autumn. Behind them, also in a row, a number of human beings sat almost as rigid as the stakes, and coloured in some fashion like the vines. For while their broad-brimmed hats were as black as their unblinking eyes, the complexions of many of them might have been made out of the dark red timber of those transatlantic forests. Many of them were smoking very long, thin black cigars; and in all that group the smoke was almost the only moving thing. The visitor would probably have described them as natives, though some of them were very proud of Spanish blood. But he was not one to draw any fine distinction between Spaniards and Red Indians, being rather disposed to dismiss people from the scene when once he had convicted them of being native to it.

He was a newspaper man from Kansas City, a lean, light-haired man with what Meredith called an adventurous nose; one could almost fancy it found its way by feeling its way and moved like the proboscis of an ant-eater. His name was Snaith, and his parents, after some obscure meditation, had called him Saul, a fact which he had the good feeling to conceal as far as possible. Indeed, he had ultimately compromised by calling himself Paul, though by no means for the same reason that had affected the Apostle of the Gentiles.[2] On the contrary, so far as he had any views on such things, the name of the persecutor would have been more appropriate; for he regarded organised religion with the conventional contempt which can be learnt more easily from Ingersoll than from Voltaire.[3] And this was, as it happened, the not very important side of his character which he turned towards the mission-station and the groups in front of the veranda. Something in their shameless repose and indifference inflamed his own fury of efficiency; and, as he could get no particular answer to his first questions, he began to do all the talking himself.

Standing out there in the strong sunshine, a spick-and-span figure in his Panama hat and neat clothes, his grip-sack held in a steely grip, he began to shout at the people in the shadow. He began to explain to them very loudly why they were lazy and filthy, and bestially ignorant and lower than the beasts that perish, in case this problem should have previously exercised their minds. In his opinion it was the deleterious influence of priests that had made them so miserably poor and so hopelessly oppressed that they were able to sit in the shade and smoke and do nothing.

"And a mighty soft crowd you must be at that," he said, "to be bullied by these stuck-up josses because they walk about in their mitres and their tiaras and their gold copes and other glad rags, looking down on everybody else like dirt—being bamboozled by crowns and canopies and sacred umbrellas like a kid at a pantomime; just because a pompous old High Priest of Mumbo-Jumbo looks as if he

[2] A reference to Saint Paul, who, as Saul of Tarsus, was an early persecutor of Christians; after his sudden conversion, he became known as Paul (Acts 13:9), Christianity's most dynamic missionary.

[3] Though a superb orator, the American freethinker Robert Ingersoll (1833–1899) had neither the intellect nor the scholarship of the brilliant French rationalist Voltaire (1694–1778).

was the lord of the earth. What about you? What do you look like, you poor simps? I tell you, that's why you're way-back in barbarism and can't read or write and—"

At this point the High Priest of Mumbo-Jumbo came in an undignified hurry out of the door of the mission-house, not looking very like a lord of the earth, but rather like a bundle of black second-hand clothes buttoned round a short bolster in the semblance of a guy.[4] He was not wearing his tiara, supposing him to possess one, but a shabby broad hat not very dissimilar from those of the Spanish Indians, and it was thrust to the back of his head with a gesture of botheration. He seemed just about to speak to the motionless natives when he caught sight of the stranger and said quickly:

"Oh, can I be of any assistance? Would you like to come inside?"

Mr. Paul Snaith came inside; and it was the beginning of a considerable increase of that journalist's information on many things. Presumably his journalistic instinct was stronger than his prejudices, as, indeed, it often is in clever journalists; and he asked a good many questions, the answers to which interested and surprised him. He discovered that the Indians could read and write, for the simple reason that the priest had taught them; but that they did not read or write any more than they could help, from a natural preference for more direct communications. He learned that these strange people, who sat about in heaps on the veranda without stirring a hair, could work quite hard on their own patches of land; especially those of them who were more than half Spanish; and he learned

---

[4] The priest's shabby appearance resembles the straw-stuffed effigies burned all over England on Guy Fawkes Day, November 5, to celebrate the exposure of the infamous "Gunpowder Plot" of 1605.

with still more astonishment that they all had patches of land that were really their own. That much was part of a stubborn tradition that seemed quite native to natives. But in that also the priest had played a certain part, and by doing so had taken perhaps what was his first and last part in politics, if it was only local politics. There had recently swept through that region one of those fevers of atheist and almost anarchist Radicalism which break out periodically in countries of the Latin culture, generally beginning in a secret society and generally ending in a civil war and in very little else. The local leader of the iconoclastic party was a certain Alvarez, a rather picturesque adventurer of Portuguese nationality but, as his enemies said, of partly Negro origin, the head of any number of lodges and temples of initiation of the sort that in such places clothe even atheism with something mystical. The leader on the more conservative side was a much more commonplace person, a very wealthy man named Mendoza, the owner of many factories and quite respectable, but not very exciting. It was the general opinion that the cause of law and order would have been entirely lost if it had not adopted a more popular policy of its own, in the form of securing land for the peasants; and this movement had mainly originated from the little mission station of Father Brown.

While he was talking to the journalist, Mendoza, the Conservative leader, came in. He was a stout, dark man, with a bald head like a pear and a round body also like a pear; he was smoking a very fragrant cigar, but he threw it away, perhaps a little theatrically, when he came into the presence of the priest, as if he had been entering church; and bowed with a curve that in so corpulent a gentleman seemed quite improbable. He was always exceedingly serious in his social gestures, especially towards religious institutions. He was one of those laymen who are much more ecclesiastical than ecclesiastics. It embarrassed Father Brown a good deal, especially when carried thus into private life.

"I think I am an anti-clerical," Father Brown would say with a faint smile; "but there wouldn't be half so much clericalism if they would only leave things to the clerics."

"Why, Mr. Mendoza," exclaimed the journalist with a new animation, "I think we have met before. Weren't you at the Trade Congress in Mexico last year?"

The heavy eyelids of Mr. Mendoza showed a flutter of recognition, and he smiled in his slow way. "I remember."

"Pretty big business done there in an hour or two," said Snaith with relish. "Made a good deal of difference to you, too, I guess."

"I have been very fortunate," said Mendoza modestly.

"Don't you believe it!" cried the enthusiastic Snaith. "Good fortune comes to the people who know when to catch hold; and you caught hold good and sure. But I hope I'm not interrupting your business?"

"Not at all," said the other. "I often have the honour of calling on the padre for a little talk. Merely for a little talk."

It seemed as if this familiarity between Father Brown and a successful and even famous man of business completed the reconciliation between the priest and the practical Mr. Snaith. He felt, it might be supposed, a new respectability clothe the station and the mission, and was ready to overlook such occasional reminders of the existence of religion as a chapel and a presbytery can seldom wholly avoid. He became quite enthusiastic about the priest's programme—at least on its secular and social side—and announced himself ready at any moment to act in the capacity of a live wire for its communication to the world at large. And it was at this point that Father Brown began to find the journalist rather more troublesome in his sympathy than in his hostility.

Mr. Paul Snaith set out vigorously to feature Father Brown. He sent long and loud eulogies on him across the continent to his newspaper in the Middle West. He took snapshots of the unfortunate cleric in the most common-place occupations and exhibited them in gigantic photographs in the gigantic Sunday papers of the United States. He turned his sayings into slogans, and was continually presenting the world with "A Message" from the reverend gentleman in South America. Any stock less strong and strenuously receptive than the American race would have become very much bored with Father Brown. As it was, he received handsome and eager offers to go on a lecturing tour in the States; and when he declined, the terms were raised with expressions of respectful wonder. A series of stories about him, like the stories of Sherlock Holmes, were, by the instrumentality of Mr. Snaith, planned out and put before the hero with requests for his assistance and encouragement. As the priest found they had started, he could offer no suggestion except that they should stop. And this in turn was taken by Mr. Snaith as the text for a discussion on whether Father Brown should disappear temporarily over a cliff, in the manner of Dr. Watson's hero.[5] To all these demands the priest had patiently to reply in writing, saying that he would consent on such terms to the temporary cessation of the stories and begging that a considerable interval might occur before they began again. The notes he wrote grew shorter and shorter; and as he wrote the last of them, he sighed.

[5] A reference to "The Final Problem" (1892), in which Dr. Watson chronicles the seemingly fatal plunge of Sherlock Holmes at Reichenbach Falls; but Holmes survived, and his further adventures were published after an interval of ten years.

Needless to say, this strange boom in the North reacted on the little outpost in the South where he had expected to live in so lonely an exile. The considerable English and American population already on the spot began to be proud of possessing so widely advertised a person. American tourists, of the sort who land with a loud demand for Westminster Abbey, landed on that distant coast with a loud demand for Father Brown. They were within measurable distance of running excursion trains named after him, and bringing crowds to see him as if he were a public monument. He was especially troubled by the active and ambitious new traders and shopkeepers of the place, who were perpetually pestering him to try their wares and to give them testimonials. Even if the testimonials were not forthcoming, they would prolong the correspondence for the purpose of collecting autographs. As he was a good-natured person they got a good deal of what they wanted out of him; and it was in answer to a particular request from a Frankfort wine-merchant named Eckstein that he wrote hastily a few words on a card, which were to prove a terrible turning-point in his life.

Eckstein was a fussy little man with fuzzy hair and pince-nez, who was wildly anxious that the priest should not only try some of his celebrated medicinal port, but should let him know where and when he would drink it, in acknowledging its receipt. The priest was not particularly surprised at the request, for he was long past surprise at the lunacies of advertisement. So he scribbled something down and turned to other business which seemed a little more sensible. He was again interrupted, by a note from no less a person than his political enemy Alvarez, asking him to come to a conference at which it was hoped that a compromise on an outstanding question might be reached; and suggesting an appointment that evening at a café just

outside the walls of the little town. To this also he sent
a message of acceptance by the rather florid and military
messenger who was waiting for it; and then, having an hour
or two before him, sat down to attempt to get through a
little of his own legitimate business. At the end of the time
he poured himself out a glass of Mr. Eckstein's remarkable
wine and, glancing at the clock with a humorous expression, drank it and went out into the night.

Strong moonlight lay on the little Spanish town, so that
when he came to the picturesque gateway, with its rather
rococo arch and the fantastic fringe of palms beyond it, it
looked rather like a scene in a Spanish opera. One long
leaf of palm with jagged edges, black against the moon,
hung down on the other side of the arch, visible through
the archway, and had something of the look of the jaw
of a black crocodile. The fancy would not have lingered
in his imagination but for something else that caught his
naturally alert eye. The air was deathly still, and there was
not a stir of wind; but he distinctly saw the pendent palm-
leaf move.

He looked around him and realised that he was alone.
He had left behind the last houses, which were mostly
closed and shuttered, and was walking between two
long blank walls built of large and shapeless but flattened
stones, tufted here and there with the queer prickly weeds
of that region—walls which ran parallel all the way to
the gateway. He could not see the lights of the café outside the gate; probably it was too far away. Nothing could
be seen under the arch but a wider expanse of large-flagged
pavement, pale in the moon, with the straggling prickly
pear here and there. He had a strong sense of the smell of
evil; he felt queer physical oppression; but he did not think
of stopping. His courage, which was considerable, was
perhaps even less strong a part of him than his curiosity.

All his life he had been led by an intellectual hunger for the truth, even of trifles. He often controlled it in the name of proportion; but it was always there. He walked straight through the gateway, and on the other side a man sprang like a monkey out of the tree-top and struck at him with a knife. At the same moment another man came crawling swiftly along the wall and, whirling a cudgel round his head, brought it down. Father Brown turned, staggered, and sank in a heap, but as he sank there dawned on his round face an expression of mild and immense surprise.

There was living in the same little town at this time another young American, particularly different from Mr. Paul Snaith. His name was John Adams Race, and he was an electrical engineer, employed by Mendoza to fit out the old town with all the new conveniences. He was a figure far less familiar in satire and international gossip than that of the American journalist. Yet, as a matter of fact, America contains a million men of the moral type of Race to one of the moral type of Snaith. He was exceptional in being exceptionally good at his job, but in every other way he was very simple. He had begun life as a druggist's assistant in a Western village and risen by sheer work and merit; but he still regarded his home town as the natural heart of the habitable world. He had been taught a very Puritan, or purely Evangelical, sort of Christianity from the Family Bible at his mother's knee; and in so far as he had time to have any religion, that was still his religion. Amid all the dazzling lights of the latest and even wildest discoveries, when he was at the very edge and extreme of experiment, working miracles of light and sound like a god creating new stars and solar systems, he never for a moment doubted that the things "back home" were the best things in the world; his mother and the Family Bible and the quiet and quaint morality of his village. He had as

serious and noble a sense of the sacredness of his mother
as if he had been a frivolous Frenchman. He was quite
sure the Bible religion was really the right thing; only
he vaguely missed it wherever he went in the modern
world. He could hardly be expected to sympathise with
the religious externals of Catholic countries; and in a
dislike of mitres and croziers he sympathised with Mr.
Snaith, though not in so cocksure a fashion. He had no
liking for the public bowings and scrapings of Mendoza
and certainly no temptation to the masonic mysticism of
the atheist Alvarez. Perhaps all that semi-tropical life was
too coloured for him, shot with Indian red and Spanish
gold. Anyhow, when he said there was nothing to touch
his home town, he was not boasting. He really meant
that there was somewhere something plain and unpretentious and touching, which he really respected more than
anything else in the world. Such being the mental attitude
of John Adams Race in a South American station, there
had been growing on him for some time a curious feeling,
which contradicted all his prejudices and for which he
could not account. For the truth was this: that the only
thing he had ever met in his travels that in the least
reminded him of the old wood-pile and the provincial
proprieties and the Bible on his mother's knee was (for
some inscrutable reason) the round face and black clumsy
umbrella of Father Brown.

He found himself insensibly watching that commonplace and even comic black figure as it went bustling
about; watching it with an almost morbid fascination, as
if it were a walking riddle or contradiction. He had found
something he could not help liking in the heart of everything he hated; it was as if he had been horribly tormented
by lesser demons and then found that the Devil was quite
an ordinary person.

Thus it happened that, looking out of his window on that moonlit night, he saw the Devil go by, the demon of unaccountable blamelessness, in his broad black hat and long black coat, shuffling along the street towards the gateway, and saw it with an interest which he could not himself understand. He wondered where the priest was going, and what he was really up to; and remained gazing out into the moonlit street long after the little black figure had passed. And then he saw something else that intrigued him further. Two other men whom he recognised passed across his window as across a lighted stage. A sort of blue limelight of the moon ran in a spectral halo round the big bush of hair that stood erect on the head of little Eckstein, the wine-seller, and it outlined a taller and darker figure with an eagle profile and a queer old-fashioned and very top-heavy black hat, which seemed to make the whole outline still more bizarre, like a shape in a shadow pantomime. Race rebuked himself for allowing the moon to play such tricks with his fancy; for on a second glance he recognised the black Spanish sidewhiskers and high-featured face of Dr. Calderon, a worthy medical man of the town, whom he had once found attending professionally on Mendoza. Still, there was something in the way the men were whispering to each other and peering up the street that struck him as peculiar. On a sudden impulse he leapt over the low window-sill and himself went bareheaded up the road, following their trail. He saw them disappear under the dark archway, and a moment after there came a dreadful cry from beyond; curiously loud and piercing, and all the more blood-curdling to Race because it said something very distinctly in some tongue that he did not know.

The next moment there was a rushing of feet, more cries, and then a confused roar of rage or grief that shook the turrets and tall palm trees of the place; there was a movement in the mob that had gathered, as if they were sweeping backwards through the gateway. And then the dark archway resounded with a new voice, this time intelligible to him and falling with the note of doom, as someone shouted through the gateway:

"Father Brown is dead!"

He never knew what prop gave way in his mind, or why something on which he had been counting suddenly failed him; but he ran towards the gateway and was just in time to meet his countryman, the journalist Snaith, coming out of the dark entrance, deadly pale and snapping his fingers nervously.

"It's quite true," said Snaith, with something which for him approached to reverence. "He's a goner. The doctor's been looking at him, and there's no hope. Some of these damned Dagos clubbed him as he came through the gate—God knows why. It'll be a great loss to the place."

Race did not or perhaps could not reply, but ran on under the arch to the scene beyond. The small black figure lay where it had fallen on the wilderness of wide stones starred here and there with green thorn; and the great crowd was being kept back, chiefly by the mere gestures of one gigantic figure in the foreground. For there were many there who swayed hither and thither at the mere movement of his hand, as if he had been a magician.

Alvarez, the dictator and demagogue, was a tall, swaggering figure, always rather flamboyantly clad, and on this occasion he wore a green uniform with embroideries like silver snakes crawling all over it, with an order round his neck hung on a very vivid maroon ribbon. His close curling hair was already grey, and in contrast his complexion, which his friends called olive and his foes octoroon, looked almost literally golden, as if it were a mask moulded in gold. But his large-featured face, which was powerful and humorous, was at this moment properly grave and grim. He had been waiting, he explained, for Father Brown at the café, when he had heard a rustle and a fall and, coming out, had found the corpse lying on the flagstones.

"I know what some of you are thinking," he said, looking round proudly, "and if you are afraid of me—as you are—I will say it for you. I am an atheist; I have no god to call on for those who will not take my word. But I tell you in the name of every root of honour that may be left to a soldier and a man, that I had no part in this. If I had the men here that did it, I would rejoice to hang them on that tree."

"Naturally we are glad to hear you say so," said old Mendoza stiffly and solemnly, standing by the body of his fallen coadjutor. "This blow has been too appalling for us to say what else we feel at present. I suggest that it will be more decent and proper if we remove my friend's body and break up this irregular meeting. I understand," he added gravely to the doctor, "that there is unfortunately no doubt."

"There is no doubt," said Dr. Calderon.

John Race went back to his lodgings sad and with a singular sense of emptiness. It seemed impossible that he should miss a man whom he never knew. He learned that the funeral was to take place next day; for all felt that the crisis should be past as quickly as possible, for fear of riots that were hourly growing more probable. When Snaith had seen the row of Red Indians sitting on the veranda, they might have been a row of ancient Aztec images carved in red wood. But he had not seen them as they were when they heard that the priest was dead.

Indeed they would certainly have risen in revolution and lynched the republican leader, if they had not been immediately blocked by the direct necessity of behaving respectfully to the coffin of their own religious leader. The actual assassins, whom it would have been most natural to lynch, seemed to have vanished into thin air. Nobody knew their names; and nobody would ever know whether the dying man had even seen their faces. That strange look of surprise that was apparently his last look on earth might have been the recognition of their faces. Alvarez repeated violently that it was no work of his, and attended the funeral, walking behind the coffin in his splendid silver and green uniform with a sort of bravado of reverence.

Behind the veranda a flight of stone steps scaled a very steep green bank, fenced by a cactus-hedge, and up this the coffin was laboriously lifted to the ground above, and placed temporarily at the foot of the great gaunt crucifix that dominated the road and guarded the consecrated ground. Below in the road were great seas of people lamenting and telling their beads—an orphan population that had lost a father. Despite all these symbols that were provocative enough to him, Alvarez behaved with restraint and respect; and all would have gone well—as Race told himself—had the others only let him alone.

Race told himself bitterly that old Mendoza had always looked like an old fool and had now very conspicuously and completely behaved like an old fool. By a custom common in simpler societies, the coffin was left open and the face uncovered, bringing the pathos to the point of agony for all those simple people. This, being consonant to tradition, need have done no harm; but some officious person had added to it the custom of the French free-thinkers, of having speeches by the graveside. Mendoza proceeded to make a speech—a rather long speech, and the longer it was, the longer and lower sank John Race's spirits and sympathies with the religious ritual involved.

A list of saintly attributes, apparently of the most antiquated sort, was rolled out with the dilatory dullness of
an after-dinner speaker who does not know how to sit
down. That was bad enough; but Mendoza had also the
ineffable stupidity to start reproaching and even taunting
his political opponents. In three minutes he had succeeded
in making a scene and a very extraordinary scene it was.

"We may well ask," he said, looking around him
pompously, "we may well ask where such virtues can
be found among those who have madly abandoned the
creed of their fathers. It is when we have atheists among
us, atheist leaders, nay sometimes even atheist rulers, that
we find their infamous philosophy bearing fruit in crimes
like this. If we ask who murdered this holy man, we shall
assuredly find—"

Africa of the forests looked out of the eyes of Alvarez
the hybrid adventurer; and Race fancied he could see
suddenly that the man was after all a barbarian, who could
not control himself to the end; one might guess that all his
"illuminated" transcendentalism had a touch of Voodoo.[6]
Anyhow, Mendoza could not continue, for Alvarez had
sprung up and was shouting back at him and shouting him
down, with infinitely superior lungs.

"Who murdered him?" he roared. "Your God
murdered him! His own God murdered him! According
to you, he murders all his faithful and foolish servants—as
he murdered *that* one," and he made a violent gesture, not
towards the coffin but the crucifix.

Seeming to control himself a little, he went on in a
tone still angry but more argumentative: "I don't believe
it, but you do. Isn't it better to have no God than one that

---

[6] Voodoo is a mix of ritual magic and totemism that derived from Africa and
still survives in Haiti, the West Indies, and other parts of the Americas.

robs you in this fashion? I, at least, am not afraid to say that there is none. There is no power in all this blind and brainless universe that can hear your prayer or return your friend. Though you beg Heaven to raise him, he will not rise. Though I dare Heaven to raise him, he will not rise. Here and now I will put it to the test—I defy the God who is not there to waken the man who sleeps for ever."

There was a shock of silence, and the demagogue had made his sensation.

"We might have known," cried Mendoza in a thick gobbling voice, "when we allowed such men as you—"

A new voice cut into his speech; a high and shrill voice with a Yankee accent.

"Stop! Stop!" cried Snaith the journalist, "something's up! I swear I saw him move."

He went racing up the steps and rushed to the coffin, while the mob below swayed with indescribable frenzies. The next moment he had turned a face of amazement over his shoulder and made a signal with his finger to Dr. Calderon, who hastened forward to confer with him. When the two men stepped away again from the coffin, all could see that the position of the head had altered. A roar of excitement rose from the crowd and seemed to stop suddenly, as if cut off in mid-air; for the priest in the coffin gave a groan and raised himself on one elbow, looking with bleared and blinking eyes at the crowd.

John Adams Race, who had hitherto known only miracles of science, never found himself able in after years to describe the topsy-turvydom of the next few days. He seemed to have burst out of the world of time and space, and to be living in the impossible. In half an hour the whole of that town and district had been transformed into something never known for a thousand years; a medieval people turned to a mob of monks by a staggering miracle;

a Greek city where the god had descended among men. Thousands prostrated themselves in the road; hundreds took vows on the spot; and even the outsiders, like the two Americans, were able to think and speak of nothing but the prodigy. Alvarez himself was shaken, as well he might be; and sat down, with his head upon his hands.

And in the midst of all this tornado of beatitude was a little man struggling to be heard. His voice was small and faint, and the noise was deafening. He made weak little gestures that seemed more those of irritation than anything else. He came to the edge of the parapet above the crowd, waving it to be quiet, with movements rather like the flap of the short wings of a penguin. There was something a little more like a lull in the noise; and then Father Brown for the first time reached the utmost stretch of the indignation that he could launch against his children.

"Oh, you *silly* people," he said in a high and quavering voice. "Oh, you silly, *silly* people."

Then he suddenly seemed to pull himself together, made a bolt for the steps with his more normal gait, and began hurriedly to descend.

"Where are you going, Father?" said Mendoza, with more than his usual veneration.

"To the telegraph office," said Father Brown hastily. "What? No; of course it's not a miracle. Why should there be a miracle? Miracles are not so cheap as all that."

And he came tumbling down the steps, the people flinging themselves before him to implore his blessing.

"Bless you, bless you," said Father Brown hastily. "God bless you all and give you more sense."

And he scuttled away with extraordinary rapidity to the telegraph office, where he wired to his Bishop's secretary: "There is some mad story about a miracle here; hope his lordship not give authority. Nothing in it."

As he turned away from his effort, he tottered a little with the reaction, and John Race caught him by the arm.

"Let me see you home," he said; "you deserve more than these people are giving you."

John Race and the priest were seated in the presbytery; the table was still piled up with the papers with which the latter had been wrestling the day before; the bottle of wine and the emptied wine-glass still stood where he had left them.

"And now," said Father Brown almost grimly, "I can begin to think."

"I shouldn't think too hard just yet," said the American. "You must be wanting a rest. Besides, what are you going to think about?"

"I have pretty often had the task of investigating murders, as it happens," said Father Brown. "Now I have got to investigate my own murder."

"If I were you," said Race, "I should take a little wine first."

Father Brown stood up and filled himself another glass, lifted it, looked thoughtfully into vacancy, and put it down again. Then he sat down once more and said:

"Do you know what I felt like when I died? You may not believe it, but my feeling was one of overwhelming astonishment."

"Well," answered Race, "I suppose you were astonished at being knocked on the head."

Father Brown leaned over to him and said in a low voice:

"I was astonished at not being knocked on the head."

Race looked at him for a moment as if he thought the knock on the head had been only too effective; but he only said: "What do you mean?"

"I mean that when that man brought his bludgeon down with a great swipe, it stopped at my head and did not even touch it. In the same way, the other fellow made as if to strike me with a knife, but he never gave me a scratch. It was just like play-acting. I think it was. But then followed the extraordinary thing."

He looked thoughtfully at the papers on the table for a moment and then went on:

"Though I had not even been touched with knife or stick, I began to feel my legs doubling up under me and my very life failing. I knew I was being struck down by something, but it was not by those weapons. Do you know what I think it was?"

And he pointed to the wine on the table.

Race picked up the wine-glass and looked at it and smelt it.

"I think you are right," he said. "I began as a druggist and studied chemistry. I couldn't say for certain without an analysis, but I think there's something very unusual in this stuff. There are drugs by which the Asiatics produce a temporary sleep that looks like death."

"Quite so," said the priest calmly. "The whole of this miracle was faked, for some reason or other. That funeral scene was staged—and timed. I think it is part of that raving madness of publicity that has got hold of Snaith; but I can hardly believe he would go quite so far, merely for that. After all, it's one thing to make copy out of me and run me as a sort of sham Sherlock Holmes, and—"

Even as the priest spoke his face altered. His blinking eyelids shut suddenly and he stood up as if he were choking. Then he put one wavering hand as if groping his way towards the door.

"Where are you going?" asked the other in some wonder.

"If you ask me," said Father Brown, who was quite white, "I was going to pray. Or rather, to praise."

"I'm not sure I understand. What is the matter with you?"

"I was going to praise God for having so strangely and so incredibly saved me—saved me by an inch."

"Of course," said Race, "I am not of your religion; but believe me, I have religion enough to understand that. Of course, you would thank God for saving you from death."

'No," said the priest. "Not from death. From disgrace."

The other sat staring; and the priest's next words broke out of him with a sort of cry.

"And if it had only been my disgrace! But it was the disgrace of all I stand for; the disgrace of the Faith that they went about to encompass. What it might have been! The most huge and horrible scandal ever launched against us since the last lie was choked in the throat of Titus Oates."[7]

"What on earth are you talking about?" demanded his companion.

"Well, I had better tell you at once," said the priest; and sitting down, he went on more composedly: "It came to me in a flash when I happened to mention Snaith and Sherlock Holmes. Now I happen to remember what I wrote about his absurd scheme; it was the natural thing to write, and yet I think they had ingeniously manoeuvred me into writing just those words. They were something like 'I am ready to die and come to life again like Sherlock Holmes, if that is the best way.' And the moment I thought of that, I realised that I had been made to write all sorts of

[7]Father Brown is referring to the Titus Oates who, in 1678, invented the details of a "Popish Plot" to murder the king, burn London, and massacre Protestants. Not until 1681, after thirty-five Catholics had been executed for treason, was the conspiracy exposed as a fraud.

things of that kind, all pointing to the same idea. I wrote, as if to an accomplice, saying that I would drink the drugged wine at a particular time. Now, don't you see?"

Race sprang to his feet still staring: "Yes," he said, "I think I began to see."

"*They* would have boomed the miracle. Then *they* would have bust up the miracle. And what is the worst, they would have proved that *I* was in the conspiracy. It would have been *our* sham miracle. That's all there is to it; and about as near hell as you and I will ever be, I hope."

Then he said, after a pause, in quite a mild voice:

"They certainly would have got quite a lot of good copy out of me."

Race looked at the table and said darkly: "How many of these brutes were in it?"

Father Brown shook his head. "More than I like to think of," he said; "but I hope some of them were only tools. Alvarez might think that all's fair in war, perhaps; he has a queer mind. I'm very much afraid that Mendoza is an old hypocrite; I never trusted him and he hated my action in an industrial matter. But all that will wait; I have only got to thank God for the escape. And especially that I wired at once to the Bishop."

John Race appeared to be very thoughtful.

"You've told me a lot I didn't know," he said at last, "and I feel inclined to tell you the only thing you don't know. I can imagine how those fellows calculated well enough. They thought any man alive, waking up in a coffin to find himself canonised like a saint, and made into a walking miracle for everyone to admire, would be swept along with his worshippers and accept the crown of glory that fell on him out the sky. And I reckon their calculation was pretty practical psychology, as men go. I've seen all sorts of men in all sorts of places; and I tell you frankly I don't believe there's one man in a thousand who could wake up like that with all his wits about him; and while he was still almost talking in his sleep, would have the sanity and the simplicity and the humility to—" He was much surprised to find himself moved, and his level voice wavering.

Father Brown was gazing abstractedly, and in a rather cockeyed fashion, at the bottle on the table. "Look here," he said, "what about a bottle of real wine?"

"Remember the sabbath day, to keep it holy."

The Salad of Colonel Cray

Father Brown was walking home from Mass on a white weird morning when the mists were slowly lifting—one of those mornings when the very element of light appears as something mysterious and new. The scattered trees outlined themselves more and more out of the vapour, as if they were first drawn in grey chalk and then in charcoal. At yet more distant intervals appeared the houses upon the broken fringe of the suburb; their outlines became clearer and clearer until he recognised many in which he had chance acquaintances, and many more the names of whose owners he knew. But all the windows and doors were sealed; none of the people were of the sort that would be up at such a time, or still less on such an errand. But as he passed under the shadow of one handsome villa with verandas and wide ornate gardens, he heard a noise that made him almost involuntarily stop. It was the unmistakable noise of a pistol or carbine or some light firearm discharged; but it was not this that puzzled him most. The first full noise was immediately followed by a series of fainter noises—as he counted them, about six. He supposed it must be the echo; but the odd thing was that the echo was not in the least like the original sound. It was not like anything else that he

"The Salad of Colonel Cray" first appeared in the July 1914 issue of *Pall Mall Magazine*.

could think of; the three things nearest to it seemed to be the noise made by siphons of soda-water, one of the many noises made by an animal, and the noise made by a person attempting to conceal laughter. None of which seemed to make much sense.

Father Brown was made of two men. There was a man of action, who was as modest as a primrose and as punctual as a clock; who went his small round of duties and never dreamed of altering it. There was also a man of reflection, who was much simpler but much stronger, who could not easily be stopped; whose thought was always (in the only intelligent sense of the words) free thought. He could not help, even unconsciously, asking himself all the questions that there were to be asked, and answering as many of them as he could; all that went on like his breathing or circulation. But he never consciously carried his actions outside the sphere of his own duty; and in this case the two attitudes were aptly tested. He was just about to resume his trudge in the twilight, telling himself it was no affair of his, but instinctively twisting and untwisting twenty theories about what the odd noises might mean. Then the grey sky-line brightened into silver, and in the broadening light he realised that he had been to the house which belonged to an Anglo-Indian Major named Putnam; and that the Major had a native cook from Malta who was of his communion. He also began to remember that pistol-shots are sometimes serious things; accompanied with consequences with which he was legitimately concerned. He turned back and went in at the garden gate, making for the front door.

Half-way down one side of the house stood out a projection like a very low shed; it was, as he afterwards discovered, a large dustbin. Round the corner of this came a figure, at first a mere shadow in the haze, apparently bending and peering about. Then, coming nearer, it solidified into a figure that was, indeed, rather unusually solid. Major Putnam was a bald-headed, bull-necked man, short and very broad, with one of those rather apoplectic faces that are produced by a prolonged attempt to combine the oriental climate with the occidental luxuries. But the face was a good-humoured one, and even now, though evidently puzzled and inquisitive, wore a kind of innocent grin. He had a large palm-leaf hat on the back of his head (suggesting a halo that was by no means appropriate to the face), but otherwise he was clad only in a very vivid suit of striped scarlet and yellow pyjamas; which, though glowing enough to behold, must have been, on a fresh morning, pretty chilly to wear. He had evidently come out of his house in a hurry, and the priest was not surprised when he called out without further ceremony: "Did you hear that noise?"

"Yes," answered Father Brown; "I thought I had better look in, in case anything was the matter."

The Major looked at him rather queerly with his good-humoured gooseberry eyes. "What do you think the noise was?" he asked.

"It sounded like a gun or something," replied the other, with some hesitation; "but it seemed to have a singular sort of echo."

The Major was still looking at him quietly, but with protruding eyes, when the front door was flung open, releasing a flood of gaslight on the face of the fading mist; and another figure in pyjamas sprang or tumbled out into the garden. The figure was much longer, leaner, and more athletic; the pyjamas, though equally tropical, were comparatively tasteful, being of white with a light lemon-yellow stripe. The man was haggard, but handsome, more sunburned than the other; he had an aquiline profile and rather deep-sunken eyes, and a slight air of oddity arising from the combination of coal-black hair with a much lighter moustache. All this Father Brown absorbed in detail more at leisure. For the moment he only saw one thing about the man: which was the revolver in his hand.

"Cray!" exclaimed the Major, staring at him, "did you fire that shot?"

"Yes, I did," retorted the black-haired gentleman hotly, "and so would you in my place. If you were chased everywhere by devils and nearly—"

The Major seemed to intervene rather hurriedly. "This is my friend Father Brown," he said. And then to Brown: "I don't know whether you've met Colonel Cray of the Royal Artillery."

"I have heard of him, of course," said the priest innocently. "Did you—did you hit anything?"

"I thought so," answered Cray with gravity.

"Did he—" asked Major Putnam in a lowered voice, "did he fall or cry out, or anything?"

Colonel Cray was regarding his host with a strange and steady stare. "I'll tell you exactly what he did," he said. "He sneezed."

Father Brown's hand went half-way to his head, with the gesture of a man remembering somebody's name. He knew now what it was that was neither soda-water nor the snorting of a dog.

"Well," ejaculated the staring Major, "I never heard before that a service revolver was a thing to be sneezed at."

"Nor I," said Father Brown faintly. "It's lucky you didn't turn your artillery on him or you might have given him quite a bad cold." Then, after a bewildered pause, he said: "Was it a burglar?"

"Let us go inside," said Major Putnam, rather sharply, and led the way into his house.

The interior exhibited a paradox often to be marked in such morning hours: that the rooms seemed brighter than the sky outside; even after the Major had turned out the one gaslight in the front hall. Father Brown was surprised to see the whole dining-table set out as for a festive meal, with napkins in their rings, and wine-glasses of some six unnecessary shapes set beside every plate. It was common enough, at that time of the morning, to find the remains of a banquet overnight; but to find it freshly spread so early was unusual.

While he stood wavering in the hall Major Putnam rushed past him and sent a raging eye over the whole oblong of the tablecloth. At last he spoke, spluttering: "All the silver gone!" he gasped. "Fish-knives and forks gone. Old cruet-stand gone. Even the old silver cream-jug gone. And now, Father Brown, I am ready to answer your question of whether it was a burglar."

"They're simply a blind," said Cray stubbornly. "I know better than you why people persecute this house; I know better than you why——"

The Major patted him on the shoulder with a gesture almost peculiar to the soothing of a sick child, and said: "It was a burglar. Obviously it was a burglar."

"A burglar with a bad cold," observed Father Brown, "that might assist you to trace him in the neighbourhood."

The Major shook his head in a sombre manner. "He must be far beyond trace now, I fear," he said.

Then, as the restless man with the revolver turned again towards the door in the garden, he added in a husky, confidential voice: "I doubt whether I should send for the police, for fear my friend here has been a little too free with his bullets, and got on the wrong side of the law. He's lived in very wild places; and, to be frank with you, I think he sometimes fancies things."

"I think you once told me," said Brown, "that he believes some Indian secret society is pursuing him."

Major Putnam nodded, but at the same time shrugged his shoulders. "I suppose we'd better follow him outside," he said. "I don't want any more—shall we say, sneezing?"

They passed out into the morning light, which was now even tinged with sunshine, and saw Colonel Cray's tall figure bent almost double, minutely examining the condition of gravel and grass. While the Major strolled unobtrusively towards him, the priest took an equally indolent turn, which took him round the next corner of the house to within a yard or two of the projecting dustbin.

He stood regarding this dismal object for some minute and a half—then he stepped towards it, lifted the lid and put his head inside. Dust and other discolouring matter shook upwards as he did so; but Father Brown never observed his own appearance, whatever else he observed. He remained thus for a measurable period, as if engaged in some mysterious prayers. Then he came out again, with some ashes on his hair, and walked unconcernedly away.

By the time he came round to the garden door again he found a group there which seemed to roll away morbidities as the sunlight had already rolled away the mists. It was in no way rationally reassuring; it was simply broadly comic, like a cluster of Dickens's characters. Major Putnam had managed to slip inside and plunge into a proper shirt and trousers, with a crimson cummerbund, and a light square jacket over all; thus normally set off, his red festive face seemed bursting with a commonplace cordiality. He was indeed emphatic, but then he was talking to his cook—the swarthy son of Malta, whose lean, yellow and rather careworn face contrasted quaintly with his snow-white cap and costume. The cook might well be careworn, for cookery was the Major's hobby. He was one of those amateurs who always know more than the professional. The only other person he even admitted to be a judge of an omelette was his friend Cray—and as Brown remembered this, he turned to look for the other officer. In the new presence of daylight and people clothed and in their right mind, the sight of him was rather a shock. The taller and more elegant man was still in his night-garb, with tousled black hair, and now crawling about the garden on his hands and knees, still looking for traces of the burglar; and now and again, to all appearance, striking the ground with his hand in anger at not finding him. Seeing him thus quadrupedal in the grass, the priest raised his eyebrows rather sadly; and for the first time guessed that "fancies things" might be an euphemism.

The third item in the group of the cook and the epicure was also known to Father Brown; it was Audrey Watson, the Major's ward and housekeeper; and at this moment, to judge by her apron, tucked-up sleeves and resolute manner, much more the housekeeper than the ward.

"It serves you right," she was saying: "I always told you not to have that old-fashioned cruet-stand."

"I prefer it," said Putnam, placably. "I'm old-fashioned myself; and the things keep together."

"And vanish together, as you see," she retorted. "Well, if you are not going to bother about the burglar, I shouldn't bother about the lunch. It's Sunday, and we can't send for vinegar and all that in the town; and you Indian gentlemen can't enjoy what you call a dinner without a lot of hot things. I wish to goodness now you hadn't asked Cousin Oliver to take me to the musical service. It isn't over till half-past twelve, and the Colonel has to leave by then. I don't believe you men can manage alone."

"Oh yes, we can, my dear," said the Major, looking at her very amiably. "Marco has all the sauces, and we've often done ourselves well in very rough places, as you might know by now. And it's time you had a treat, Audrey; you mustn't be a housekeeper every hour of the day; and I know you want to hear the music."

"I want to go to church," she said, with rather severe eyes.

She was one of those handsome women who will always be handsome, because the beauty is not in an air or a tint, but in the very structure of the head and features. But though she was not yet middle-aged and her auburn hair was of a Titianesque fullness in form and colour, there was a look in her mouth and around her eyes which suggested that some sorrows wasted her, as winds waste at last the edges of a Greek temple. For indeed the little domestic difficulty of which she was now speaking so decisively was rather comic than tragic. Father Brown gathered, from the course of the conversation, that Cray, the other *gourmet*, had to leave before the usual lunch-time; but that Putnam, his host, not to be done out of a final feast with an old crony, had arranged for a special *déjeuner* to be set out and consumed in the course of the morning, while Audrey and other graver persons were at morning service. She was going there under the escort of a relative and old friend of hers, Dr. Oliver Oman, who, though a scientific man of a somewhat bitter type, was enthusiastic for music, and would go even to church to get it. There was nothing in all this that could conceivably concern the tragedy in Miss Watson's face; and by a half conscious instinct, Father Brown turned again to the seeming lunatic grubbing about in the grass.

When he strolled across to him, the black, unbrushed head was lifted abruptly, as if in some surprise at his continued presence. And indeed, Father Brown, for reasons best known to himself, had lingered much longer than politeness required; or even, in the ordinary sense, permitted.

"Well!" cried Cray, with wild eyes. "I suppose you think I'm mad, like the rest?"

"I have considered the thesis," answered the little man, composedly. "And I incline to think you are not."

"What do you mean?" snapped Cray quite savagely.

"Real madmen," explained Father Brown, "always encourage their own morbidity. They never strive against it. But you are trying to find traces of the burglar; even when there aren't any. You are struggling against it. You want what no madman ever wants."

"And what is that?"

"You want to be proved wrong," said Brown.

During the last words Cray had sprung or staggered to his feet and was regarding the cleric with agitated eyes. "By hell, but that is a true word!" he cried. "They are all at me here that the fellow was only after the silver— as if I shouldn't be only too pleased to think so! She's been at me," and he tossed his tousled black head towards Audrey, but the other had no need of the direction, "she's been at me today about how cruel I was to shoot a poor harmless house-breaker, and how I have the devil in me against poor harmless natives. But I was a good-natured man once—as good-natured as Putnam."

After a pause he said: "Look here, I've never seen you before; but you shall judge of the whole story. Old Putnam and I were friends in the same mess; but, owing to some accidents on the Afghan border, I got my command much sooner than most men; only we were both invalided home for a bit. I was engaged to Audrey out there; and we all travelled back together. But on the journey back things happened. Curious things. The result of them was that Putnam wants it broken off, and even Audrey keeps it hanging on—and I know what they mean. I know what they think I am. So do you.

"Well, these are the facts. The last day we were in an Indian city I asked Putnam if I could get some Trichinopoli cigars; he directed me to a little place opposite his lodgings. I have since found he was quite right; but 'opposite' is a dangerous word when one decent house stands opposite five or six squalid ones; and I must have mistaken the door. It opened with difficulty, and then only on darkness; but as I turned back, the door behind me sank back and settled into its place with a noise as of innumerable bolts. There was nothing to do but to walk forward; which I did through passage after passage, pitch-dark. Then I came to a flight of steps, and then to a blind door, secured by a latch of elaborate Eastern ironwork, which I could only trace by touch, but which I loosened at last. I came out again upon gloom, which was half turned into a greenish twilight by a multitude of small but steady lamps below. They showed merely the feet or fringes of some huge and empty architecture. Just in front of me was something that looked like a mountain. I confess I nearly fell on the great stone platform on which I had emerged, to realise that it was an idol. And worst of all, an idol with its back to me.

"It was hardly half human, I guessed; to judge by the small squat head, and still more by a thing like a tail or extra limb turned up behind and pointing, like a loathsome large finger, at some symbol graven in the centre of the vast stone back. I had begun, in the dim light, to guess at the hieroglyphic, not without horror, when a more horrible thing happened. A door opened silently in the temple wall behind me and a man came out, with a brown face and a black coat. He had a carved smile on his face, of copper flesh and ivory teeth; but I think the most hateful thing about him was that he was in European dress. I was prepared, I think, for shrouded priests or naked fakirs. But this seemed to say that the devilry was over all the earth. As indeed I found it to be.

"'If you had only seen the Monkey's Feet,' he said, smiling steadily, and without other preface, 'we should have been very gentle—you would only be tortured and die. If you had seen the Monkey's Face, still we should be very moderate, very tolerant—you would only be tortured and live. But as you have seen the Monkey's Tail, we must pronounce the worst sentence, which is—Go Free.'

"When he said the words I heard the elaborate iron latch with which I had struggled, automatically unlock itself: and then, far down the dark passages I had passed, I heard the heavy street-door shifting its own bolts backwards.

"'It is vain to ask for mercy; you must go free,' said the smiling man. 'Henceforth a hair shall slay you like a sword, and a breath shall bite you like an adder; weapons shall come against you out of nowhere; and you shall die many times.' And with that he was swallowed once more in the wall behind; and I went out into the street."

Cray paused; and Father Brown unaffectedly sat down on the lawn and began to pick daisies.

Then the soldier continued: "Putnam, of course, with his jolly common sense, pooh-poohed all my fears; and from that time dates his doubt of my mental balance. Well, I'll simply tell you, in the fewest words, the three things that have happened since; and you shall judge which of us is right.

"The first happened in an Indian village on the edge of the jungle, but hundreds of miles from the temple, or town, or type of tribes and customs where the curse had been put on me. I woke in black midnight, and lay thinking of nothing in particular, when I felt a faint tickling thing, like a thread or a hair, trailed across my throat. I shrank back out of its way, and could not help thinking of the words in the temple. But when I got up and sought lights and a mirror, the line across my neck was a line of blood.

"The second happened in a lodging in Port Said, later, on our journey home together. It was a jumble of tavern and curiosity-shop; and though there was nothing there remotely suggesting the cult of the Monkey, it is, of course, possible that some of its images or talismans were in such a place. Its curse was there, anyhow. I woke again in the dark with a sensation that could not be put in colder or more literal words than that a breath bit like an adder. Existence was an agony of extinction; I dashed my head against walls until I dashed it against a window; and fell rather than jumped into the garden below. Putnam, poor fellow, who had called the other thing a chance scratch, was bound to take seriously the fact of finding me half insensible on the grass at dawn. But I fear it was my mental state he took seriously; and not my story.

"The third happened in Malta. We were in a fortress there; and as it happened our bedrooms overlooked the open sea, which almost came up to our window-sills, save for a flat white outer wall as bare as the sea. I woke up again; but it was not dark. There was a full moon, as I walked to the window; I could have seen a bird on the bare battlement, or a sail on the horizon. What I did see was a sort of stick or branch circling, self-supported, in the empty sky. It flew straight in at my window and smashed the lamp beside the pillow I had just quitted. It was one of those queer-shaped war-clubs some Eastern tribes use. But it had come from no human hand."

Father Brown threw away a daisy-chain he was making, and rose with a wistful look. "Has Major Putnam," he asked, "got any Eastern curios, idols, weapons and so on, from which one might get a hint?"

"Plenty of those, though not much use, I fear," replied Cray; "but by all means come into his study."

As they entered they passed Miss Watson buttoning her gloves for church, and heard the voice of Putnam downstairs still giving a lecture on cookery to the cook. In the Major's study and den of curios they came suddenly on a third party, silk-hatted and dressed for the street, who was poring over an open book on the smoking-table—a book which he dropped rather guiltily, and turned.

Cray introduced him civilly enough, as Dr. Oman, but he showed such disfavour in his very face that Brown guessed the two men, whether Audrey knew it or not, were rivals. Nor was the priest wholly unsympathetic with the prejudice. Dr. Oman was a very well-dressed gentleman indeed; well-featured, though almost dark enough for an Asiatic. But Father Brown had to tell himself sharply that one should be in charity even with those who wax their pointed beards, who have small gloved hands, and who speak with perfectly modulated voices.

Cray seemed to find something specially irritating in the small prayer-book in Oman's dark-gloved hand. "I didn't know that was in your line," he said rather rudely.

Oman laughed mildly, but without offence. "This is more so, I know," he said, laying his hand on the big book he had dropped, "a dictionary of drugs and such things. But it's rather too large to take to church." Then he closed the larger book, and there seemed again the faintest touch of hurry and embarrassment.

"I suppose," said the priest, who seemed anxious to change the subject, "all these spears and things are from India?"

"From everywhere," answered the doctor. "Putnam is an old soldier, and has been in Mexico and Australia, and the Cannibal Islands for all I know."

"I hope it was not in the Cannibal Islands," said Brown, "that he learnt the art of cookery." And he ran his eyes over the stew-pots or other strange utensils on the wall.

At this moment the jolly subject of their conversation thrust his laughing, lobsterish face into the room. "Come along, Cray," he cried. "Your lunch is just coming in. And the bells are ringing for those who want to go to church."

Cray slipped upstairs to change; Dr. Oman and Miss Watson betook themselves solemnly down the street, with a string of other churchgoers; but Father Brown noticed that the doctor twice looked back and scrutinised the house; and even came back to the corner of the street to look at it again.

The priest looked puzzled. "*He* can't have been at the dustbin," he muttered. "Not in those clothes. Or was he there earlier today?"

Father Brown, touching other people, was as sensitive as a barometer; but today he seemed about as sensitive as a rhinoceros. By no social law, rigid or implied, could he be supposed to linger round the lunch of the Anglo-Indian friends; but he lingered, covering his position with torrents of amusing but quite needless conversation. He was the more puzzling because he did not seem to want any lunch. As one after another of the most exquisitely balanced kedgerees of curries, accompanied with their appropriate vintages, were laid before the other two, he only repeated that it was one of his fast-days, and munched a piece of bread and sipped and then left untasted a tumbler of cold water. His talk, however, was exuberant.

"I'll tell you what I'll do for you," he cried—"I'll mix you a salad! I can't eat it, but I'll mix it like an angel! You've got a lettuce there."

"Unfortunately it's the only thing we have got," answered the good-humoured Major. "You must remember that mustard, vinegar, oil and so on vanished with the cruet and the burglar."

"I know," replied Brown, rather vaguely. "That's what I've always been afraid would happen. That's why I always carry a cruet-stand about with me. I'm so fond of salads."

And to the amazement of the two men he took a pepper-pot out of his waistcoat pocket and put it on the table.

"I wonder why the burglar wanted mustard, too," he went on, taking a mustard-pot from another pocket. "A mustard plaster, I suppose. And vinegar"—and producing that condiment—"haven't I heard something about vinegar and brown paper? As for oil, which I think I put in my left—"

His garrulity was an instant arrested; for lifting his eyes, he saw what no one else saw—the black figure of Dr. Oman standing on the sunlit lawn and looking steadily into the room. Before he could quite recover himself Cray had cloven in.

"You're an astounding card," he said, staring. "I shall come and hear your sermons, if they're as amusing as your manners." His voice changed a little, and he leaned back in his chair.

"Oh, there are sermons in a cruet-stand, too," said Father Brown, quite gravely. "Have you heard of faith like a grain of mustard-seed; or charity that anoints with oil? And as for vinegar, can any soldiers forget that solitary soldier, who, when the sun was darkened—"

Colonel Cray leaned forward a little and clutched the tablecloth.

Father Brown, who was making the salad, tipped two spoonfuls of the mustard into the tumbler of water beside him; stood up and said in a new, loud and sudden voice—"Drink that!"

At the same moment the motionless doctor in the garden came running, and bursting open a window cried: "Am I wanted? Has he been poisoned?"

"Pretty near," said Brown, with the shadow of a smile; for the emetic had very suddenly taken effect. And Cray lay in a deck-chair, gasping as for life, but alive.

Major Putnam had sprung up, his purple face mottled. "A crime!" he cried hoarsely. "I will go for the police!"

The priest could hear him dragging down his palm-leaf hat from the peg and tumbling out of the front door; he heard the garden gate slam. But he only stood looking at Cray; and after a silence said quietly:

"I shall not talk to you much; but I will tell you what you want to know. There is no curse on you. The Temple of the Monkey was either a coincidence or a part of the trick; the trick was the trick of a white man. There is only one weapon that will bring blood with that mere feathery touch: a razor held by a white man. There is one way of making a common room full of invisible, overpowering poison: turning on the gas—the crime of a white man. And there is only one kind of club that can be thrown out of a window, turn in mid-air and come back to the window next to it: the Australian boomerang. You'll see some of them in the Major's study."

With that he went outside and spoke for a moment to the doctor. The moment after, Audrey Watson came rushing into the house and fell on her knees beside Cray's chair. He could not hear what they said to each other; but their faces moved with amazement, not unhappiness. The doctor and the priest walked slowly towards the garden gate.

"I suppose the Major was in love with her, too," he said with a sigh; and when the other nodded, observed: "You were very generous, doctor. You did a fine thing. But what made you suspect?"

"A very small thing," said Oman; "but it kept me restless in church till I came back to see that all was well. That book on his table was a work on poisons; and was put down open at the place where it stated that a certain Indian poison, though deadly and difficult to trace, was particularly easily reversible by the use of the commonest emetics. I suppose he read that at the last moment—"

"And remembered that there were emetics in the cruet-stand," said Father Brown. "Exactly. He threw the cruet in the dustbin—where I found it, along with other silver—for the sake of a burglary blind. But if you look at that pepper-pot I put on the table, you'll see a small hole. That's where Cray's bullet struck, shaking up the pepper and making the criminal sneeze."

There was a silence. Then Dr. Oman said grimly: "The Major is a long time looking for the police."

"Or the police in looking for the Major?" said the priest. "Well, good-bye."

"Honor your father and your mother."

The Worst Crime in the World

Father Brown was wandering through a picture gallery with an expression that suggested that he had not come there to look at the pictures. Indeed, he did not want to look at the pictures, though he liked pictures well enough. Not that there was anything immoral or improper about those highly modern pictorial designs. He would indeed be of an inflammable temperament who was stirred to any of the more pagan passions by the display of interrupted spirals, inverted cones and broken cylinders with which the art of the future inspired or menaced mankind. The truth is that Father Brown was looking for a young friend who had appointed that somewhat incongruous meeting-place, being herself of a more futuristic turn. The young friend was also a young relative; one of the few relatives that he had. Her name was Elizabeth Fane, simplified into Betty, and she was the child of a sister who had married into a race of refined but impoverished squires. As the squire was dead as well as impoverished, Father Brown stood in the relation of a protector as well as a priest, and in some sense a guardian as well as an uncle. At the moment, however, he was blinking about at the groups in the gallery without catching sight of the familiar brown hair and bright face of

"The Worst Crime in the World" first appeared in America in *Harper's Magazine* in October 1925.

his niece. Nevertheless, he saw some people he knew and a number of people he did not know, including some that, as a mere matter of taste, he did not much want to know.

Among the people the priest did not know and who yet aroused his interest was a lithe and alert young man, very beautifully dressed and looking rather like a foreigner, because, while his beard was cut in a spade shape like an old Spaniard's, his dark hair was cropped so close as to look like a tight black skull-cap. Among the people the priest did not particularly want to know was a very dominant-looking lady, sensationally clad in scarlet, with a mane of yellow hair too long to be called bobbed, but too loose to be called anything else. She had a powerful and rather heavy face of a pale and rather unwholesome complexion, and when she looked at anybody she cultivated the fascinations of a basilisk.[1] She towed in attendance behind her a short man with a big beard and a very broad face, with long sleepy slits of eyes. The expression of his face was beaming and benevolent, if only partially awake; but his bull neck, when seen from behind, looked a little brutal.

Father Brown gazed at the lady, feeling that the appearance and approach of his niece would be an agreeable contrast. Yet he continued to gaze, for some reason, until he reached the point of feeling that the appearance of anybody would be an agreeable contrast. It was therefore with a certain relief, though with a slight start as of awakening, that he turned at the sound of his name and saw another face that he knew.

It was the sharp but not unfriendly face of a lawyer named Granby, whose patches of grey hair might almost have been the powder from a wig, so incongruous were they with his youthful energy of movement. He was one

[1] The basilisk was a mythical serpent whose mere glance was fatal to travelers.

of those men in the City who run about like schoolboys in and out of their offices. He could not run round the fashionable picture gallery quite in that fashion; but he looked as if he wanted to, and fretted as he glanced to left and right, seeking somebody he knew.

"I didn't know," said Father Brown, smiling, "that you were a patron of the New Art."

"I didn't know that you were," retorted the other. "I came here to catch a man."

"I hope you will have good sport," answered the priest. "I'm doing much the same."

"Said he was passing through to the Continent," snorted the solicitor, "and could I meet him in this cranky place." He ruminated a moment, and said abruptly: "Look here, I know you can keep a secret. Do you know Sir John Musgrave?"

"No," answered the priest; "but I should hardly have thought he was a secret, though they say he does hide himself in a castle. Isn't he the old man they tell all those tales about—how he lives in a tower with a real portcullis and drawbridge, and generally refuses to emerge from the Dark Ages? Is he one of your clients?"

"No," replied Granby shortly: "it's his son, Captain Musgrave, who has come to us. But the old man counts for a good deal in the affair, and I don't know him; that's the point. Look here, this is confidential, as I say, but I can confide in you." He dropped his voice and drew his friend apart into a side gallery containing representations of various real objects, which was comparatively empty.

"This young Musgrave," he said, "wants to raise a big sum from us on a *post obit*[2] on his old father in Northumberland. The old man's long past seventy and presumably

_____

[2] *Post obit* (shortened from the Latin *post obitum*) is a legal term for that going into effect "after death".

will *obit* some time or other; but what about the *post*, so to speak? What will happen afterwards to his cash and castles and portcullises and all the rest? It's a very fine old estate, and still worth a lot, but strangely enough it isn't entailed. So you see how we stand. The question is, as the man said in Dickens, is the old man friendly?"[3]

"If he's friendly to his son you'll feel all the friendlier," observed Father Brown. "No, I'm afraid I can't help you. I never met Sir John Musgrave, and I understand very few people do meet him nowadays. But it seems obvious you have a right to an answer on that point before you lend the young gentleman your firm's money. Is he the sort that people cut off with a shilling?"

"Well, I'm doubtful," answered the other. "He's very popular and brilliant and a great figure in society; but he's a great deal abroad, and he's been a journalist."

"Well," said Father Brown, "that's not a crime. At least not always."

"Nonsense!" said Granby curtly. "You know what I mean—he's rather a rolling stone, who's been a journalist and a lecturer and an actor, and all sorts of things. I've got to know where I stand.... Why, there he is."

And the solicitor, who had been stamping impatiently about the emptier gallery, turned suddenly and darted into the more crowded room at a run. He was running towards the tall and well-dressed young man with the short hair and the foreign-looking beard.

The two walked away together talking, and for some moments afterwards Father Brown followed them with his screwed, short-sighted eyes. His gaze was shifted and recalled, however, by the breathless and even boisterous arrival of his niece, Betty. Rather to the surprise of her

---

[3] From the novel *The Old Curiosity Shop* by popular nineteenth-century English author Charles Dickens.

uncle, she led him back into the emptier room and planted him on a seat that was like an island in that sea of floor.

"I've got something I must tell you," she said. "It's so silly that nobody else will understand it."

"You overwhelm me," said Father Brown. "Is it about this business your mother started telling me about? Engagements and all that; not what the military historians call a general engagement."

"You know," she said, "that she wants me to be engaged to Captain Musgrave."

"I didn't," said Father Brown with resignation; "but Captain Musgrave seems to be quite a fashionable topic."

"Of course we're very poor," she said, "and it's no good saying it makes no difference."

"Do you want to marry him?" asked Father Brown, looking at her through his half-closed eyes.

She frowned at the floor, and answered in a lower tone:

"I thought I did. At least I think I thought I did. But I've just had rather a shock."

"Then tell us all about it."

"I heard him laugh," she said.

"It is an excellent social accomplishment," he replied.

"You don't understand," said the girl. "It wasn't social at all. That was just the point of it—that it wasn't social."

She paused a moment, and then went on firmly: "I came here quite early, and saw him sitting quite alone in the middle of that gallery with the new pictures, that was quite empty then. He had no idea I or anybody was near; he was sitting quite alone, and he laughed."

"Well, no wonder," said Father Brown. "I'm not an art critic myself, but as a general view of the pictures taken as a whole—"

"Oh, you won't understand," she said almost angrily. "It wasn't a bit like that. He wasn't looking at the pictures.

He was staring right up at the ceiling; but his eyes seemed to be turned inwards, and he laughed so that my blood ran cold."

The priest had risen and was pacing the room with his hands behind him. "You mustn't be hasty in a case of this sort," he began. "There are two kinds of men—but we can hardly discuss him just now, for here he is."

Captain Musgrave entered the room swiftly and swept it with a smile. Granby, the lawyer, was just behind him, and his legal face bore a new expression of relief and satisfaction.

"I must apologise for everything I said about the Captain," he said to the priest as they drifted together towards the door. "He's a thoroughly sensible fellow and quite sees my point. He asked me himself why I didn't go north and see his old father; I could hear from the old man's own lips how it stood about the inheritance. Well, he couldn't say fairer than that, could he? But he's so anxious to get the thing settled that he offered to take me up in his own car to Musgrave Moss. That's the name of the estate. I suggested that, if he was so kind, we might go together; and we're starting to-morrow morning."

As they spoke Betty and the Captain came through the doorway together, making in that framework at least a sort of picture that some would be sentimental enough to prefer to cones and cylinders. Whatever their other affinities, they were both very good-looking; and the lawyer was moved to a remark on the fact, when the picture abruptly altered.

Captain James Musgrave looked out into the main gallery, and his laughing and triumphant eyes were riveted on something that seemed to change him from head to foot. Father Brown looked round as under an advancing shadow of premonition; and he saw the lowering, almost livid face of the large woman in scarlet under its leonine yellow hair. She always stood with a slight stoop, like a bull lowering its horns, and the expression of her pale pasty face was so oppressive and hypnotic that they hardly saw the little man with the large beard standing beside her.

Musgrave advanced into the centre of the room towards her, almost like a beautifully dressed wax-work wound up to walk. He said a few words to her that could not be heard. She did not answer; but they turned away together, walking down the long gallery as if in debate, the short, bull-necked man with the beard bringing up the rear like some grotesque goblin page.

"Heaven help us!" muttered Father Brown, frowning after them. "Who in the world is that woman?"

"No pal of mine, I'm happy to say," replied Granby with grim flippancy. "Looks as if a little flirtation with her might end fatally, doesn't it?"

"I don't think he's flirting with her," said Father Brown.

Even as he spoke the group in question turned at the end of the gallery and broke up, and Captain Musgrave came back to them in hasty strides.

"Look here," he cried, speaking naturally enough, though they fancied his colour was changed. "I'm awfully sorry, Mr. Granby, but I find I can't come north with you tomorrow. Of course, you will take the car all the same. Please do; I shan't want it. I—I have to be in London for some days. Take a friend with you if you like."

"My friend, Father Brown—" began the lawyer.

"If Captain Musgrave is really so kind," said Father Brown gravely. "I may explain that I have some status in Mr. Granby's inquiry, and it would be a great relief to my mind if I could go."

Which was how it came about that a very elegant car, with an equally elegant chauffeur, shot north the next day over the Yorkshire moors, bearing the incongruous burden of a priest who looked rather like a black bundle, and a lawyer who had the habit of running about on his feet instead of racing on somebody else's wheels.

They broke their journey very agreeably in one of the great dales of the West Riding, dining and sleeping at a comfortable inn, and starting early next day, began to run along the Northumbrian coast till they reached a country that was a maze of sand dunes and rank sea meadows, somewhere in the heart of which lay the old Border castle which had remained so unique and yet so secretive a monument of the old Border wars. They found it at last, by following a path running beside a long arm of the sea that ran inland, and turned eventually into a sort of rude canal ending in the moat of the castle. The castle really was a castle, of the square, embattled plan that the Normans built everywhere from Galilee to the Grampians. It did really and truly have a portcullis and a drawbridge, and they were very realistically reminded of the fact by an accident that delayed their entrance.

They waded amid long coarse grass and thistle to the bank of the moat which ran in a ribbon of black with dead leaves and scum upon it, like ebony inlaid with a pattern of gold. Barely a yard or two beyond the black ribbon was the other green bank and the big stone pillars of the gateway. But so little, it would seem, had this lonely fastness been approached from outside that when the impatient Granby halloed across to the dim figures behind the portcullis, they seemed to have considerable difficulty even in lowering the great rusty drawbridge. It started on its way, turning over like a great falling tower above them, and then stuck, sticking out in mid-air at a threatening angle.

The impatient Granby, dancing upon the bank, called out to his companion:

"Oh, I can't stand these stick-in-the-mud ways! Why, it'd be less trouble to jump."

And with characteristic impetuosity he did jump, landing with a slight stagger in safety on the inner shore. Father Brown's short legs were not adapted to jumping. But his temper was more adapted than most people's to falling with a splash into very muddy water. By the promptitude of his companion he escaped falling in very far. But as he was being hauled up the green, slimy bank, he stopped with bent head, peering at a particular point upon the grassy slope.

"Are you botanising?" asked Granby irritably. "We've got no time for you to collect rare plants after your last attempt as a diver among the wonders of the deep. Come on, muddy or no, we've got to present ourselves before the baronet."

When they had penetrated into the castle, they were received courteously enough by an old servant, the only one in sight, and after indicating their business were shown into a long oak-panelled room with latticed windows of antiquated pattern. Weapons of many different centuries hung in balanced patterns on the dark walls, and a complete suit of fourteenth-century armour stood like a sentinel beside the large fireplace. In another long room beyond could be seen, through the half-open door, the dark colours of the rows of family portraits.

"I feel as if I'd got into a novel instead of a house," said the lawyer. "I'd no idea anybody did really keep up the 'Mysteries of Udolpho' in this fashion."[4]

"Yes; the old gentleman certainly carries out his historical craze consistently," answered the priest; "and these

[4] *The Mysteries of Udolpho* is the title of a novel penned by the American novelist Ann Radcliffe in 1794.

things are not fakes, either. It's not done by somebody who thinks all medieval people lived at the same time. Sometimes they make up suits of armour out of different bits; but that suit all covered one man, and covered him very completely. You see it's the late sort of tilting-armour."

"I think he's a late sort of host, if it comes to that," grumbled Granby. "He's keeping us waiting the devil of a time."

"You must expect everything to go slowly in a place like this," said Father Brown. "I think it's very decent of him to see us at all: two total strangers come to ask him highly personal questions."

And, indeed, when the master of the house appeared they had no reason to complain of their reception; but rather became conscious of something genuine in the traditions of breeding and behaviour that could retain their native dignity without difficulty in that barbarous solitude, and after those long years of rustication and moping. The baronet did not seem either surprised or embarrassed at the rare visitation; though they suspected that he had not had a stranger in his house for a quarter of a life-time, he behaved as if he had been bowing out duchesses a moment before. He showed neither shyness nor impatience when they touched on the very private matter of their errand; after a little leisurely reflection he seemed to recognise their curiosity as justified under the circumstances. He was a thin, keen-looking old gentleman, with black eyebrows and a long chin, and though the carefully-curled hair he wore was undoubtedly a wig, he had the wisdom to wear the grey wig of an elderly man.

"As regards the question that immediately concerns you," he said, "the answer is very simple indeed. I do most certainly propose to hand on the whole of my property to my son, as my father handed it on to me; and nothing—I say advisedly, nothing—would induce me to take any other course."

"I am most profoundly grateful for the information," answered the lawyer. "But your kindness encourages me to say that you are putting it very strongly. I would not suggest that it is in the least likely that your son would do anything to make you doubt his fitness for the charge. Still, he might—"

"Exactly," said Sir John Musgrave dryly, "he might. It is rather an under-statement to say that he might. Will you be good enough to step into the next room with me for a moment."

He led them into the further gallery, of which they had already caught a glimpse, and gravely paused before a row of the blackened and lowering portraits.

"This is Sir Roger Musgrave," he said, pointing to a long-faced person in a black periwig. "He was one of the lowest liars and rascals in the rascally time of William of Orange, a traitor to two kings and something like the murderer of two wives. That is his father, Sir Robert, a perfectly honest old cavalier. That is his son, Sir James, one of the noblest of the Jacobite martyrs and one of the first men to attempt some reparation to the Church and the poor. Does it matter that the House of Musgrave, the power, the honour, the authority, descended from one good man to another good man through the interval of a bad one? Edward I governed England well. Edward III covered England with glory. And yet the second glory came from the first glory through the infamy and im-becility of Edward II, who fawned upon Gaveston and ran away from Bruce. Believe me, Mr. Granby, the greatness of a great house and history is something more than these accidental individuals who carry it on, even though they do not grace it. From father to son our heritage has come down, and from father to son it shall continue. You may assure yourselves, gentlemen, and you may assure my son, that I shall not leave my money to a home for lost cats. Musgrave shall leave it to Musgrave till the heavens fall."

"Yes," said Father Brown thoughtfully; "I see what you mean."

"And we shall be only too glad," said the solicitor, "to convey such a happy assurance to your son."

"You may convey the assurance," said their host gravely. "He is secure in any event of having the castle, the title, the land and the money. There is only a small and merely private addition to that arrangement. Under no circumstances whatever will I ever [see or] speak to him as long as I live."

The lawyer remained in the same respectful attitude, but he was now respectfully staring.

"Why, what on earth has he—"

"I am a private gentleman," said Musgrave, "as well as the custodian of a great inheritance. And my son did something so horrible that he has ceased to be—I will not say a gentleman—but even a human being. It is the worst crime in the world. Do you remember what Douglas said when Marmion, his guest, offered to shake hands with him?"

"Yes," said Father Brown.

"'My castles are my king's alone, from turret to foundation stone,'" said Musgrave. "'The hand of Douglas is his own.'"

He turned towards the other room and showed his rather dazed visitors back into it.

"I hope you will take some refreshment," he said, in the same equable fashion. "If you have any doubt about your movements, I should be delighted to offer you the hospitality of the castle for the night."

"Thank you, Sir John," said the priest in a dull voice, "but I think we had better go."

"I will have the bridge lowered at once," said their host; and in a few moments the creaking of that huge and absurdly antiquated apparatus filled the castle like the grinding of a mill. Rusty as it was, however, it worked successfully this time, and they found themselves standing once more on the grassy bank beyond the moat.

Granby was suddenly shaken by a shudder.

"What in hell was it that his son did?" he cried.

Father Brown made no answer. But when they had driven off again in their car and pursued their journey to a village not far off, called Graystones, where they alighted at the inn of the Seven Stars, the lawyer learned with a little mild surprise that the priest did not propose to travel much farther; in other words, that he had apparently every intention of remaining in the neighbourhood.

"I cannot bring myself to leave it like this," he said gravely. "I will send back the car, and you, of course, may very naturally want to go with it. Your question is answered; it is simply whether your firm can afford to lend money on young Musgrave's prospects. But my question isn't answered; it is whether he is a fit husband for Betty. I must try to discover whether he's really done something dreadful, or whether it's the delusion of an old lunatic."

"But," objected the lawyer, "if you want to find out about him, why don't you go after him? Why should you hang about in this desolate hole where he hardly ever comes?"

"What would be the use of my going after him?" asked the other. "There's no sense in going up to a fashionable young man in Bond Street and saying: 'Excuse me, but have you committed a crime too horrible for a human being?' If he's bad enough to do it, he's certainly bad enough to deny it. And we don't even know what it is. No, there's only one man that knows, and may tell, in some further outburst of dignified eccentricity. I'm going to keep near him for the present."

And in truth Father Brown did keep near the eccentric baronet, and did actually meet him on more than one occasion, with the utmost politeness on both sides. For the baronet, in spite of his years, was very vigorous and a great walker, and could often be seen stumping through the village, and along the country lanes. Only the day after their arrival, Father Brown, coming out of the inn on to the cobbled market-place, saw the dark and distinguished figure stride past in the direction of the post office. He was very quietly dressed in black, but his strong face was even more arresting in the strong sunlight; with his silvery hair, swarthy eyebrows and long chin, he had something of a reminiscence of Henry Irving, or some other famous actor. In spite of his hoary hair, his figure as well as his face suggested strength, and he carried his stick more like a cudgel than a crutch. He saluted the priest, and spoke with the same air of coming fearlessly to the point which had marked his revelations of yesterday.

"If you are still interested in my son," he said, using the term with an icy indifference, "you will not see very much of him. He has just left the country. Between ourselves, I might say fled the country."

"Indeed," said Father Brown with a grave stare.

"Some people I never heard of, called Grunov, have been pestering me, of all people, about his whereabouts," said Sir John; "and I've just come in to send off a wire to tell them that, so far as I know, he's living in the Poste Restante, Riga.[5] Even that has been a nuisance. I came

[5] His mail is to be held at the central post office in Riga (the capital of Latvia).

in yesterday to do it, but was five minutes too late for the post office. Are you staying long? I hope you will pay me another visit."

When the priest recounted to the lawyer his little interview with old Musgrave in the village, the lawyer was both puzzled and interested. "Why has the Captain bolted?" he asked. "Who are the other people who want him? Who on earth are the Grunovs?"

"For the first, I don't know," replied Father Brown. "Possibly his mysterious sin has come to light. I should rather guess that the other people are blackmailing him about it. For the third, I think I do know. That horrible fat woman with yellow hair is called Madame Grunov, and that little man passes as her husband."

The next day Father Brown came in rather wearily, and threw down his black bundle of an umbrella with the air of a pilgrim laying down his staff. He had an air of some depression. But it was as it was so often in his criminal investigations. It was not the depression of failure, but the depression of success.

"It's rather a shock," he said in a dull voice; "but I ought to have guessed it. I ought to have guessed it when I first went in and saw the thing standing there."

"When you saw what?" asked Granby impatiently.

"When I saw there was only one suit of armour," answered Father Brown. There was a silence during which the lawyer only stared at his friend, and then the friend resumed.

"Only the other day I was just going to tell my niece that there are two types of men who can laugh when they are alone. One might almost say the man who does it is either very good or very bad. You see, he is either confiding the joke to God or confiding it to the Devil. But anyhow he has an inner life. Well, there really is a kind of man who confides the joke to the Devil. He does not mind if nobody sees the joke; if nobody can safely be allowed even to know the joke. The joke is enough in itself, if it is sufficiently sinister and malignant."

"But what are you talking about?" demanded Granby. "Whom are you talking about? Which of them, I mean? Who is this person who is having a sinister joke with his Satanic Majesty?"

Father Brown looked across at him with a ghastly smile.

"Ah," he said, "that's the joke."

There was another silence, but this time the silence seemed to be rather full and oppressive than merely empty; it seemed to settle down on them like the twilight that was gradually turning from dusk to dark. Father Brown went on speaking in a level voice, sitting stolidly with his elbows on the table.

"I've been looking up the Musgrave family," he said. "They are vigorous and long-lived stock, and even in the ordinary way I should think you would wait a good time for your money."

"We're quite prepared for that," answered the solicitor; "but anyhow it can't last indefinitely. The old man is nearly eighty, though he still walks about, and the people at the inn here laugh and say they don't believe he will ever die."

Father Brown jumped up with one of his rare but rapid movements, but remained with his hands on the table, leaning forward and looking his friend in the face.

"That's it," he cried in a low but excited voice. "That's the only problem. That's the only real difficulty. How will he die? How on earth is he to die?"

"What on earth do you mean?" asked Granby.

"I mean," came the voice of the priest out of the darkening room, "that I know the crime that James Musgrave committed."

His tones had such a chill in them that Granby could hardly repress a shiver; he murmured a further question.

"It was really the worst crime in the world," said Father Brown. "At least, many communities and civilisations have accounted it so. It was always from the earliest times marked out in tribe and village for tremendous punishment. But anyhow, I know now what young Musgrave really did and why he did it."

"And what did he do?" asked the lawyer.

"He killed his father," answered the priest.

The lawyer in his turn rose from his seat and gazed across the table with wrinkled brows.

"But his father is at the castle," he cried in sharp tones.

"His father is in the moat," said the priest, "and I was a fool not to have known it from the first when something bothered me about that suit of armour. Don't you remember the look of that room? How very carefully it was arranged and decorated? There were two crossed battle-axes hung on one side of the fire-place, two crossed battle-axes on the other. There was a round Scottish shield on one wall, a round Scottish shield on the other. And there was a stand of armour guarding one side of the hearth, and an empty space on the other. Nothing will make me believe that a man who arranged all the rest of that room with that exaggerated symmetry left that one feature of it lopsided. There was almost certainly another man in armour. And what has become of him?"

He paused a moment, and then went on in a more matter-of-fact tone; "When you come to think of it, it's a very good plan for a murder, and meets the permanent problem of the disposal of the body. The body could stand inside that complete tilting-armour for hours, or even days, while servants came and went, until the murderer could simply drag it out in the dead of night and lower it into the moat, without even crossing the bridge. And then what a good chance he ran! As soon as the body was at all decayed in the stagnant water there would sooner or later be nothing but a skeleton in fourteenth-century armour, a thing very likely to be found in the moat of an old Border castle. It was unlikely that anybody would look for anything there, but if they did, that would soon be all they would find. And I got some confirmation of that. That was when you said I was looking for a rare plant; it was a plant in a good many senses, if you'll excuse the jest. I saw the marks of two feet sunk so deep into the solid bank I was sure that the man was either very heavy or was carrying something very heavy. Also, by the way, there's another moral from that little incident when I made my celebrated graceful and cat-like leap."

"My brain is rather reeling," said Granby, "but I begin to have some notion of what all this nightmare is about. What about you and your cat-like leap?"

"At the post office to-day," said Father Brown, "I casually confirmed the statement the baronet made to me yesterday, that he had been there just after closing-time on the day previous—that is, not only on the very day we arrived, but at the very time we arrived. Don't you see what that means? It means that he was actually out when we called, and came back while we were waiting; and that was why we had to wait so long. And when I saw that, I suddenly saw a picture that told the whole story."

"Well," asked the other impatiently, "and what about it?"

"An old man of eighty can walk," said Father Brown. "An old man can even walk a good deal, pottering about in country lanes. But an old man can't jump. He would be an even less graceful jumper than I was. Yet, if the baronet came back while we were waiting, he must have come in as we came in—by jumping the moat—for the bridge wasn't lowered till later. I rather guess he had hampered it himself to delay inconvenient visitors, to judge by the rapidity with which it was repaired. But that doesn't matter. When I saw that fancy picture of the black figure with the grey hair taking a flying leap across the moat I knew instantly that it was a young man dressed up as an old man. And there you have the whole story."

"You mean," said Granby slowly, "that this pleasing youth killed his father, hid the corpse first in the armour and then in the moat, disguised himself and so on?"

"They happened to be almost exactly alike," said the priest. "You could see from the family portraits how strong the likeness ran. And then you talk of his disguising himself. But in a sense everybody's dress is a disguise. The old man disguised himself in a wig, and the young man in a foreign beard. When he shaved and put the wig on his cropped head he was exactly like his father, with a little make-up. Of course, you understand now why he was so very polite about getting you to come up next day here by car. It was because he himself was coming up that night by train. He got in front of you, committed his crime, assumed his disguise, and was ready for the legal negotiations."

"Ah," said Granby thoughtfully, "the legal negotiations! You mean, of course, that the real old baronet would have negotiated very differently."

"He would have told you plainly that the Captain would never get a penny," said Father Brown. "The plot, queer as it sounds, was really the only way of preventing his telling you so. But I want you to appreciate the cunning of what the fellow did tell you. His plan answered several purposes at once. He was being blackmailed by these Russians for some villainy; I suspect for treason during the war. He escaped from them at a stroke, and probably sent them chasing off to Riga after him. But the most beautiful refinement of all was that theory he enunciated about recognising his son as an heir, but not as a human being. Don't you see that while it secured the *post obit*, it also provided some sort of answer to what would soon be the greatest difficulty of all?"

"I see several difficulties," said Granby; "which one do you mean?"

"I mean that if the son was not even disinherited, it would look rather odd that the father and son never met. The theory of a private repudiation answered that. So there only remained one difficulty, as I say, which is probably perplexing the gentleman now. How on earth is the old man to die?"

"I know how he ought to die," said Granby.

Father Brown seemed to be a little bemused, and went on in a more abstracted fashion.

"And yet there is something more in it than that," he said. "There was something about that theory that he liked in a way that is more—well, more theoretical. It gave him an insane intellectual pleasure to tell you in one character that he had committed a crime in another character—when he really had. That is what I mean by the infernal irony; by the joke shared with the Devil. Shall I tell you something that sounds like what they call a paradox? Sometimes it is a joy in the very heart of hell to tell the truth. And above all, to tell it so that everybody misunderstands it. That is why he liked that antic of pretending to be somebody else, and then painting himself as black—as he was. And that was why my niece heard him laughing to himself all alone in the picture gallery."

Granby gave a slight start, like a person brought back to common things with a bump.

"Your niece," he cried. "Didn't her mother want her to marry Musgrave? A question of wealth and position, I suppose."

"Yes," said Father Brown dryly; "her mother was all in favour of a prudent marriage."

"You shall not kill."

The Sign of the Broken Sword

The thousand arms of the forest were grey, and its million
fingers silver. In a sky of dark green-blue-like slate the stars
were bleak and brilliant like splintered ice. All that thickly
wooded and sparsely tenanted countryside was stiff with
a bitter and brittle frost. The black hollows between the
trunks of the trees looked like bottomless, black caverns
of that Scandinavian hell, a hell of incalculable cold.[1]
Even the square stone tower of the church looked northern to the point of heathenry, as if it were some barbaric
tower among the sea rocks of Iceland. It was a queer night
for anyone to explore a churchyard. But, on the other
hand, perhaps it was worth exploring. It rose abruptly
out of the ashen wastes of forest in a sort of hump or
shoulder of green turf that looked grey in the starlight.
Most of the graves were on a slant, and the path leading
up to the church was as steep as a staircase. On the top
of the hill, in the one flat and prominent place, was the
monument for which the place was famous. It contrasted
strangely with the featureless graves all round, for it was the

"The Sign of the Broken Sword" first appeared in America in the *Saturday
Evening Post*, January 7, 1911.
[1] The hell referred to is Niflheim ("mist-home"), the icy netherworld of
Norse mythology.

work of one of the greatest sculptors of modern Europe; and yet his fame was at once forgotten in the fame of the man whose image he had made. It showed, by touches of the small silver pencil of starlight, the massive metal figure of a soldier recumbent, the strong hands sealed in an ever-lasting worship, the great head pillowed upon a gun. The venerable face was bearded, or rather whiskered, in the old, heavy Colonel Newcome fashion. The uniform, though suggested with the few strokes of simplicity, was that of modern war. By his right side lay a sword, of which the tip was broken off; on the left side lay a Bible. On glowing summer afternoons wagonettes came full of Americans and cultured suburbans to see the sepulchre; but even then they felt the vast forest land with its one dumpy dome of churchyard and church as a place oddly dumb and neglected. In this freezing darkness of mid-winter one would think he might be left alone with the stars. Never-theless, in the stillness of those stiff woods a wooden gate creaked, and two dim figures dressed in black climbed up the little path to the tomb.

So faint was that frigid starlight that nothing could have been traced about them except that while they both wore black, one man was enormously big, and the other (perhaps by contrast) almost startlingly small. They went up to the great graven tomb of the historic warrior, and stood for a few minutes staring at it. There was no human, perhaps no living, thing for a wide circle; and a morbid fancy might well have wondered if they were human themselves. In any case, the beginning of their conversa-tion might have seemed strange. After the first silence the small man said to the other:

"Where does a wise man hide a pebble?"

And the tall man answered in a low voice: "On the beach."

The small man nodded, and after a short silence said: "Where does a wise man hide a leaf?"

And the other answered: "In the forest."

There was another stillness, and then the tall man resumed: "Do you mean that when a wise man has to hide a real diamond he has been known to hide it among sham ones?"

"No, no," said the little man with a laugh, "we will let bygones be bygones."

He stamped his cold feet for a second or two, and then said: "I'm not thinking of that at all, but of something else; something rather peculiar. Just strike a match, will you?"

The big man fumbled in his pocket, and soon a scratch and a flare painted gold the whole flat side of the monument. On it was cut in black letters the well-known words which so many Americans had reverently read: "Sacred to the Memory of General Sir Arthur St. Clare, Hero and Martyr, who Always Vanquished his Enemies and Always Spared Them, and Was Treacherously Slain by Them at Last. May God in Whom he Trusted both Reward and Revenge him."

The match burnt the big man's fingers, blackened, and dropped. He was about to strike another, but his small companion stopped him. "That's all right, Flambeau, old man; I saw what I wanted. Or, rather, I didn't see what I didn't want. And now we must walk a mile and a half along the road to the next inn, and I will try to tell you all about it. For Heaven knows a man should have a fire and ale when he dares tell such a story."

They descended the precipitous path, they relatched the rusty gate, and set off at a stamping, ringing walk down the frozen forest road. They had gone a full quarter of a mile before the smaller man spoke again. He said: "Yes; the wise man hides a pebble on the beach. But what does he do if there is no beach? Do you know anything of that great St. Clare trouble?"

"I know nothing about English generals, Father Brown," answered the large man, laughing, "though a little about English policemen. I only know that you have dragged me a precious long dance to all the shrines of this fellow, whoever he is. One would think he got buried in six different places. I've seen a memorial to General St. Clare in Westminster Abbey. I've seen a ramping equestrian statue of General St. Clare on the Embankment. I've seen a medallion of St. Clare in the street he was born in, and another in the street he lived in; and now you drag me after dark to his coffin in the village churchyard. I am beginning to be a bit tired of his magnificent personality, especially as I don't in the least know who he was. What are you hunting for in all these crypts and effigies?"

"I am only looking for one word," said Father Brown. "A word that isn't there."

"Well," asked Flambeau; "are you going to tell me anything about it?"

"I must divide it into two parts," remarked the priest. "First there is what everybody knows; and then there is what I know. Now, what everybody knows is short and plain enough. It is also entirely wrong."

"Right you are," said the big man called Flambeau cheerfully. "Let's begin at the wrong end. Let's begin with what everybody knows, which isn't true."

"If not wholly untrue, it is at least very inadequate," continued Brown; "for in point of fact, all that the public knows amounts precisely to this: The public knows that Arthur St. Clare was a great and successful English general. It knows that after splendid yet careful campaigns both in India and Africa he was in command against Brazil when the great Brazilian patriot Olivier issued his ultimatum. It knows that on that occasion St. Clare with a very small force attacked Olivier with a very large one, and was captured after heroic resistance. And it knows that after his capture, and to the abhorrence of the civilised world, St. Clare was hanged on the nearest tree. He was found swinging there after the Brazilians had retired, with his broken sword hung round his neck."

"And that popular story is untrue?" suggested Flambeau.

"No," said his friend quietly, "that story is quite true, so far as it goes."

"Well, I think it goes far enough!" said Flambeau; "but if the popular story is true, what is the mystery?"

They had passed many hundreds of grey and ghostly trees before the little priest answered. Then he bit his finger reflectively and said: "Why, the mystery is a mystery of psychology. Or, rather, it is a mystery of two psychologies. In that Brazilian business two of the most famous men of modern history acted flat against their characters. Mind you, Olivier and St. Clare were both heroes—the old thing, and no mistake; it was like the fight between Hector and Achilles. Now, what would you say to an affair in which Achilles was timid and Hector was treacherous?"

"Go on," said the large man impatiently as the other bit his finger again.

"Sir Arthur St. Clare was a soldier of the old religious type—the type that saved us during the Mutiny," continued Brown. "He was always more for duty than for dash; and with all his personal courage was decidedly a prudent commander, particularly indignant at any needless waste of soldiers. Yet in this last battle he attempted something that a baby could see was absurd. One need not be a strategist to see it was as wild as wind; just as one need not be a strategist to keep out of the way of a motor-bus. Well, that is the first mystery; what had become of the English general's head? The second riddle is, what had become of the Brazilian general's heart? President Olivier might be called a visionary or a nuisance; but even his enemies admitted that he was magnanimous to the point of knight errantry. Almost every other prisoner he had ever captured had been set free or even loaded with benefits. Men who had really wronged him came away touched by his simplicity and sweetness. Why the deuce should he diabolically revenge himself only once in his life; and that for the one particular blow that could not have hurt him? Well, there you have it. One of the wisest men in the world acted like an idiot for no reason. One of the best men in the world acted like a fiend for no reason. That's the long and the short of it; and I leave it to you, my boy."

"No, you don't," said the other with a snort. "I leave it to you; and you jolly well tell me all about it."

"Well," resumed Father Brown, "it's not fair to say that the public impression is just what I've said, without adding that two things have happened since. I can't say they threw a new light; for nobody can make sense of them. But they threw a new kind of darkness; they threw the darkness in new directions. The first was this. The family physician of the St. Clares quarrelled with that family, and began publishing a violent series of articles, in which he said that the late general was a religious maniac; but as far as the tale went, this seemed to mean little more than a religious man. Anyhow, the story fizzled out. Everyone knew, of course, that St. Clare had some of the eccentricities of puritan piety. The second incident was much more arresting. In the luckless and unsupported regiment which made that rash attempt at the Black River there was a certain Captain Keith, who was at that time engaged to St. Clare's daughter, and who afterwards married her.

He was one of those who were captured by Olivier, and, like all the rest except the general, appears to have been bounteously treated and promptly set free. Some twenty years afterwards this man, then Lieutenant-Colonel Keith, published a sort of autobiography called 'A British Officer in Burmah and Brazil.' In the place where the reader looks eagerly for some account of the mystery of St. Clare's disaster may be found the following words: 'Everywhere else in this book I have narrated things exactly as they occurred, holding as I do the old-fashioned opinion that the glory of England is old enough to take care of itself. The exception I shall make is in this matter of the defeat by the Black River; and my reasons, though private, are honourable and compelling. I will, however, add this in justice to the memories of two distinguished men. General St. Clare has been accused of incapacity on this occasion; I can at least testify that this action, properly understood, was one of the most brilliant and sagacious of his life. President Olivier by similar report is charged with savage injustice. I think it due to the honour of an enemy to say that he acted on this occasion with even more than his characteristic good feeling. To put the matter popularly, I can assure my countrymen that St. Clare was by no means such a fool nor Olivier such a brute as he looked. This is all I have to say; nor shall any earthly consideration induce me to add a word to it.' "

A large frozen moon like a lustrous snowball began to show through the tangle of twigs in front of them, and by its light the narrator had been able to refresh his memory of Captain Keith's text from a scrap of printed paper. As he folded it up and put it back in his pocket Flambeau threw up his hand with a French gesture.

"Wait a bit, wait a bit," he cried excitedly. "I believe I can guess it at the first go."

He strode on, breathing hard, his black head and bull neck forward, like a man winning a walking race. The little priest, amused and interested, had some trouble in trotting beside him. Just before them the trees fell back a little to left and right, and the road swept downwards across a clear, moonlit valley, till it dived again like a rabbit into the wall of another wood. The entrance to the farther forest looked small and round, like the black hole of a remote railway tunnel. But it was within some hundred yards, and gaped like a cavern before Flambeau spoke again.

"I've got it," he cried at last, slapping his thigh with his great hand. "Four minutes' thinking, and I can tell your whole story myself."

"All right," assented his friend. "You tell it."

Flambeau lifted his head, but lowered his voice. "General Sir Arthur St. Clare," he said, "came of a family in which madness was hereditary; and his whole aim was to keep this from his daughter, and even, if possible, from his future son-in-law. Rightly or wrongly, he thought the final collapse was close, and resolved on suicide. Yet ordinary suicide would blazon the very idea he dreaded. As the campaign approached the clouds came thicker on his brain; and at last in a mad moment he sacrificed his public duty to his private. He rushed rashly into battle, hoping to fall by the first shot. When he found that he had only attained capture and discredit, the sealed bomb in his brain burst, and he broke his own sword and hanged himself."

He stared firmly at the grey façade of forest in front of him, with the one black gap in it, like the mouth of the grave, into which their path plunged. Perhaps something menacing in the road thus suddenly swallowed reinforced his vivid vision of the tragedy, for he shuddered.

"A horrid story," he said.

"A horrid story," repeated the priest with bent head. "But not the real story."

Then he threw back his head with a sort of despair and cried: "Oh, I wish it had been."

The tall Flambeau faced round and stared at him.

"Yours is a clean story," cried Father Brown, deeply moved. "A sweet, pure, honest story, as open and white as that moon. Madness and despair are innocent enough. There are worse things, Flambeau."

Flambeau looked up wildly at the moon thus invoked; and from where he stood one black tree-bough curved across it exactly like a devil's horn.

"Father—Father," cried Flambeau with the French gesture and stepping yet more rapidly forward, "do you mean it was worse than that?"

"Worse than that," said the other like a grave echo. And they plunged into the black cloister of the woodland, which ran by them in a dim tapestry of trunks, like one of the dark corridors in a dream.

They were soon in the most secret entrails of the wood, and felt close about them foliage that they could not see, when the priest said again:

"Where does a wise man hide a leaf? In the forest. But what does he do if there is no forest?"

"Well, well," cried Flambeau irritably, "what does he do?"

"He grows a forest to hide it in," said the priest in an obscure voice. "A fearful sin."

"Look here," cried his friend impatiently, for the dark wood and the dark saying got a little on his nerves; "will you tell me this story or not? What other evidence is there to go on?"

"There are three more bits of evidence," said the other, "that I have dug up in holes and corners; and I will give them in logical rather than chronological order. First of all, of course, our authority for the issue and event of the battle is in Olivier's own dispatches, which are lucid enough. He was entrenched with two or three regiments on the heights that swept down to the Black River, on the other side of which was lower and more marshy ground. Beyond this again was gently rising country, on which was the first English outpost, supported by others which lay, however, considerably in its rear. The British forces as a whole were greatly superior in numbers; but this particular regiment was just far enough from its base to make Olivier consider the project of crossing the river to cut it off. By sunset, however, he had decided to retain his own position, which was a specially strong one. At daybreak next morning he was thunderstruck to see that this stray handful of English, entirely unsupported from their rear, had flung themselves across the river, half by a bridge to the right, and the other half by a ford higher up, and were massed upon the marshy bank below him.

"That they should attempt an attack with such numbers against such a position was incredible enough; but Olivier noticed something yet more extraordinary. For instead of attempting to seize more solid ground, this mad regiment, having put the river in its rear by one wild charge, did nothing more, but stuck there in the mire like flies in treacle. Needless to say, the Brazilians blew great gaps in them with artillery, which they could only return with spirited but lessening rifle fire. Yet they never broke; and Olivier's curt account ends with a strong tribute of admiration for the mystic valour of these imbeciles. 'Our line then advanced finally,' writes Olivier, 'and drove them into the river; we captured General St. Clare himself and several other officers. The colonel and the major had both fallen in the battle. I cannot resist saying that few finer

sights can have been seen in history than the last stand of
this extraordinary regiment; wounded officers picking up
the rifles of dead soldiers, and the general himself facing us
on horseback bareheaded and with a broken sword.' On
what happened to the general afterwards Olivier is as silent
as Captain Keith."

"Well," grunted Flambeau, "get on to the next bit of
evidence."

"The next evidence," said Father Brown, "took some
time to find, but it will not take long to tell. I found at
last in an almshouse down in the Lincolnshire Fens an old
soldier who not only was wounded at the Black River,
but had actually knelt beside the colonel of the regiment
when he died. This latter was a certain Colonel Clancy,
a big bull of an Irishman; and it would seem that he died
almost as much of rage as of bullets. He, at any rate, was
not responsible for that ridiculous raid; it must have been
imposed on him by the general. His last edifying words,
according to my informant, were these: 'And there goes
the damned old donkey with the end of his sword knocked
off. I wish it was his head.' You will remark that everyone
seems to have noticed this detail about the broken sword
blade, though most people regard it somewhat more reverently than did the late Colonel Clancy. And now for the
third fragment."

Their path through the woodland began to go upward,
and the speaker paused a little for breath before he went
on. Then he continued in the same business-like tone:

"Only a month or two ago a certain Brazilian official
died in England, having quarrelled with Olivier and left his
country. He was a well-known figure both here and on the
Continent, a Spaniard named Espado; I knew him myself,
a yellow-faced old dandy, with a hooked nose. For various
private reasons I had permission to see the documents he

had left; he was a Catholic, of course, and I had been with him towards the end. There was nothing of his that lit up any corner of the black St. Clare business, except five or six common exercise books filled with the diary of some English soldier. I can only suppose that it was found by the Brazilians on one of those that fell. Anyhow, it stopped abruptly the night before the battle.

"But the account of that last day in the poor fellow's life was certainly worth reading. I have it on me; but it's too dark to read it here, and I will give you a résumé. The first part of that entry is full of jokes, evidently flung about among the men, about somebody called the Vulture. It does not seem as if this person, whoever he was, was one of themselves, nor even an Englishman; neither is he exactly spoken of as one of the enemy. It sounds rather as if he were some local go-between and non-combatant; perhaps a guide or a journalist. He has been closeted with old Colonel Clancy; but is more often seen talking to the major. Indeed, the major is somewhat prominent in this soldier's narrative; a lean, dark-haired man, apparently, of the name of Murray—a north of Ireland man and a Puritan. There are continual jests about the contrast between this Ulsterman's austerity and the conviviality of Colonel Clancy. There is also some joke about the Vulture wearing bright-coloured clothes.

"But all these levities are scattered by what may well be called the note of a bugle. Behind the English camp and almost parallel to the river ran one of the few great roads of that district. Westward the road curved round towards the river, which it crossed by the bridge before mentioned. To the east the road swept backwards into the wilds, and some two miles along it was the next English outpost. From this direction there came along the road that evening a glitter and clatter of light cavalry, in which even the simple diarist could recognise with astonishment the general with his staff. He rode the great white horse which you have seen so often in illustrated papers and Academy pictures; and you may be sure that the salute they gave him was not merely ceremonial. He, at least, wasted no time on ceremony, but, springing from the saddle immediately, mixed with the group of officers, and fell into emphatic though confidential speech. What struck our friend the diarist most was his special disposition to discuss matters with Major Murray; but, indeed, such a selection, so long as it was not marked, was in no way unnatural. The two men were made for sympathy; they were men who 'read their Bibles'; they were both the old Evangelical type of officer. However this may be, it is certain that when the general mounted again he was still talking earnestly to Murray; and that as he walked his horse slowly down the road towards the river, the tall Ulsterman still walked by his bridle rein in earnest debate. The soldiers watched the two until they vanished behind a clump of trees where the road turned towards the river. The colonel had gone back to his tent, and the men to their pickets; the man with the diary lingered for another four minutes, and saw a marvellous sight.

"The great white horse which had marched slowly down the road, as it had marched in so many processions, flew back, galloping up the road towards them as if it were mad to win a race. At first they thought it had run away with the man on its back; but they soon saw that the general, a fine rider, was himself urging it to full speed. Horse and man swept up to them like a whirlwind; and then, reining up the reeling charger, the general turned on them a face like flame, and called for the colonel like the trumpet that wakes the dead.

"I conceive that all the earthquake events of that catastrophe tumbled on top of each other rather like lumber in the minds of men such as our friend with the diary. With the dazed excitement of a dream, they found themselves falling—literally falling—into their ranks, and learned that an attack was to be led at once across the river. The general and the major, it was said, had found out something at the bridge, and there was only just time to strike for life. The major had gone back at once to call up the reserve along the road behind; it was doubtful if even with that prompt appeal help could reach them in time. But they must pass the stream that night, and seize the heights by morning. It is with the very stir and throb of that romantic nocturnal march that the diary suddenly ends."

Father Brown had mounted ahead; for the woodland path grew smaller, steeper, and more twisted, till they felt as if they were ascending a winding staircase. The priest's voice came from above out of the darkness.

"There was one other little and enormous thing. When the general urged them to their chivalric charge he half drew his sword from the scabbard; and then, as if ashamed of such melodrama, thrust it back again. The sword again, you see."

A half-light broke through the network of boughs above them, flinging the ghost of a net about their feet; for they were mounting again to the faint luminosity of the naked night. Flambeau felt truth all round him as an atmosphere, but not as an idea. He answered with bewildered brain: "Well, what's the matter with the sword? Officers generally have swords, don't they?"

"They are not often mentioned in modern war," said the other dispassionately; "but in this affair one falls over the blessed sword everywhere."

"Well, what is there in that?" growled Flambeau; "it was a twopence coloured sort of incident; the old man's blade breaking in his last battle. Anyone might bet the papers would get hold of it, as they have. On all these tombs and things it's shown broken at the point. I hope you haven't dragged me through this Polar expedition merely because two men with an eye for a picture saw St. Clare's broken sword."

"No," cried Father Brown, with a sharp voice like a pistol shot; "but who saw his unbroken sword?"

"What do you mean?" cried the other, and stood still under the stars. They had come abruptly out of the grey gates of the wood.

"I say, who saw his unbroken sword?" repeated Father Brown obstinately. "Not the writer of the diary, anyhow; the general sheathed it in time."

Flambeau looked about him in the moonlight, as a man struck blind might look in the sun; and his friend went on, for the first time with eagerness:

"Flambeau," he cried, "I cannot prove it, even after hunting through the tombs. But I am sure of it. Let me add just one more tiny fact that tips the whole thing over. The colonel, by a strange chance, was one of the first struck by a bullet. He was struck long before the troops came to close quarters. But he saw St. Clare's sword broken. Why was it broken? How was it broken? My friend, it was broken before the battle."

"Oh!" said his friend, with a sort of forlorn jocularity; "and pray where is the other piece?"

"I can tell you," said the priest promptly. "In the northeast corner of the cemetery of the Protestant Cathedral at Belfast."

"Indeed?" inquired the other. "Have you looked for it?"

"I couldn't," replied Brown, with frank regret. "There's a great marble monument on top of it; a monument to the heroic Major Murray, who fell fighting gloriously at the famous Battle of the Black River."

Flambeau seemed suddenly galvanised into existence. "You mean," he cried hoarsely, "that General St. Clare hated Murray, and murdered him on the field of battle because—"

"You are still full of good and pure thoughts," said the other. "It was worse than that."

"Well," said the large man, "my stock of evil imagination is used up."

The priest seemed really doubtful where to begin, and at last he said again:

"Where would a wise man hide a leaf? In the forest."

The other did not answer.

"If there were no forest, he would make a forest. And if he wished to hide a dead leaf, he would make a dead forest."

There was still no reply, and the priest added still more mildly and quietly:

"And if a man had to hide a dead body, he would make a field of dead bodies to hide it in."

Flambeau began to stamp forward with an intolerance of delay in time or space; but Father Brown went on as if he were continuing the last sentence:

"Sir Arthur St. Clare, as I have already said, was a man who read his Bible. That was what was the matter with him. When will people understand that it is useless for a man to read his Bible unless he also reads everybody else's Bible? A printer reads a Bible for misprints. A Mormon reads his Bible, and finds polygamy; a Christian Scientist reads his, and finds we have no arms and legs. St. Clare was an old Anglo-Indian Protestant soldier. Now, just think what that might mean; and, for Heaven's sake, don't cant about it. It might mean a man physically formidable living under a tropic sun in an Oriental society, and soaking himself without sense or guidance in an Oriental

Book. Of course, he read the Old Testament rather than the New. Of course, he found in the Old Testament anything that he wanted—lust, tyranny, treason. Oh, I dare say he was honest, as you call it. But what is the good of a man being honest in his worship of dishonesty?

"In each of the hot and secret countries to which the man went he kept a harem, he tortured witnesses, he amassed shameful gold; but certainly he would have said with steady eyes that he did it to the glory of the Lord. My own theology is sufficiently expressed by asking which Lord? Anyhow, there is this about such evil, that it opens door after door in hell, and always into smaller and smaller chambers. This is the real case against crime, that a man does not become wilder and wilder, but only meaner and meaner. St. Clare was soon suffocated by difficulties of bribery and blackmail; and needed more and more cash. And by the time of the Battle of the Black River he had fallen from world to world to that place which Dante makes the lowest floor of the universe."

"What do you mean?" asked his friend again.

"I mean that," retorted the cleric, and suddenly pointed at a puddle sealed with ice that shone in the moon. "Do you remember whom Dante put in the last circle of ice?"

"The traitors," said Flambeau, and shuddered. As he looked around at the inhuman landscape of trees, with taunting and almost obscene outlines, he could almost fancy he was Dante, and the priest with the rivulet of a voice was, indeed, a Virgil leading him through a land of eternal sins.

The voice went on: "Olivier, as you know, was quixotic, and would not permit a secret service and spies. The thing, however, was done, like many other things, behind his back. It was managed by my old friend Espado; he was the bright-clad fop, whose hook nose got him called the

Vulture. Posing as a sort of philanthropist at the front, he felt his way through the English Army, and at last got his fingers on its one corrupt man—please God!—and that man at the top. St. Clare was in foul need of money, and mountains of it. The discredited family doctor was threatening those extraordinary exposures that afterwards began and were broken off; tales of monstrous and prehistoric things in Park Lane; things done by an English Evangelist that smelt like human sacrifice and hordes of slaves. Money was wanted, too, for his daughter's dowry; for to him the fame of wealth was as sweet as wealth itself. He snapped the last thread, whispered the word to Brazil, and wealth poured in from the enemies of England. But another man had talked to Espado the Vulture as well as he. Somehow the dark, grim young major from Ulster had guessed the hideous truth; and when they walked slowly together down that road towards the bridge Murray was telling the general that he must resign instantly, or be court-martialled and shot. The general temporised with him till they came to the fringe of tropic trees by the bridge; and there by the singing river and the sunlit palms (for I can see the picture) the general drew his sabre and plunged it through the body of the major."

The wintry road curved over a ridge in cutting frost, with cruel black shapes of bush and thicket; but Flambeau fancied that he saw beyond it faintly the edge of an aureole that was not starlight and moonlight, but some fire such as is made by men. He watched it as the tale drew to its close.

"St. Clare was a hell-hound, but he was a hound of breed. Never, I'll swear, was he so lucid and so strong as when poor Murray lay a cold lump at his feet. Never in all his triumphs, as Captain Keith said truly, was the great man so great as he was in this last world-despised defeat. He looked coolly at his weapon to wipe off the blood;

he saw the point he had planted between his victim's shoulders had broken off in the body. He saw quite calmly, as through a club windowpane, all that must follow. He saw that men must find the unaccountable corpse; must extract the unaccountable sword-point; must notice the unaccountable broken sword—or absence of sword. He had killed, but not silenced. But his imperious intellect rose against the facer; there was one way yet. He could make the corpse less unaccountable. He could create a hill of corpses to cover this one. In twenty minutes eight hundred English soldiers were marching down to their death."

The warmer glow behind the black winter wood grew richer and brighter, and Flambeau strode on to reach it. Father Brown also quickened his stride; but he seemed merely absorbed in his tale.

"Such was the valour of that English thousand, and such the genius of their commander, that if they had at once attacked the hill, even their mad march might have met some luck. But the evil mind that played with them like pawns had other aims and reasons. They must remain in the marshes by the bridge at least till British corpses should be a common sight there. Then for the last grand scene; the silver-haired soldier-saint would give up his shattered sword to save further slaughter. Oh, it was well organised for an impromptu. But I think (I cannot prove), I think that it was while they stuck there in the bloody mire that someone doubted—and someone guessed."

He was mute a moment, and then said: "There is a voice from nowhere that tells me the man who guessed was the lover ... the man to wed the old man's child."

"But what about Olivier and the hanging?" asked Flambeau.

"Olivier, partly from chivalry, partly from policy, seldom encumbered his march with captives," explained the narrator. "He released everybody in most cases. He released everybody in this case."

"Everybody but the general," said the tall man.

"Everybody," said the priest.

Flambeau knit his black brows. "I don't grasp it all yet," he said.

"There is another picture, Flambeau," said Brown in his more mystical undertone. "I can't prove it; but I can do more—I can see it. There is a camp breaking up on the bare, torrid hills at morning, and Brazilian uniforms massed in blocks and columns to march. There is the red shirt and long black beard of Olivier, which blows as he stands, his broad-brimmed hat in his hand. He is saying farewell to the great enemy he is setting free—the simple, snow-headed English veteran, who thanks him in the name of his men. The English remnant stand behind at attention; beside them are stores and vehicles for the retreat. The drums roll; the Brazilians are moving; the English are still like statues. So they abide till the last hum and flash of the enemy have faded from the tropic horizon. Then they alter their postures all at once, like dead men coming to life; they turn their fifty faces upon the general—faces not to be forgotten."

Flambeau gave a great jump. "Ah," he cried, "you don't mean—"

"Yes," said Father Brown in a deep, moving voice. "It was an English hand that put the rope round St. Clare's neck; I believe the hand that put the ring on his daughter's finger. They were English hands that dragged him up to the tree of shame; the hands of men that had adored him and followed him to victory. And they were English souls (God pardon and endure us all!) who stared at him swinging in that foreign sun on the green gallows of palm, and prayed in their hatred that he might drop off it into hell."

As the two topped the ridge there burst on them the strong scarlet light of a red-curtained English inn. It stood sideways in the road, as if standing aside in the amplitude of hospitality. Its three doors stood open with invitation; and even where they stood they could hear the hum and laughter of humanity happy for a night.

"I need not tell you more," said Father Brown. "They tried him in the wilderness and destroyed him; and then, for the honour of England and of his daughter, they took an oath to seal up for ever the story of the traitor's purse and the assassin's sword blade. Perhaps—Heaven help them—they tried to forget it. Let us try to forget it, anyhow; here is our inn."

"With all my heart," said Flambeau, and was just striding into the bright, noisy bar when he stepped back and almost fell on the road.

"Look there, in the devil's name!" he cried, and pointed rigidly at the square wooden sign that overhung the road. It showed dimly the crude shape of a sabre hilt and a shortened blade; and was inscribed in false archaic lettering, "The Sign of the Broken Sword."

"Were you not prepared?" asked Father Brown gently. "He is the god of this country; half the inns and parks and streets are named after him and his story."

"I thought we had done with the leper," cried Flambeau, and spat on the road.

"You will never have done with him in England," said the priest, looking down, "while brass is strong and stone abides. His marble statues will erect the souls of proud, innocent boys for centuries, his village tomb will smell of loyalty as of lilies. Millions who never knew him shall love him like a father—this man whom the last few that knew him dealt with like dung. He shall be a saint; and the truth shall never be told of him, because I have made up my mind at last. There is so much good and evil in breaking secrets, that I put my conduct to a test. All these newspapers will perish; the anti-Brazil boom is already over; Olivier is already honoured everywhere. But I told myself that if anywhere, by name, in metal or marble that will endure like the pyramids, Colonel Clancy, or Captain Keith, or President Olivier, or any innocent man was wrongly blamed, then I would speak. If it were only that St. Clare was wrongly praised, I would be silent. And I will."

They plunged into the red-curtained tavern, which was not only cosy, but even luxurious inside. On a table stood a silver model of the tomb of St. Clare, the silver head bowed, the silver sword broken. On the walls were coloured photographs of the same scene, and of the system of wagonettes that took tourists to see it. They sat down on the comfortable padded benches.

"Come, it's cold," cried Father Brown; "let's have some wine or beer."

"Or brandy," said Flambeau.

"You shall not commit adultery."

The Actor and the Alibi

Mr. Mundon Mandeville, the theatrical manager, walked briskly through the passages behind the scenes, or rather below the scenes. His attire was smart and festive, perhaps a little too festive; the flower in his buttonhole was festive; the very varnish on his boots was festive; but his face was not at all festive. He was a big, bull-necked, black-browed man, and at the moment his brow was blacker than usual. He had in any case, of course, the hundred botherations that besiege a man in such a position; and they ranged from large to small and from new to old. It annoyed him to pass through the passages where the old pantomime scenery was stacked; because he had successfully begun his career at that theatre with very popular pantomimes, and had since been induced to gamble in more serious and classical drama over which he had dropped a good deal of money. Hence, to see the Sapphire Gates of Blue-beard's Blue Palace, or portions of the Enchanted Grove of Golden Orange Trees, leaning up against the wall to be festooned with cobwebs or nibbled by mice, did not give him that soothing sense of a return to simplicity which we all ought to have when given a glimpse of that

"The Actor and the Alibi" first appeared in the March 1926 issue of *Cassell's Magazine*.

wonderland of our childhood. Nor had he any time to drop a tear where he had dropped the money, or to dream of this Paradise of Peter Pan; for he had been summoned hurriedly to settle a practical problem, not of the past but of the moment. It was the sort of thing that does sometimes happen in that strange world behind the scenes; but it was big enough to be serious. Miss Maroni, the talented young actress of Italian parentage, who had undertaken to act an important part in the play that was to be rehearsed that afternoon and performed that evening, had abruptly and even violently refused at the last moment to do anything of the kind. He had not even seen the exasperating lady yet; and as she had locked herself up in her dressing-room and defied the world through the door, it seemed unlikely, for the present, that he would. Mr. Mundon Mandeville was sufficiently British to explain it by murmuring that all foreigners were mad; but the thought of his good fortune in inhabiting the only sane island of the planet did not suffice to soothe him any more than the memory of the Enchanted Grove. All these things, and many more, were annoying; and yet a very intimate observer might have suspected that something was wrong with Mr. Mandeville that went beyond annoyance.

If it be possible for a heavy and healthy man to look haggard, he looked haggard. His face was full, but his eye-sockets were hollow; his mouth twitched as if it were always trying to bite the black strip of moustache that was just too short to be bitten. He might have been a man who had begun to take drugs; but even on that assumption there was something that suggested that he had a reason for doing it; that the drug was not the cause of the tragedy, but the tragedy the cause of the drug. Whatever was his deeper secret, it seemed to inhabit that dark end of the long passage where was the entrance to his own little study; and as he went along the empty corridor, he threw back a nervous glance now and then.

However, business is business; and he made his way to the opposite end of the passage where the blank green door of Miss Maroni defied the world. A group of actors and other people involved were already standing in front of it, conferring and considering, one might almost fancy, the advisability of a battering-ram. The group contained one figure, at least, who was already well enough known; whose photograph was on many mantelpieces and his autograph in many albums. For though Norman Knight was playing the hero in a theatre that was still a little provincial and old-fashioned and capable of calling him the first walking gentleman, he, at least, was certainly on the way to wider triumphs. He was a good-looking man with a long cleft chin and fair hair low on his forehead, giving him a rather Neronian look that did not altogether correspond to his impulsive and plunging movements. The group also contained Ralph Randall, who generally acted elderly character parts, and had a humorous hatchet face, blue with shaving, and discoloured with grease paint. It contained Mandeville's second walking gentleman, carrying on the not yet wholly vanished tradition of Charles's Friend,[1] a dark, curly-haired youth of somewhat Semitic profile bearing the name of Aubrey Vernon.

It included Mr. Mundon Mandeville's wife's maid or dresser, a very powerful-looking person with tight red hair and a hard wooden face. It also, incidentally, included Mandeville's wife, a quiet woman in the background, with a pale, patient face, the lines of which had not lost a classical symmetry and severity, but which looked all the paler because her very eyes were pale, and her pale

---

[1] A reference to the popular theatrical comedy *Charlie's Aunt* (1892).

yellow hair lay in two plain bands like some very archaic Madonna. Not everybody knew that she had once been a serious and successful actress in Ibsen and the intellectual drama. But her husband did not think much of problem plays; and certainly at the moment was more interested in the problem of getting a foreign actress out of a locked room; a new version of the conjuring trick of the Vanishing Lady.

"Hasn't she come out yet?" he demanded, speaking to his wife's business-like attendant rather than to his wife.

"No, sir," answered the woman—who was known as Mrs. Sands—in a sombre manner.

"We are beginning to get a little alarmed," said old Randall. "She seemed quite unbalanced, and we're afraid she might even do herself some mischief."

"Hell!" said Mandeville in his simple and artless way. "Advertisement's very good, but we don't want that sort of advertisement. Hasn't she any friends here? Has nobody any influence with her?"

"Jarvis thinks the only man who might manage her is her own priest round the corner," said Randall; "and in case she does start hanging herself on a hat peg, I really thought perhaps he'd better be here. Jarvis has gone to fetch him ... and, as a matter of fact, here he comes."

Two more figures appeared in that subterranean passage under the stage: the first was Ashton Jarvis, a jolly fellow who generally acted villains, but who had surrendered that high vocation for the moment to the curly-headed youth with the nose. The other figure was short and square and clad all in black; it was Father Brown from the church round the corner.

Father Brown seemed to take it quite naturally and even casually, that he should be called in to consider the queer conduct of one of his flock, whether she was to be regarded as a black sheep or only as a lost lamb. But he did not seem to think much of the suggestion of suicide.

"I suppose there was some reason for her flying off the handle like that," he said. "Does anybody know what it was?"

"Dissatisfied with her part, I believe," said the older actor.

"They always are," growled Mr. Mundon Mandeville. "And I thought my wife would look after those arrangements."

"I can only say," said Mrs. Mundon Mandeville rather wearily, "that I gave her what ought to be the best part. It's supposed to be what stage-struck young women want, isn't it—to act the beautiful young heroine and marry the beautiful young hero in a shower of bouquets and cheers from the gallery? Women of my age naturally have to fall back on acting respectable matrons, and I was careful to confine myself to that."

"It would be devilish awkward to alter the parts now, anyhow," said Randall.

"It's not to be thought of," declared Norman Knight firmly. "Why, I could hardly act—but anyhow it's much too late."

Father Brown had slipped forward and was standing outside the locked door listening.

"Is there no sound?" asked the manager anxiously; and then added in a lower voice: "Do you think she can have done herself in?"

"There is a certain sound," replied Father Brown calmly. "I should be inclined to deduce from the sound that she is engaged in breaking windows or looking-glasses, probably with her feet. No; I do not think there is much danger of her going on to destroy herself. Breaking looking-glasses with your feet is a very unusual prelude to suicide. If she had been a German, gone away to think quietly about metaphysics and *weltschmerz*,[2] I should be all for breaking the door down. These Italians don't really die so easily; and are not liable to kill themselves in a rage. Somebody else, perhaps—yes, possibly—it might be well to take ordinary precautions if she comes out with a leap."

"So you're not in favour of forcing the door?" asked Mandeville.

"Not if you want her to act in your play," replied Father Brown. "If you do that, she'll raise the roof and refuse to stay in the place; if you leave her alone—she'll probably come out from mere curiosity. If I were you, I should just leave somebody to guard the door, more or less, and trust to time for an hour or two."

"In that case," said Mandeville, "we can only get on with rehearsing the scenes where she doesn't appear. My wife will arrange all that is necessary for scenery just now. After all, the fourth act is the main business. You had better get on with that."

"Not a dress rehearsal," said Mandeville's wife to the others.

"Very well," said Knight, "not a dress rehearsal, of course. I wish the dresses of the infernal period weren't so elaborate."

"What is the play?" asked the priest with a touch of curiosity.

"*The School for Scandal*," said Mandeville. "It may be literature, but I want plays. My wife likes what she calls classical comedies. A long sight more classic than comic."

At this moment, the old doorkeeper known as Sam, and the solitary inhabitant of the theatre during off-hours, came waddling up to the manager with a card, to say

---

[2] *Weltschmerz* is a German concept and means "world-weariness".

that Lady Miriam Marden wished to see him. He turned away, but Father Brown continued to blink steadily for a few seconds in the direction of the manager's wife, and saw that her wan face wore a faint smile; not altogether a cheerful smile.

Father Brown moved off in company with the man who had brought him in, who happened, indeed, to be a friend and person of a similar persuasion, which is not uncommon among actors. As he moved off, however, he heard Mrs. Mandeville give quiet directions to Mrs. Sands that she should take up the post of watcher beside the closed door.

"Mrs. Mandeville seems to be an intelligent woman," said the priest to his companion, "though she keeps so much in the background."

"She was once a highly intellectual woman," said Jarvis sadly; "rather washed-out and wasted, some would say, by marrying a bounder like Mandeville. She has the very highest ideals of the drama, you know; but, of course, it isn't often she can get her lord and master to look at anything in that light. Do you know, he actually wanted a woman like that to act as a pantomime boy? Admitted that she was a fine actress, but said pantomimes paid better. That will give you about a measure of his psychological insight and sensibility. But she never complained. As she said to me once: 'Complaint always comes back in an echo from the ends of the world; but silence strengthens us.' If only she were married to somebody who understood her ideas she might have been one of the great actresses of the age; indeed, the highbrow critics still think a lot of her. As it is, she is married to that."

And he pointed to where the big black bulk of Mandeville stood with his back to them, talking to the ladies who had summoned him forth into the vestibule. Lady

Miriam was a very long and languid and elegant lady, handsome in a recent fashion largely modelled on Egyptian mummies; her dark hair cut low and square, like a sort of helmet, and her lips very painted and prominent and giving her a permanent expression of contempt. Her companion was a very vivacious lady with an ugly attractive face and hair powdered with grey. She was a Miss Theresa Talbot and she talked a great deal, while her companion seemed too tired to talk at all. Only, just as the two men passed, Lady Miriam summoned up the energy to say:

"Plays are a bore; but I've never seen a rehearsal in ordinary clothes. Might be a bit funny. Somehow, nowadays, one can never find a thing one's never seen."

"Now, Mr. Mandeville," said Miss Talbot, tapping him on the arm with animated persistence, "you simply must let us see that rehearsal. We can't come tonight, and we don't want to. We want to see all the funny people in the wrong clothes."

"Of course I can give you a box if you wish it," said Mandeville hastily. "Perhaps your ladyship would come this way." And he led them off down another corridor.

"I wonder," said Jarvis in a meditative manner, "whether even Mandeville prefers *that* sort of woman."

"Well," asked his clerical companion, "have you any reason to suppose that Mandeville does prefer her?"

Jarvis looked at him steadily for an instant before answering.

"Mandeville is a mystery," he said gravely. "Oh, yes, I know that he looks about as commonplace a cad as ever walked down Piccadilly. But he really is a mystery for all that. There's something on his conscience. There's a shadow in his life. And I doubt whether it has anything more to do with a few fashionable flirtations than it has with his poor neglected wife. If it has, there's something more in them than meets the eye. As a matter of fact, I happen to know rather more about it than anyone else does, merely by accident. But even I can't make anything of what I know, except a mystery."

He looked around him in the vestibule to see that they were alone and then added, lowering his voice:

"I don't mind telling you, because I know you are a tower of silence where secrets are concerned. But I had a curious shock the other day; and it has been repeated several times since. You know that Mandeville always works in that little room at the end of the passage, just under the stage. Well, twice over I happened to pass by there when everyone thought he was alone; and what's more, when I myself happened to be able to account for all the women in the company, and all the women likely to have to do with him, being absent or at their usual posts."

"All the women?" remarked Father Brown inquiringly.

"There was a woman with him," said Jarvis almost in a whisper. "There is some woman who is always visiting him; somebody that none of us knows. I don't even know how she comes there, since it isn't down the passage to the door; but I think I once saw a veiled or cloaked figure passing out into the twilight at the back of the theatre, like a ghost. But she can't be a ghost. And I don't believe she's even an ordinary 'affair'. I don't think it's love-making. I think it's blackmail."

"What makes you think that?" asked the other.

"Because," said Jarvis, his face turning from grave to grim, "I once heard sounds like a quarrel; and then the strange woman said in a metallic, menacing voice, four words: 'I am your wife.'"

"You think he's a bigamist," said Father Brown reflectively. "Well, bigamy and blackmail often go together, of course. But she may be bluffing as well as blackmailing.

She may be mad. These theatrical people often have monomaniacs running after them. You may be right, but I shouldn't jump to conclusions.... And talking about theatrical people, isn't the rehearsal going to begin, and aren't you a theatrical person?"

"I'm not on in this scene," said Jarvis with a smile. "They're only doing one act, you know, until your Italian friend comes to her senses."

"Talking about my Italian friend," observed the priest, "I should rather like to know whether she has come to her senses."

"We can go back and see, if you like," said Jarvis; and they descended again to the basement and the long passage, at one end of which was Mandeville's study and at the other the closed door of Signora Maroni. The door seemed to be still closed; and Mrs. Sands sat grimly outside it, as motionless as a wooden idol.

Near the other end of the passage they caught a glimpse of some of the other actors in the scene mounting the stairs to the stage just above. Vernon and old Randall went ahead, running rapidly up the stairs; but Mrs. Mandeville went more slowly, in her quietly dignified fashion, and Norman Knight seemed to linger a little to speak to her. A few words fell on the ears of the unintentional eavesdroppers as they passed.

"I tell you a woman visits him," Knight was saying violently.

"Hush!" said the lady in her voice of silver that still had in it something of steel. "You must not talk like this. Remember, he is my husband."

"I wish to God I could forget it," said Knight, and rushed up the stairs to the stage.

The lady followed him, still pale and calm, to take up her own position there.

"Somebody else knows it," said the priest quietly; "but I doubt whether it is any business of ours."

"Yes," muttered Jarvis; "it seems as if everybody knows it and nobody knows anything about it."

They proceeded along the passage to the other end, where the rigid attendant sat outside the Italian's door.

"No; she ain't come out yet," said the woman in her sullen way; "and she ain't dead, for I heard her moving about now and then. I dunno what tricks she's up to."

"Do you happen to know, ma'am," said Father Brown with abrupt politeness, "where Mr. Mandeville is just now?"

"Yes," she replied promptly. "Saw him go into his little room at the end of the passage a minute or two ago; just before the prompter called and the curtain went up. Must be there still, for I ain't seen him come out."

"There's no other door to his office, you mean," said Father Brown in an off-hand way. "Well, I suppose the rehearsal's going in full swing now, for all the Signora's sulking."

"Yes," said Jarvis after a moment's silence; "I can just hear the voices on the stage from here. Old Randall has a splendid carrying voice."

They both remained for an instant in a listening attitude, so that the booming voice of the actor on the stage could indeed be heard rolling faintly down the stairs and along the passage. Before they had spoken again or resumed their normal poise, their ears were filled with another sound. It was a dull but heavy crash and it came from behind the closed door of Mundon Mandeville's private room.

Father Brown went racing along the passage like an arrow from the bow and was struggling with the door-handle before Jarvis had wakened with a start and begun to follow him.

"The door is locked," said the priest, turning a face that was a little pale. "And I am all in favour of breaking down *this* door."

"Do you mean," asked Jarvis with a rather ghastly look, "that the unknown visitor has got in here again? Do you think it's anything serious?" After a moment he added: "I may be able to push back the bolt; I know the fastening on these doors."

He knelt down and pulled out a pocket-knife with a long steel implement, manipulated it for a moment, and the door swung open on the manager's study. Almost the first thing they noticed was that there was no other door and even no window, but a great electric lamp stood on the table. But it was not quite the first thing that they noticed; for even before that they had seen that Mandeville was lying flat on his face in the middle of the room and the blood was crawling out from under his fallen face like a pattern of scarlet snakes that glittered evilly in that unnatural subterranean light.

They did not know how long they had been staring at each other when Jarvis said, like one letting loose something that he had held back with his breath:

"If the stranger got in somehow, she has gone somehow."

"Perhaps we think too much about the stranger," said Father Brown. "There are so many strange things in this strange theatre that you rather tend to forget some of them."

"Why, which things do you mean?" asked his friend quickly.

"There are many," said the priest. "There is the other locked door, for instance."

"But the other door *is* locked," cried Jarvis staring.

"But you forgot it all the same," said Father Brown. A few moments afterwards he said thoughtfully: "That Mrs. Sands is a grumpy and gloomy sort of card."

"Do you mean," asked the other in a lowered voice, "that she's lying and the Italian did come out?"

"No," said the priest calmly; "I think I meant it more or less as a detached study of character."

"You can't mean," cried the actor, "that Mrs. Sands did it herself?"

"I didn't mean a study of *her* character," said Father Brown.

While they had been exchanging these abrupt reflections, Father Brown had knelt down by the body and ascertained that it was beyond any hope or question a dead body. Lying beside it, though not immediately visible from the doorway, was a dagger of the theatrical sort; lying as if it had fallen from the wound or from the hand of the assassin. According to Jarvis, who recognised the instrument, there was not very much to be learned from it, unless the experts could find some finger-prints. It was a property dagger; that is, it was nobody's property; it had been kicking about the theatre for a long time, and anybody might have picked it up. Then the priest rose and looked gravely round the room.

"We must send for the police," he said; "and for a doctor, though the doctor comes too late. Looking at this room, by the way, I don't see how our Italian friend could manage it."

"The Italian!" cried his friend; "I should think not. I should have thought she had an alibi, if anybody had. Two separate rooms, both locked, at opposite ends of a long passage, with a fixed witness watching it."

"No," said Father Brown. "Not quite. The difficulty is how she could have got in this end. I think she might have got out the other end."

"And why?" asked the other.

"I told you," said Father Brown, "that it sounded as if she was breaking glass—mirrors or windows. Stupidly enough I forgot something I knew quite well; that she is pretty superstitious. She wouldn't be likely to break a mirror; so I suspect she broke a window. It's true that all this is under the ground floor; but it might be a skylight or a window opening on an area. But there don't seem to be any skylights or areas here." And he stared at the ceiling very intently for a considerable time.

Suddenly he came back to conscious life again with a start. "We must go upstairs and telephone and tell everybody. It is pretty painful.... My God, can you hear those actors still shouting and ranting upstairs? The play is still going on. I suppose that's what they mean by tragic irony."

When it was fated that the theatre should be turned into a house of mourning, an opportunity was given to the actors to show many of the real virtues of their type and trade. They did, as the phrase goes, behave like gentlemen; and not only like first walking gentlemen. They had not all of them liked or trusted Mandeville, but they knew exactly the right things to say about him; they showed not only sympathy but delicacy in their attitude to his widow. She had become, in a new and very different sense, a tragedy queen—her lightest word was law and while she moved about slowly and sadly, they ran her many errands.

"She was always a strong character," said old Randall rather huskily; "and had the best brains of any of us. Of course poor Mandeville was never on her level in education and so on; but she always did her duty splendidly. It was quite pathetic the way she would sometimes say she wished she had more intellectual life; but Mandeville—well, *nil nisi bonum*,[3] as they say." And the old gentleman went away wagging his head sadly.

[3] The Latin phrase *De mortuis nihil nisi bonum* translates to "Of the dead, say nothing unless good."

"*Nil nisi bonum* indeed," said Jarvis grimly. "I don't think Randall at any rate has heard of the story of the strange lady visitor. By the way, don't you think it probably was the strange woman?"

"It depends," said the priest, "whom you mean by the strange woman."

"Oh! I don't mean the Italian woman," said Jarvis hastily. "Though, as a matter of fact, you were quite right about her, too. When they went in the skylight was smashed and the room was empty; but so far as the police can discover, she simply went home in the most harmless fashion. No, I mean the woman who was heard threatening him at that secret meeting; the woman who said she was his wife. Do you think she really was his wife?"

"It is possible," said Father Brown, staring blankly into the void, "that she really was his wife."

"That would give us the motive of jealousy over his bigamous remarriage," reflected Jarvis, "for the body was not robbed in any way. No need to poke about for thieving servants or even impecunious actors. But as for that, of course, you've noticed the outstanding and peculiar thing about the case?"

"I have noticed several peculiar things," said Father Brown. "Which one do you mean?"

"I mean the corporate alibi," said Jarvis gravely. "It's not often that practically a whole company has a public alibi like that; an alibi on a lighted stage and all witnessing to each other. As it turns out it is jolly lucky for our friends here that poor Mandeville did put those two silly society women in the box to watch the rehearsal. They can bear witness that the whole act was performed without a hitch, with the characters on the stage all the time. They began long before Mandeville was last seen going into his room. They went on at least five or ten minutes after you and I found his dead body. And, by a lucky coincidence, the moment we actually heard him fall was during the time when all the characters were on the stage together."

"Yes, that is certainly very important and simplifies everything," agreed Father Brown. "Let us count the people covered by the alibi. There was Randall: I rather fancy Randall practically hated the manager, though he is very properly covering his feelings just now. But he is ruled out; it was his voice we heard thundering over our heads from the stage. There is our *jeune premier*, Mr. Knight: I have rather good reason to suppose he was in love with Mandeville's wife and not concealing that sentiment so much as he might; but he is out of it, for he was on the stage at the same time, being thundered at. There was that amiable Jew who calls himself Aubrey Vernon, he's out of it; and there's Mrs. Mandeville, she's out of it. Their corporate alibi, as you say, depends chiefly on Lady Miriam and her friend in the box; though there is the general common-sense corroboration that the act had to be gone through and the routine of the theatre seems to have suffered no interruption. The legal witnesses, however, are Lady Miriam and her friend, Miss Talbot. I suppose you feel sure *they* are all right?"

"Lady Miriam?" said Jarvis in surprise. "Oh, yes ... I suppose you mean that she looks a queer sort of vamp. But you've no notion what even the ladies of the best families are looking like nowadays. Besides, is there any particular reason for doubting their evidence?"

"Only that it brings us up against a blank wall," said Father Brown. "Don't you see that this collective alibi practically covers everybody? Those four were the only performers in the theatre at the time; and there were scarcely any servants in the theatre; none indeed, except old Sam, who guards the only regular entrance, and the woman who guarded Miss Maroni's door. There is nobody else left available but you and me. We certainly might be accused of the crime, especially as we found the body. There seems nobody else who can be accused. You didn't happen to kill him when I wasn't looking, I suppose?"

Jarvis looked up with a slight start and stared a moment, then the broad grin returned to his swarthy face. He shook his head.

"You didn't do it," said Father Brown; "and we will assume for the moment, merely for the sake of argument, that I didn't do it. The people on the stage being out of it, it really leaves the Signora behind her locked door, the sentinel in front of her door, and old Sam. Or are you thinking of the two ladies in the box? Of course they might have slipped out of the box."

"No," said Jarvis; "I am thinking of the unknown woman who came and told Mandeville she was his wife."

"Perhaps she was," said the priest; and this time there was a note in his steady voice that made his companion start to his feet once more and lean across the table.

"We said," he observed in a low, eager voice, "that this first wife might have been jealous of the other wife."

"No," said Father Brown; "she might have been jealous of the Italian girl, perhaps, or of Lady Miriam Marden. But she was not jealous of the other wife."

"And why not?"

"Because there was no other wife," said Father Brown. "So far from being a bigamist, Mr. Mandeville seems to me to have been a highly monogamous person. His wife was almost too much with him; so much with him that you all charitably suppose that she must be somebody else. But I don't see how she could have been with him when he was killed, for we agree that she was acting all the time in front of the footlights. Acting an important part, too ..."

"Do you really mean," cried Jarvis, "that the strange woman who haunted him like a ghost was only the Mrs. Mandeville we know?" But he received no answer; for Father Brown was staring into vacancy with a blank expression almost like an idiot's. He always did look most idiotic at the instant when he was most intelligent.

The next moment he scrambled to his feet, looking very harassed and distressed. "This is awful," he said. "I'm not sure it isn't the worst business I ever had; but I've got to go through with it. Would you go and ask Mrs. Mandeville if I may speak to her in private?"

"Oh, certainly," said Jarvis, as he turned towards the door. "But what's the matter with you?"

"Only being a born fool," said Father Brown; "a very common complaint in this vale of tears. I was fool enough to forget altogether that the play was *The School for Scandal*."

He walked restlessly up and down the room until Jarvis re-appeared at the door with an altered and even alarmed face.

"I can't find her anywhere," he said. "Nobody seems to have seen her."

"They haven't seen Norman Knight either, have they?" asked Father Brown dryly. "Well, it saves me the most painful interview of my life. Saving the grace of God, I was very nearly frightened of that woman. But she was frightened of me, too; frightened of something I'd seen or said. Knight was always begging her to bolt with him. Now she's done it; and I'm devilish sorry for him."

"For him?" inquired Jarvis.

"Well, it can't be very nice to elope with a murderess," said the other dispassionately. "But as a matter of fact she was something very much worse than a murderess."

"And what is that?"

"An egoist," said Father Brown. "She was the sort of person who had looked in the mirror before looking out of the window, and it is the worst calamity of mortal life. The looking-glass was unlucky for her, all right; but rather because it wasn't broken."

"I can't understand what all this means," said Jarvis. "Everybody regarded her as a person of the most exalted ideals, almost moving on a higher spiritual plane than the rest of us ..."

"She regarded herself in that light," said the other; "and she knew how to hypnotise everybody else into it. Perhaps I hadn't known her long enough to be wrong about her. But I knew the sort of person she was five minutes after I clapped eyes on her."

"Oh, come!" cried Jarvis; "I'm sure her behaviour about the Italian was beautiful."

"Her behaviour always was beautiful," said the other. "I've heard from everybody here all about her refinements and subtleties and spiritual soarings above poor Mandeville's head. But all these spiritualities and subtleties seem to me to boil themselves down to the simple fact that she certainly was a lady and he most certainly was not a gentleman. But, do you know, I have never felt quite sure that St. Peter will make that the only test at the gate of heaven.

"As for the rest," he went on with increasing animation, "I knew from the very first words she said that she was not really being fair to the poor Italian, with all her fine airs of frigid magnanimity. And again, I realised it when I knew that the play was *The School for Scandal.*"

"You are going rather too fast for me," said Jarvis in some bewilderment. "What does it matter what the play was?"

"Well," said the priest, "she said she had given the girl the part of the beautiful heroine and had retired into the background herself with the older part of a matron. Now that might have applied to almost any play; but it falsifies the facts about that particular play. She can only have meant that she gave the other actress the part of Maria, which is hardly a part at all. And the part of the obscure and self-effacing married woman, if you please, must have been the part of Lady Teazle, which is the only part any actress wants to act. If the Italian was a first-rate actress who had been promised a first-rate part, there was really some excuse, or at least some cause, for her mad Italian rage. There generally is for mad Italian rages: Latins are logical and have a reason for going mad. But that one little thing let in daylight for me on the meaning of her mag-nanimity. And there was another thing, even then. You laughed when I said that the sulky look of Mrs. Sands was a study in character; but not in the character of Mrs. Sands. But it was true. If you want to know what a lady is really like, don't look at her; for she may be too clever for you. Don't look at the men round her, for they may be too silly about her. But look at some other woman who is always near to her, and especially one who is under her. You will see in that mirror her real face, and the face mirrored in Mrs. Sands was very ugly.

"And as for all the other impressions, what were they? I heard a lot about the unworthiness of poor old Man-deville; but it was all about his being unworthy of her, and I am pretty certain it came indirectly from her. And, even so, it betrayed itself. Obviously, from what every man said, she had confided in every man about her con-founded intellectual loneliness. You yourself said she never complained; and then quoted her about how her uncomplaining silence strengthened her soul. And that is just the note; that's the unmistakable style. People who complain are just jolly, human Christian nuisances; I don't mind them. But people who complain that they never

complain are the devil. They are really the devil; isn't
that swagger of stoicism the whole point of the Byronic
cult of Satan?[4] I heard all this; but for the life of me I
couldn't hear of anything tangible she had to complain
of. Nobody pretended that her husband drank, or beat
her, or left her without money, or even was unfaithful,
until the rumour about the secret meetings, which were
simply her own melodramatic habit of pestering him with
curtain-lectures in his own business office. And when one
looked at the facts, apart from the atmospheric impression
of martyrdom she contrived to spread, the facts were really
quite the other way. Mandeville left off making money
on pantomimes to please her; he started losing money on
classical drama to please her. She arranged the scenery and
furniture as she liked. She wanted Sheridan's play and she
had it; she wanted the part of Lady Teazle and she had it;
she wanted a rehearsal without costume at that particular
hour and she had it. It may be worth remarking on the
curious fact that she wanted that."

"But what is the use of all this tirade?" asked the actor,
who had hardly ever heard his clerical friend make so
long a speech before. "We seem to have got a long way
from the murder in all this psychological business. She
may have eloped with Knight; she may have bamboozled
Randall; she may have bamboozled me. But she can't have
murdered her husband—for everyone agrees she was on
the stage through the whole scene. She may be wicked;
but she isn't a witch."

"Well, I wouldn't be so sure," said Father Brown, with
a smile. "But she didn't need to use any witchcraft in this
case. I know now that she did it, and very simply indeed."

[4]Lord Byron (1788–1824) was an English poet who attempted in his writings
to make a hero of the fallen angel Satan, the arch-villain of the Bible and
Christian tradition.

"Why are you so sure of that?" asked Jarvis, looking at him in a puzzled way.

"Because the play was *The School for Scandal*," replied Father Brown, "and that particular act of *The School for Scandal*. I should like to remind you, as I said just now, that she always arranged the furniture how she liked. I should also like to remind you that this stage was built and used for pantomimes; it would naturally have trap-doors and trick exits of that sort. And when you say that witnesses could attest to having seen all the performers on the stage, I should like to remind you that in the principal scene of *The School for Scandal* one of the principal performers remains for a considerable time on the stage, but is *not* seen. She is technically 'on,' but she might practically be very much 'off.' That is the Screen of Lady Teazle and the Alibi of Mrs. Mandeville."

There was a silence and then the actor said: "You think she slipped through a trap-door behind a screen down to the floor below, where the manager's room was?"

"She certainly slipped away in some fashion; and that is the most probable fashion," said the other. "I think it all the more probable because she took the opportunity of an undress rehearsal, and even indeed arranged for one. It is a guess; but I fancy if it had been a dress rehearsal it might have been more difficult to get through a trap-door in the hoops of the eighteenth century. There are many little difficulties, of course, but I think they could all be met in time and in turn."

"What I can't meet is the big difficulty," said Jarvis, putting his head on his hand with a sort of groan. "I simply can't bring myself to believe that a radiant and serene creature like that could so lose, so to speak, her bodily balance, to say nothing of her moral balance. Was any motive strong enough? Was she very much in love with Knight?"

"I hope so," replied his companion; "for really it would be the most human excuse. But I'm sorry to say that I have my doubts. She wanted to get rid of her husband, who was an old-fashioned, provincial hack, not even making much money. She wanted to have a career as the brilliant wife of a brilliant and rapidly-rising actor. But she didn't want in that sense to act in *The School for Scandal*. She wouldn't have run away with a man except in the last resort. It wasn't a human passion with her, but a sort of hellish respectability. She was always dogging her husband in secret and badgering him to divorce himself or otherwise get out of the way; and as he refused he paid at last for his refusal. There's another thing you've got to remember. You talk about these highbrows having a higher art and a more philosophical drama. But remember what a lot of the philosophy is! Remember what sort of conduct those highbrows often present to the highest! All about the Will to Power and the Right to Live and the Right to Experience—damned nonsense and more than damned nonsense—nonsense that can damn."

Father Brown frowned, which he did very rarely; and there was still a cloud on his brow as he put on his hat and went out into the night.

"You shall not steal."

The Head of Caesar

There is somewhere in Brompton or Kensington an inter-
minable avenue of tall houses, rich but largely empty, that
looks like a terrace of tombs. The very steps up to the
dark front doors seem as steep as the side of pyramids;
one would hesitate to knock at the door, lest it should be
opened by a mummy. But a yet more depressing feature
in the grey façade is its telescopic length and changeless
continuity. The pilgrim walking down it begins to think
he will never come to a break or a corner; but there is one
exception—a very small one, but hailed by the pilgrim
almost with a shout. There is a sort of mews between two
of the tall mansions, a mere slit like the crack of a door by
comparison with the street, but just large enough to permit
a pigmy ale-house or eating-house, still allowed by the
rich to their stable-servants, to stand in the angle. There is
something cheery in its very dinginess, and something free
and elfin in its very insignificance. At the feet of those grey
stone giants it looks like a lighted house of dwarfs.

Anyone passing the place during a certain autumn
evening, itself almost fairylike, might have seen a hand
pull aside the red half-blind which (along with some large
white lettering) half hid the interior from the street, and a

"The Head of Caesar" first appeared in the June 1913 issue of *Pall Mall*
magazine.

face peer out not unlike a rather innocent goblin's. It was, in fact, the face of one with the harmless human name of Brown, formerly priest of Cobhole in Essex, and now working in London. His friend, Flambeau, a semi-official investigator, was sitting opposite him, making his last notes of a case he had cleared up in the neighbourhood. They were sitting at a small table, close up to the window, when the priest pulled the curtain back and looked out. He waited till a stranger in the street had passed the window, to let the curtain fall into its place again. Then his round eyes rolled to the large white lettering on the window above his head, and then strayed to the next table, at which sat only a navvy[1] with beer and cheese, and a young girl with red hair and a glass of milk. Then (seeing his friend put away the pocket-book), he said softly:

"If you've got ten minutes, I wish you'd follow that man with the false nose."

Flambeau looked up in surprise; but the girl with the red hair also looked up, and with something that was stronger than astonishment. She was simply and even loosely dressed in light brown sacking stuff; but she was a lady, and even, on a second glance, a rather needlessly haughty one. "The man with the false nose!" repeated Flambeau. "Who's he?"

"I haven't a notion," answered Father Brown. "I want you to find out; I ask it as a favour. He went down there"—and he jerked his thumb over his shoulder in one of his undistinguished gestures—"and can't have passed three lamp-posts yet. I only want to know the direction."

Flambeau gazed at his friend for some time, with an expression between perplexity and amusement; and then,

[1] In England, "navvy" is short for "navigator", a manual laborer working on civil engineering projects.

rising from the table; squeezed his huge form out of the little door of the dwarf tavern, and melted into the twilight.

Father Brown took a small book out of his pocket and began to read steadily; he betrayed no consciousness of the fact that the red-haired lady had left her own table and sat down opposite him. At last she leaned over and said in a low, strong voice: "Why do you say that? How do you know it's false?"

He lifted his rather heavy eyelids, which fluttered in considerable embarrassment. Then his dubious eye roamed again to the white lettering on the glass front of the public-house. The young woman's eyes followed his, and rested there also, but in pure puzzledom.

"No," said Father Brown, answering her thoughts. "It doesn't say 'Sela', like the thing in the Psalms;[2] I read it like that myself when I was wool-gathering just now; it says 'Ales.'"

"Well?" inquired the staring young lady. "What does it matter what it says?"

His ruminating eye roved to the girl's light canvas sleeve, round the wrist of which ran a very slight thread of artistic pattern, just enough to distinguish it from a working-dress of a common woman and make it more like the working-dress of a lady art-student. He seemed to find much food for thought in this; but his reply was very slow and hesitant. "You see, madam," he said, "from outside the place looks—well, it is a perfectly decent place—but ladies like you don't—don't generally think so. They never go into such places from choice, except—"

"Well?" she repeated.

"Except an unfortunate few who don't go in to drink milk."

---

[2] *Selah* is a Hebrew word found throughout the biblical Psalms and indicates a pause (for reflection).

"You are a most singular person," said the young lady. "What is your object in all this?"

"Not to trouble you about it," he replied, very gently. "Only to arm myself with knowledge enough to help you, if ever you freely ask my help."

"But why should I need help?"

He continued his dreamy monologue. "You couldn't have come in to see *protégées*, humble friends, that sort of thing, or you'd have gone through into the parlour ... and you couldn't have come in because you were ill, or you'd have spoken to the woman of the place, who's obviously respectable ... besides, you don't look ill in that way, but only unhappy.... This street is the only original long lane that has no turning; and the houses on both sides are shut up.... I could only suppose that you'd seen somebody coming whom you didn't want to meet; and found the public-house was the only shelter in this wilderness of stone.... I don't think I went beyond the licence of a stranger in glancing at the only man who passed immediately after.... And as I thought he looked like the wrong sort ... and you looked like the right sort.... I held myself ready to help if he annoyed you; that is all. As for my friend, he'll be back soon; and he certainly can't find out anything by stumping down a road like this.... I didn't think he could."

"Then why did you send him out?" she cried, leaning forward with yet warmer curiosity. She had the proud, impetuous face that goes with reddish colouring and a Roman nose as it did in Marie Antoinette.

He looked at her steadily for the first time, and said: "Because I hoped you would speak to me."

She looked back at him for some time with a heated face, in which there hung a red shadow of anger; then, despite her anxieties, humour broke out of her eyes and the corners of her mouth, and she answered almost grimly: "Well, if you're so keen on my conversation, perhaps

you'll answer my question." After a pause she added: "I
had the honour to ask you why you thought the man's
nose was false."

"The wax always spots like that just a little in this
weather," answered Father Brown with entire simplicity,

"But it's such a *crooked* nose," remonstrated the red-
haired girl.

The priest smiled in his turn. "I don't say it's the sort of
nose one would wear out of mere foppery," he admitted.
"This man, I think, wears it because his real nose is so
much nicer."

"But why?" she insisted.

"What is the nursery-rhyme?" observed Brown absentmindedly. "There was a crooked man and he went
a crooked mile.... That man, I fancy, has gone a very
crooked road—by following his nose."

"Why, what's he done?" she demanded, rather shakily.

"I don't want to force your confidence by a hair," said
Father Brown, very quietly. "But I think you could tell
me more about that than I can tell you."

The girl sprang to her feet and stood quite quietly, but
with clenched hands, like one about to stride away; then
her hands loosened slowly, and she sat down again. "You
are more of a mystery than all the others," she said desper-
ately, "but I feel there might be a heart in your mystery."

"What we all dread most," said the priest in a low voice,
"is a maze with *no* centre. That is why atheism is only a
nightmare."

"I will tell you everything," said the red-haired girl
doggedly, "except why I am telling you; and that I don't
know."

She picked at the darned table-cloth and went on: "You
look as if you knew what isn't snobbery as well as what
is; and when I say that ours is a good old family, you'll

understand it is a necessary part of the story; indeed, my chief danger is in my brother's high-and-dry notions, *noblesse oblige*[3] and all that. Well, my name is Christabel Carstairs; and my father was that Colonel Carstairs you've probably heard of, who made the famous Carstairs Collection of Roman coins. I could never describe my father to you; the nearest I can say is that he was very like a Roman coin himself. He was as handsome and as genuine and as valuable and as metallic and as out-of-date. He was prouder of his Collection than of his coat-of-arms—nobody could say more than that. His extraordinary character came out most in his will. He had two sons and one daughter. He quarrelled with one son, my brother Giles, and sent him to Australia on a small allowance. He then made a will leaving the Carstairs Collection, actually with a yet smaller allowance, to my brother Arthur. He meant it as a reward, as the highest honour he could offer, in acknowledgement of Arthur's loyalty and rectitude and the distinctions he had already gained in mathematics and economics at Cambridge. He left me practically all his pretty large fortune; and I am sure he meant it in contempt.

"Arthur, you may say, might well complain of this; but Arthur is my father over again. Though he had some differences with my father in early youth, no sooner had he taken over the Collection than he became like a pagan priest dedicated to a temple. He mixed up these Roman halfpence with the honour of the Carstairs family in the same stiff, idolatrous way as his father before him. He acted as if Roman money must be guarded by all the Roman virtues. He took no pleasures; he spent nothing on himself; he lived for the Collection. Often he would not trouble

---

[3] *Noblesse oblige* is a French phrase meaning "nobility obliges" and that nobility requires the person of status to fulfill social responsibilities.

to dress for his simple meals; but pattered about among the corded brown-paper parcels (which no one else was allowed to touch) in an old brown dressing-gown. With its rope and tassel and his pale, thin, refined face, it made him look like an old ascetic monk. Every now and then, though, he would appear dressed like a decidedly fashionable gentleman; but that was only when he went up to the London sales or shops to make an addition to the Carstairs Collection.

"Now, if you've known any young people, you won't be shocked if I say that I got into rather a low frame of mind with all this; the frame of mind in which one begins to say that the Ancient Romans were all very well in their way. I'm not like my brother Arthur; I can't help enjoying enjoyment. I got a lot of romance and rubbish where I got my red hair, from the other side of the family. Poor Giles was the same; and I think the atmosphere of coins might count in excuse for him; though he really did wrong and nearly went to prison. But he didn't behave any worse than I did; as you shall hear.

"I come now to the silly part of the story. I think a man as clever as you can guess the sort of thing that would begin to relieve the monotony for an unruly girl of seventeen placed in such a position. But I am so rattled with more dreadful things that I can hardly read my own feeling; and don't know whether I despise it now as a flirtation or bear it as a broken heart. We lived then at a little seaside watering-place in South Wales, and a retired sea-captain living a few doors off had a son about five years older than myself, who had been a friend of Giles before he went to the Colonies. His name does not affect my tale; but I tell you it was Philip Hawker, because I am telling you everything. We used to go shrimping together, and said and thought we were in love with each other; at least he certainly said he was, and I certainly thought I was. If I tell you he had bronzed curly hair and a falconish sort of face, bronzed by the sea also, it's not for his sake, I assure you, but for the story; for it was the cause of a very curious coincidence.

"One summer afternoon, when I had promised to go shrimping along the sands with Philip, I was waiting rather impatiently in the front drawing-room, watching Arthur handle some packets of coins he had just purchased and slowly shunt them, one or two at a time, into his own dark study and museum which was at the back of the house. As soon as I heard the heavy door close on him finally, I made a bolt for my shrimping-net and tam-o'-shanter and was just going to slip out, when I saw that my brother had left behind him one coin that lay gleaming on the long bench by the window. It was a bronze coin, and the colour, combined with the exact curve of the Roman nose and something in the very lift of the long, wiry neck, made the head of Caesar on it the almost precise portrait of Philip Hawker. Then I suddenly remembered Giles telling Philip of a coin that was like him, and Philip wishing he had it. Perhaps you can fancy the wild, foolish thoughts with which my head went round; I felt as if I had had a gift from the fairies. It seemed to me that if I could only run away with this, and give it to Philip like a wild sort of wedding-ring, it would be a bond between us for ever; I felt a thousand such things at once. Then there yawned under me, like the pit, the enormous, awful notion of what I was doing; above all, the unbearable thought, which was like touching hot iron, of what Arthur would think of it. A Carstairs a thief; and a thief of the Carstairs treasure! I believe my brother could see me burned like a witch for such a thing. But then, the very thought of such fanatical cruelty heightened my old hatred of his dingy old antiquarian fussiness and my longing for the youth and liberty that called to me from the sea. Outside was strong sunlight with a wind; and a yellow head of some broom or gorse in the garden rapped against the glass of the window. I thought of that living and growing gold calling to me from all the heaths of the world—and then of that dead, dull gold and bronze and brass of my brother's growing dustier and dustier as life went by. Nature and the Carstairs Collection had come to grips at last.

"Nature is older than the Carstairs Collection. As I ran down the streets to the sea, the coin clenched tight in my fist, I felt all the Roman Empire on my back as well as the Carstairs pedigree. It was not only the old lion argent that was roaring in my ear, but all the eagles of the Caesars seemed flapping and screaming in pursuit of me. And yet my heart rose higher and higher like a child's kite, until I came over the loose, dry sand-hills and to the flat, wet sands, where Philip stood already up to his ankles in the shallow shining water, some hundred yards out to sea. There was a great red sunset; and the long stretch of low water, hardly rising over the ankle for half a mile, was like a lake of ruby flame. It was not till I had torn off my shoes and stockings and waded to where he stood, which was well away from the dry land, that I turned and looked round. We were quite alone in a circle of sea-water and wet sand, and I gave him the head of Caesar.

"At the very instant I had a shock of fancy: that a man far away on the sand-hills was looking at me intently. I must have felt immediately after that it was a mere leap of unreasonable nerves; for the man was only a dark dot in the distance, and I could only just see that he was standing quite still and gazing, with his head a little on one side. There was no earthly logical evidence that he was looking at me; he might have been looking at a ship, or the sunset, or the sea-gulls, or at any of the people who still strayed here and there on the shore between us. Nevertheless, whatever my start sprang from was prophetic; for, as I gazed, he started walking briskly in a bee-line towards us across the wide wet sands. As he drew nearer and nearer I saw that he was dark and bearded, and that his eyes were marked with dark spectacles. He was dressed poorly but respectably in black, from the old black top hat on his head to the solid black boots on his feet. In spite of these he walked straight into the sea without a flash of hesitation, and came on at me with the steadiness of a travelling bullet.

"I can't tell you the sense of monstrosity and miracle I had when he thus silently burst the barrier between land and water. It was as if he had walked straight off a cliff and still marched steadily in mid-air. It was as if a house had flown up into the sky or a man's head had fallen off. He was only wetting his boots; but he seemed to be a demon disregarding a law of Nature. If he had hesitated an instant at the water's edge it would have been nothing. As it was, he seemed to look so much at me alone as not to notice the ocean. Philip was some yards away with his back to me, bending over his net. The stranger came on till he stood within two yards of me, the water washing half-way up to his knees. Then he said, with a clearly modulated and rather mincing articulation: 'Would it discommode you to contribute elsewhere a coin with a somewhat different superscription?'

"With one exception there was nothing definably abnormal about him. His tinted glasses were not really opaque, but of a blue kind common enough, nor were the eyes behind them shifty, but regarded me steadily. His dark beard was not really long or wild—but he looked rather hairy, because the beard began very high up in his face, just under the cheek-bones. His complexion was neither sallow nor livid, but on the contrary rather clear and youthful; yet this gave a pink-and-white wax look which somehow (I don't know why) rather increased the horror. The only oddity one could fix was that his nose, which was otherwise of a good shape, was just slightly turned sideways at the tip; as if, when it was soft, it had been tapped on one side with a toy hammer. The thing was hardly a deformity; yet I cannot tell you what a living nightmare it was to me. As he stood there in the sunset-stained water he affected me as some hellish sea-monster just risen roaring out of a sea like blood. I don't know why a touch on the nose should affect my imagination so much. I think it seemed as if he could move his nose like a finger. And as if he had just that moment moved it.

"'Any little assistance,' he continued with the same queer, priggish accent, 'that may obviate the necessity of my communicating with the family.'

"Then it rushed over me that I was being blackmailed for the theft of the bronze piece; and all my merely super-stitious fears and doubts were swallowed up in one over-powering, practical question. How could he have found out? I had stolen the thing suddenly and on impulse; I was certainly alone; for I always made sure of being unob-served when I slipped out to see Philip in this way. I had not, to all appearance, been followed in the street; and if I had, they could not 'X-ray' the coin in my closed hand. The man standing on the sand-hills could no more have seen what I gave Philip than shoot a fly in one eye, like the man in the fairy-tale.

"'Philip,' I cried helplessly, 'ask this man what he wants.'

"When Philip lifted his head at last from mending his net he looked rather red, as if sulky or ashamed; but it may have been only the exertion of stooping and the

red evening light; I may have only had another of the
morbid fancies that seemed to be dancing about me. He
merely said gruffly to the man: 'You clear out of this.'
And, motioning me to follow, set off wading shoreward
without paying further attention to him. He stepped on to
a stone breakwater that ran out from among the roots of
the sand-hills, and so struck homeward, perhaps thinking
our incubus would find it less easy to walk on such rough
stones, green and slippery with seaweed, than we, who
were young and used to it. But my persecutor walked as
daintily as he talked; and he still followed me, picking his
way and picking his phrases. I heard his delicate, detestable
voice appealing to me over my shoulder, until at last, when
we had crested the sand-hills, Philip's patience (which was
by no means so conspicuous on most occasions) seemed to
snap. He turned suddenly, saying, 'Go back. I can't talk
to you now.' And as the man hovered and opened his
mouth, Philip struck him a buffet on it that sent him flying
from the top of the tallest sand-hill to the bottom. I saw
him crawling out below, covered with sand.

"This stroke comforted me somehow, though it might
well increase my peril; but Philip showed none of his usual
elation at his own prowess. Though as affectionate as ever,
he still seemed cast down; and before I could ask him
anything fully, he parted with me at his own gate, with
two remarks that struck me as strange. He said that, all
things considered, I ought to put the coin back in the Collection; but that he himself would keep it 'for the present'.
And then he added quite suddenly and irrelevantly: 'You
know Giles is back from Australia?'"

The door of the tavern opened and the gigantic shadow
of the investigator Flambeau fell across the table. Father
Brown presented him to the lady in his own slight, per-
suasive style of speech, mentioning his knowledge and

sympathy in such cases; and almost without knowing, the girl was soon reiterating her story to two listeners. But Flambeau, as he bowed and sat down, handed the priest a small slip of paper. Brown accepted it with some surprise and read on it: "Cab to Wagga Wagga, 379, Mafeking Avenue, Putney." The girl was going on with her story.

"I went up the steep street to my own house with my head in a whirl; it had not begun to clear when I came to the doorstep, on which I found a milk-can—and the man with the twisted nose. The milk-can told me the servants were all out; for, of course, Arthur, browsing about in his brown dressing-gown in a brown study, would not hear or answer a bell. Thus there was no one to help me in the house, except my brother, whose help must be my ruin. In desperation I thrust two shillings into the horrid thing's hand, and told him to call again in a few days, when I had thought it out. He went off sulking, but more sheepishly than I had expected—perhaps he had been shaken by his fall—and I watched the star of sand splashed on his back receding down the road with a horrid vindictive pleasure. He turned a corner some six houses down.

"Then I let myself in, made myself some tea, and tried to think it out. I sat at the drawing-room window looking on to the garden, which still glowed with the last full evening light. But I was too distracted and dreamy to look at the lawns and flower-pots and flower-beds with any concentration. So I took the shock the more sharply because I'd seen it so slowly.

"The man or monster I'd sent away was standing quite still in the middle of the garden. Oh, we've all read a lot about pale-faced phantoms in the dark; but this was more dreadful than anything of that kind could ever be. Because, though he cast a long evening shadow, he still stood in warm sunlight. And because his face was not pale, but had that waxen bloom still upon it that belongs to a barber's dummy. He stood quite still, with his face towards me; and I can't tell you how horrid he looked among the tulips and all those tall, gaudy, almost hothouse-looking flowers. It looked as if we'd stuck up a waxwork instead of a statue in the centre of our garden.

"Yet almost the instant he saw me move in the window he turned and ran out of the garden by the back gate, which stood open and by which he had undoubtedly entered. This renewed timidity on his part was so different from the impudence with which he had walked into the sea, that I felt vaguely comforted. I fancied, perhaps, that he feared confronting Arthur more than I knew. Anyhow, I settled down at last, and had a quiet dinner alone (for it was against the rules to disturb Arthur when he was rearranging the museum), and, my thoughts, a little released, fled to Philip and lost themselves, I suppose. Anyhow, I was looking blankly, but rather pleasantly than otherwise, at another window, uncurtained, but by this time black as a slate with the final nightfall. It seemed to me that something like a snail was on the outside of the window-pane. But when I stared harder, it was more like a man's thumb pressed on the pane; it had that curled look that a thumb has. With my fear and courage re-awakened together, I rushed at the window and then recoiled with a strangled scream that any man but Arthur must have heard.

"For it was not a thumb, any more than it was a snail. It was the tip of a crooked nose, crushed against the glass; it looked white with the pressure; and the staring face and eyes behind it were at first invisible and afterwards grey like a ghost. I slammed the shutters together somehow, rushed up to my room and locked myself in. But, even as I passed, I could swear I saw a second black window with something on it that was like a snail.

"It might be best to go to Arthur after all. If the thing was crawling close all around the house like a cat, it might have purposes worse even than blackmail. My brother might cast me out and curse me for ever, but he was a gentleman, and would defend me on the spot. After ten minutes' curious thinking, I went down, knocked on the door and then went in: to see the last and worst sight.

"My brother's chair was empty, and he was obviously out. But the man with the crooked nose was sitting waiting for his return, with his hat still insolently on his head, and actually reading one of my brother's books under my brother's lamp. His face was composed and occupied, but his nose-tip still had the air of being the most mobile part of his face, as if it had just turned from left to right like an elephant's proboscis. I had thought him poisonous enough while he was pursuing and watching me; but I think his unconsciousness of my presence was more frightful still.

"I think I screamed loud and long; but that doesn't matter. What I did next does matter: I gave him all the money I had, including a good deal in paper which, though it was mine, I dare say I had no right to touch. He went off at last, with hateful, tactful regrets all in long words; and I sat down, feeling ruined in every sense. And yet I was saved that very night by a pure accident. Arthur had gone off suddenly to London, as he so often did, for bargains; and returned, late but radiant, having nearly secured a treasure that was an added splendour even to the family Collection. He was so resplendent that I was almost emboldened to confess the abstraction of the lesser gem—but he bore down all other topics with his overpowering projects. Because the bargain might still misfire any moment, he insisted on my packing at once and going up with him to lodgings he had already taken in Fulham, to be near the curio-shop in question. Thus in spite of myself, I fled from my foe almost in the dead of night—but

from Philip also.... My brother was often at the South
Kensington Museum, and, in order to make some sort of
secondary life for myself, I paid for a few lessons at the Art
Schools. I was coming back from them this evening, when
I saw the abomination of desolation walking alive down
the long straight street and the rest is as this gentleman
has said.

"I've got only one thing to say. I don't deserve to be
helped; and I don't question or complain of my punishment; it is just, it ought to have happened. But I still
question, with bursting brains, how it can have happened.
Am I punished by miracle? or how can anyone but Philip
and myself know I gave him a tiny coin in the middle of
the sea?"

"It is an extraordinary problem," admitted Flambeau.

"Not so extraordinary as the answer," remarked Father
Brown rather gloomily. "Miss Carstairs, will you be at
home if we call at your Fulham place in an hour and a half
hence?"

The girl looked at him, and then rose and put her gloves
on. "Yes," she said, "I'll be there"; and almost instantly left
the place.

That night the detective and the priest were still talking
of the matter as they drew near the Fulham house, a
tenement strangely mean even for a temporary residence
of the Carstairs family.

"Of course the superficial, on reflection," said Flambeau,
"would think first of this Australian brother who's been in
trouble before, who's come back so suddenly and who's
just the man to have shabby confederates. But I can't see
how he can come into the thing by any process of thought,
unless ..."

"Well?" asked his companion patiently.

Flambeau lowered his voice. "Unless the girl's lover
comes in, too, and he would be the blacker villain. The

Australian chap did know that Hawker wanted the coin. But I can't see how on earth he could know that Hawker had got it, unless Hawker signalled to him or his representative across the shore."

"That is true," assented the priest, with respect.

"Have you noted another thing?" went on Flambeau eagerly; "this Hawker hears his love insulted, but doesn't strike till he's got to the soft sand-hills, where he can be victor in a mere sham-fight. If he'd struck amid rocks and sea, he might have hurt his ally."

"That is true again," said Father Brown, nodding.

"And now, take it from the start. It lies between few people, but at least three. You want one person for suicide; two people for murder; but at least three people for blackmail."

"Why?" asked the priest softly.

"Well, obviously," cried his friend, "there must be one to be exposed; one to threaten exposure; and one at least whom exposure would horrify."

After a long ruminant pause, the priest said: "You miss a logical step. Three persons are needed as ideas. Only two are needed as agents."

"What can you mean?" asked the other.

"Why shouldn't a blackmailer," asked Brown, in a low voice, "threaten his victim with himself? Suppose a wife became a rigid teetotaller in order to frighten her husband into concealing his pub-frequenting, and then wrote him blackmailing letters in another hand, threatening to tell his wife! Why shouldn't it work? Suppose a father forbade a son to gamble and then, following him in a good disguise, threatened the boy with his own sham paternal strictness! Suppose—but, here we are, my friend."

"My God!" cried Flambeau; "you don't mean—"

An active figure ran down the steps of the house and showed under the golden lamplight the unmistakable head that resembled the Roman coin. "Miss Carstairs," said Hawker without ceremony, "wouldn't go in till you came."

"Well," observed Brown confidently, "don't you think it's the best thing she can do to stop outside—with you to look after her? You see, I rather guess you have guessed it all yourself."

"Yes," said the young man, in an undertone, "I guessed on the sands and now I know; that was why I let him fall soft."

Taking a latchkey from the girl and the coin from Hawker, Flambeau let himself and his friend into the empty house and passed into the outer parlour. It was empty of all occupants but one. The man whom Father Brown had seen pass the tavern was standing against the wall as if at bay; unchanged, save that he had taken off his black coat and was wearing a brown dressing-gown.

"We have come," said Father Brown politely, "to give back this coin to its owner." And he handed it to the man with the nose.

Flambeau's eyes rolled. "Is this man a coin-collector?" he asked.

"This man is Mr. Arthur Carstairs," said the priest positively, "and he is a coin-collector of a somewhat singular kind."

The man changed colour so horribly that the crooked nose stood out on his face like a separate and comic thing. He spoke, nevertheless, with a sort of despairing dignity. "You shall see, then," he said, "that I have not lost all the family qualities." And he turned suddenly and strode into an inner room, slamming the door.

"Stop him!" shouted Father Brown, bounding and half falling over a chair; and, after a wrench or two, Flambeau had the door open. But it was too late. In dead silence Flambeau strode across and telephoned for doctor and police.

An empty medicine bottle lay on the floor. Across the table the body of the man in the brown dressing-gown lay amid his burst and gaping brown-paper parcels; out of which poured and rolled, not Roman, but very modern English coins.

The priest held up the bronze head of Caesar. "This," he said, "was all that was left of the Carstairs Collection."

After a silence he went on, with more than common gentleness: "It was a cruel will his wicked father made, and you see he did resent it a little. He hated the Roman money he had, and grew fonder of the real money denied him. He not only sold the Collection bit by bit, but sank bit by bit to the basest ways of making money—even to blackmailing his own family in a disguise. He blackmailed his brother from Australia for his little forgotten crime (that is why he took the cab to Wagga Wagga in Putney), he blackmailed his sister for the theft he alone could have noticed. And that, by the way, is why she had that supernatural guess when he was away on the sand-dunes. Mere figure and gait, however distant, are more likely to remind us of somebody than a well-made-up face quite close."

There was another silence. "Well," growled the detective, "and so this great numismatist and coin-collector was nothing but a vulgar miser."

"Is there so great a difference?" asked Father Brown, in the same strange, indulgent tone. "What is there wrong about a miser that is not often as wrong about a collector? What is wrong, except ... thou shalt not make to thyself any graven image; thou shalt not bow down to them nor serve them, for I ... but we must go and see how the poor young people are getting on."

"I think," said Flambeau, "that in spite of everything, they are probably getting on very well."

"You shall not bear false witness against your neighbor."

The Scandal of Father Brown

It would not be fair to record the adventures of Father Brown, without admitting that he was once involved in a grave scandal. There still are persons, perhaps even of his own community, who would say that there was a sort of blot upon his name. It happened in a picturesque Mexican road-house of rather loose repute, as appeared later; and to some it seemed that for once the priest had allowed a romantic streak in him, and his sympathy for human weakness, to lead him into loose and unorthodox action. The story in itself was a simple one; and perhaps the whole surprise of it consisted in its simplicity.

Burning Troy began with Helen; this disgraceful story began with the beauty of Hypatia Potter. Americans have a great power, which Europeans do not always appreciate, of creating institutions from below; that is by popular initiative. Like every other good thing, it has its lighter aspects; one of which, as has been remarked by Mr. Wells and others, is that a person may become a public institution without becoming an official institution. A girl of great beauty or brilliancy will be a sort of uncrowned queen, even if she is not a Film Star or the original of a Gibson Girl. Among those who had the fortune, or misfortune,

"The Scandal of Father Brown" first appeared in the November 1933 issue of *Story Teller* magazine.

to exist beautifully in public in this manner, was a certain
Hypatia Hard, who had passed through the preliminary
stage of receiving florid compliments in society paragraphs
of the local press, to the position of one who is actually
interviewed by real pressmen. On War and Peace and
Patriotism and Prohibition and Evolution and the Bible
she had made her pronouncements with a charming smile;
and if none of them seemed very near to the real grounds
of her own reputation, it was almost equally hard to say
what the grounds of her reputation really were. Beauty,
and being the daughter of a rich man, are things not rare
in her country; but to these she added whatever it is that
attracts the wandering eye of journalism. Next to none of
her admirers had even seen her, or even hoped to do so;
and none of them could possibly derive any sordid benefit
from her father's wealth. It was simply a sort of popular
romance, the modern substitute for mythology; and it laid
the first foundations of the more turgid and tempestuous
sort of romance in which she was to figure later on; and in
which many held that the reputation of Father Brown, as
well as of others, had been blown to rags.

It was accepted, sometimes romantically, sometimes
resignedly, by those whom American satire has named the
Sob Sisters,[1] that she had already married a very worthy
and respectable business man of the name of Potter. It was
even possible to regard her for a moment as Mrs. Potter,
on the universal understanding that her husband was only
the husband of Mrs. Potter.

Then came the Great Scandal, by which her friends
and enemies were horrified beyond their wildest hopes.
Her name was coupled (as the queer phrase goes) with a
literary man living in Mexico; in status an American, but

[1] "Sob sister" was a slang term of the day for a sentimental woman journalist.

in spirit a very Spanish American. Unfortunately his vices resembled her virtues, in being good copy. He was no less a person than the famous or infamous Rudel Romanes; the poet whose works had been so universally popularised by being vetoed by libraries or prosecuted by the police. Anyhow, her pure and placid star was seen in conjunction with this comet. He was of the sort to be compared to a comet, being hairy and hot; the first in his portraits, the second in his poetry. He was also destructive; the comet's tail was a trail of divorces, which some called his success as a lover and some his prolonged failure as a husband. It was hard on Hypatia; there are disadvantages in conducting the perfect private life in public; like a domestic interior in a shop-window. Interviewers reported doubtful utterances about Love's Larger Law of Supreme Self-Realisation. The Pagans applauded. The Sob Sisterhood permitted themselves a note of romantic regret; some having even the hardened audacity to quote from the poem of Maud Mueller, to the effect that of all the words of tongue or pen, the saddest are "It might have been." And Mr. Agar P. Rock, who hated the Sob Sisterhood with a holy and righteous hatred, said that in this case he thoroughly agreed with Bret Harte's emendation of the poem: "More sad are those we daily see; it is, but it hadn't ought to be."

For Mr. Rock was very firmly and rightly convinced that a very large number of things hadn't ought to be. He was a slashing and savage critic of national degeneration, on the *Minneapolis Meteor*, and a bold and honest man. He had perhaps come to specialise too much in the spirit of indignation, but it had had a healthy enough origin in his reaction against sloppy attempts to confuse right and wrong in modern journalism and gossip. He expressed it first in the form of a protest against an unholy halo of romance being thrown round the gunman and

the gangster. Perhaps he was rather too much inclined to
assume, in robust impatience, that all gangsters were Dagos
and that all Dagos were gangsters. But his prejudices, even
when they were a little provincial, were rather refreshing
after a certain sort of maudlin and unmanly hero-worship,
which was ready to regard a professional murderer as a
leader of fashion, so long as the pressmen reported that his
smile was irresistible or his tuxedo was all right. Anyhow,
the prejudices did not boil the less in the bosom of Mr.
Rock, because he was actually in the land of the Dagos
when this story opens; striding furiously up a hill beyond
the Mexican border, to the white hotel, fringed with orna-
mental palms, in which it was supposed that the Potters
were staying and that the mysterious Hypatia now held
her court. Agar Rock was a good specimen of a Puritan,
even to look at; he might even have been a virile Puritan
of the seventeenth century, rather than the softer and more
sophisticated Puritan of the twentieth. If you had told him
that his antiquated black hat and habitual black frown, and
fine flinty features, cast a gloom over the sunny land of
palms and vines, he would have been very much gratified.
He looked to right and left with eyes bright with universal
suspicions. And, as he did so, he saw two figures on the
ridge above him, outlined against the clear sub-tropical
sunset; figures in a momentary posture which might have
made even a less suspicious man suspect something.

One of the figures was rather remarkable in itself. It
was poised at the exact angle of the turning road above
the valley, as if by an instinct for the site as well as the
attitude of statuary. It was wrapt in a great black cloak,
in the Byronic manner, and the head that rose above it in
swarthy beauty was remarkably like Byron's. This man
had the same curling hair and curling nostrils; and he
seemed to be snorting something of the same scorn and

indignation against the world. He grasped in his hand a rather long cane or walking-stick, which having a spike of the sort used for mountaineering, carried at the moment a fanciful suggestion of a spear. It was rendered all the more fanciful by something comically contradictory in the figure of the other man, who carried an umbrella. It was indeed a new and neatly-rolled umbrella, very different, for instance, from Father Brown's umbrella: and he was neatly clad like a clerk in light holiday clothes; a stumpy stoutish bearded man; but the prosaic umbrella was raised and even brandished at an acute angle of attack. The taller man thrust back at him, but in a hasty defensive manner; and then the scene rather collapsed into comedy; for the umbrella opened of itself and its owner almost seemed to sink behind it, while the other man had the air of pushing his spear through a great grotesque shield. But the other man did not push it, or the quarrel, very far; he plucked out the point, turned away impatiently and strode down the road; while the other, rising and carefully refolding his umbrella, turned in the opposite direction towards the hotel. Rock had not heard any of the words of the quarrel, which must have immediately preceded this brief and rather absurd bodily conflict; but as he went up the road in the track of the short man with the beard, he revolved many things. And the romantic cloak and rather operatic good looks of the one man, combined with the sturdy self-assertion of the other, fitted in with the whole story which he had come to seek; and he knew that he could have fixed those two strange figures with their names: Romanes and Potter.

His view was in every way confirmed when he entered the pillared porch; and heard the voice of the bearded man raised high in altercation or command. He was evidently speaking to the manager or staff of the hotel, and Rock

heard enough to know that he was warning them of a wild
and dangerous character in the neighbourhood.

"If he's really been to the hotel already," the little man
was saying, in answer to some murmur, "all I can say is
that you'd better not let him in again. Your police ought
to be looking after a fellow of that sort, but anyhow, I
won't have the lady pestered with him."

Rock listened in grim silence and growing conviction;
then he slid across the vestibule to an alcove where he
saw the hotel register and turning to the last page, saw
"the fellow" had indeed been to the hotel already. There
appeared the name of "Rudel Romanes", that romantic
public character, in very large and florid foreign lettering;
and after a space under it, rather close together, the names
of Hypatia Potter and Ellis T. Potter, in a correct and quite
American handwriting.

Agar Rock looked moodily about him, and saw in the
surroundings and even the small decorations of the hotel
everything that he hated most. It is perhaps unreasonable
to complain of oranges growing on orange-trees, even
in small tubs; still more of their only growing on thread-
bare curtains or faded wallpapers as a formal scheme of
ornament. But to him those red and golden moons, deco-
ratively alternated with silver moons, were in a queer way
the quintessence of all moonshine. He saw in them all that
sentimental deterioration which his principles deplored
in modern manners, and which his prejudices vaguely
connected with the warmth and softness of the South. It
annoyed him even to catch sight of a patch of dark canvas,
half-showing a Watteau shepherd with a guitar, or a blue
tile with a common-place design of a Cupid on a dolphin.
His common sense would have told him that he might
have seen these things in a shop-window on Fifth Avenue;
but where they were, they seemed like a taunting siren

voice of the Paganism of the Mediterranean. And then suddenly, the look of all these things seemed to alter, as a still mirror will flicker when a figure has flashed past it for a moment; and he knew the whole room was full of a challenging presence. He turned almost stiffly, and with a sort of resistance, and knew that he was facing the famous Hypatia, of whom he had read and heard for so many years.

Hypatia Potter, *née* Hard, was one of those people to whom the word "radiant" really does apply definitely and derivatively. That is, she allowed what the papers called her Personality to go out from her in rays. She would have been equally beautiful, and to some tastes more attractive, if she had been self-contained; but she had always been taught to believe that self-containment was only selfishness. She would have said that she had lost Self in Service; it would perhaps be truer to say that she had asserted Self in Service; but she was quite in good faith about the service. Therefore her outstanding starry blue eyes really struck outwards, as in the old metaphor that made eyes like Cupid's darts, killing at a distance; but with an abstract conception of conquest beyond any mere coquetry. Her pale fair hair, though arranged in a saintly halo, had a look of almost electric radiation. And when she understood that the stranger before her was Mr. Agar Rock, of the *Minneapolis Meteor*, her eyes took on themselves the range of long searchlights, sweeping the horizon of the States.

But in this the lady was mistaken; as she sometimes was. For Agar Rock was not Agar Rock of the *Minneapolis Meteor*. He was at that moment merely Agar Rock; there had surged up in him a great and sincere moral impulsion, beyond the coarse courage of the interviewer. A feeling profoundly mixed of a chivalrous and national sensibility to beauty, with an instant itch for moral action of some definite sort, which was also national, nerved him to face a great scene; and to deliver a noble insult. He remembered the original Hypatia, the beautiful Neo-Platonist, and how he had been thrilled as a boy by Kingsley's romance in which the young monk denounces her for harlotries and idolatries. He confronted her with an iron gravity and said:

"If you'll pardon me. Madam, I should like to have a word with you in private."

"Well," she said, sweeping the room with her splendid gaze, "I don't know whether you consider this place private."

Rock also gazed round the room and could see no sign of life less vegetable than the orange trees, except what looked like a large black mushroom, which he recognised as the hat of some native priest or other, stolidly smoking a black local cigar, and otherwise as stagnant as any vegetable. He looked for a moment at the heavy, expressionless features, noting the rudeness of that peasant type from which priests so often come, in Latin and especially Latin-American countries; and lowered his voice a little as he laughed.

"I don't imagine that Mexican padre knows our language," he said. "Catch those lumps of laziness learning any language but their own. Oh, I can't swear he's a Mexican; he might be anything; mongrel Indian or nigger, I suppose. But I'll answer for it he's not an American. Our ministries don't produce that debased type."

"As a matter of fact," said the debased type, removing his black cigar, "I'm English and my name is Brown. But pray let me leave you if you wish to be private."

"If you're English,' said Rock warmly, "you ought to have some normal Nordic instinct for protesting against all this nonsense. Well, it's enough to say now that I'm in a position to testify that there's a pretty dangerous fellow hanging round this place; a tall fellow in a cloak, like those pictures of crazy poets."

"Well, you can't go much by that," said the priest mildly; "a lot of people round here use those cloaks, because the chill strikes very suddenly after sunset."

Rock darted a dark and doubtful glance at him; as if suspecting some evasion in the interests of all that was symbolised to him by mushroom hats and moonshine. "It wasn't only the cloak," he growled, "though it was partly the way he wore it. The whole look of the fellow was theatrical, down to his damned theatrical good looks. And if you'll forgive me, Madam, I strongly advise you to have nothing to do with him, if he comes bothering here. Your husband has already told the hotel people to keep him out—"

Hypatia sprang to her feet and, with a very unusual gesture, covered her face, thrusting her fingers into her hair. She seemed to be shaken, possibly with sobs, but by the time she had recovered they had turned into a sort of wild laughter.

"Oh, you are all too funny," she said, and, in a way very unusual with her, ducked and darted to the door and disappeared.

"Bit hysterical when they laugh like that," said Rock uncomfortably; then, rather at a loss, and turning to the little priest: "as I say, if you're English, you ought really to be on my side against these Dagos, anyhow. Oh, I'm not one of those who talk tosh about Anglo-Saxons; but there is such a thing as history. You can always claim that America got her civilisation from England."

"Also, to temper our pride," said Father Brown, "we must always admit that England got her civilisation from Dagos."

Again there glowed in the other's mind the exasperated sense that his interlocutor was fencing with him, and fencing on the wrong side, in some secret and evasive way; and he curtly professed a failure to comprehend.

"Well, there was a Dago, or possibly a Wop, called Julius Caesar," said Father Brown; "he was afterwards killed in a stabbing match; you know these Dagos always use knives. And there was another one called Augustine, who brought Christianity to our little island; and really, I don't think we should have had much civilisation without those two."

"Anyhow, that's all ancient history," said the somewhat irritated journalist, "and I'm very much interested in modern history. What I see is that these scoundrels are bringing Paganism to our country, and destroying all the Christianity there is. Also destroying all the common sense there is. All settled habits, all solid social order, all the way in which the farmers who were our fathers and grandfathers did manage to live in the world, melted into a hot mush by sensations and sensualities about film stars who divorced every month or so, and make every silly girl think that marriage is only a way of getting divorced."

"You are quite right," said Father Brown. "Of course I quite agree with you there. But you must make some allowances. Perhaps these Southern people are a little prone to that sort of fault. You must remember that Northern people have other kinds of faults. Perhaps these surroundings do encourage people to give too rich an importance to mere romance."

The whole integral indignation of Agar Rock's life rose up within him at the word.

"I hate Romance," he said, hitting the little table before him. "I've fought the papers I worked for for forty years about the infernal trash. Every blackguard bolting with a barmaid is called a romantic elopement or something; and now our own Hypatia Hard, a daughter of a decent people, may get dragged into some rotten romantic divorce case, that will be trumpeted to the whole world as happily as a royal wedding. This mad poet Romanes is hanging round her; and you bet the spotlight will follow him, as if he were any rotten little Dago who is called the Great Lover on the films. I saw him outside; and he's got the regular spotlight face. Now my sympathies are with decency and common sense. My sympathies are with poor Potter, a plain straightforward broker from Pittsburgh, who thinks he has a right to his own home. And he's making a fight for it, too. I heard him hollering at the management, telling them to keep that rascal out; and quite right too. The people here seem a sly and slinky lot; but I rather fancy he's put the fear of God into them already."

"As a matter of fact," said Father Brown, "I rather agree with you about the manager and the men in this hotel; but you mustn't judge all Mexicans by them. Also I fancy the gentleman you speak of has not only hollered, but handed round dollars enough to get the whole staff on his side. I saw them locking doors and whispering most excitedly. By the way, your plain straightforward friend seems to have a lot of money."

"I've no doubt his business does well," said Rock. "He's quite the best type of sound business man. What do you mean?"

"I fancied it might suggest another thought to you," said Father Brown; and, rising with rather heavy civility, he left the room.

Rock watched the Potters very carefully that evening at dinner; and gained some new impressions, though none that disturbed his deep sense of the wrong that probably threatened the peace of the Potter home. Potter himself proved worthy of somewhat closer study; though the journalist had at first accepted him as prosaic and unpretentious, there was a pleasure in recognising finer lines in what he considered the hero or victim of a tragedy. Potter had really rather a thoughtful and distinguished face, though worried and occasionally petulant. Rock got an impression that the man was recovering from an illness; his faded hair was thin but rather long, as if it had been lately neglected, and his rather unusual beard gave the onlooker the same notion. Certainly he spoke once or twice to his wife in a rather sharp and acid manner, fussing about tablets or some detail of digestive science; but his real worry was doubtless concerned with the danger from without. His wife played up to him in the splendid if somewhat condescending manner of a Patient Griselda; but her eyes also roamed continually to the doors and shutters, as if in half-hearted fear of an invasion. Rock had only too good reason to dread, after her curious outbreak, the fact that her fear might turn out to be only half-hearted.

It was in the middle of the night that the extraordinary event occurred. Rock, imagining himself to be the last to go up to bed, was surprised to find Father Brown still tucked obscurely under an orange-tree in the hall, and placidly reading a book. He returned the other's farewell without further words, and the journalist had his foot on the lowest step of the stair, when suddenly the outer door sprang on its hinges and shook and rattled under the shock of blows planted from without; and a great voice louder than the blows was heard violently demanding admission. Somehow the journalist was certain that the blows had been struck with a pointed stick like an alpenstock. He looked back at the darkened lower floor, and saw the servants of the hotel sliding here and there to see that the doors were locked; and not unlocking them. Then he slowly mounted to his room, and sat down furiously to write his report.

He described the siege of the hotel; the evil atmosphere; the shabby luxury of the place; the shifty evasions of the priest; above all, that terrible voice crying without, like a wolf prowling round the house. Then, as he wrote, he heard a new sound and sat up suddenly. It was a long repeated whistle, and in his mood he hated it doubly, because it was like the signal of a conspirator and like the love-call of a bird. There followed an utter silence, in which he sat rigid; then he rose abruptly; for he had heard yet another noise. It was a faint swish followed by a sharp rap or rattle; and he was almost certain that somebody was throwing something at the window. He walked stiffly downstairs, to the floor which was now dark and deserted; or nearly deserted. For the little priest was still sitting under the orange shrub, lit by a low lamp; and still reading his book.

"You seem to be sitting up late," he said harshly.

"Quite a dissipated character," said Father Brown, looking up with a broad smile, "reading *Economics of Usury* at all wild hours of the night."

"The place is locked up," said Rock.

"Very thoroughly locked up," replied the other. "Your friend with the beard seems to have taken every precaution. By the way, your friend with the beard is a little rattled; I thought he was rather cross at dinner."

"Natural enough," growled the other, "if he thinks savages in this savage place are out to wreck his home life."

"Wouldn't it be better," said Father Brown, "if a man tried to make his home life nice inside, while he was protecting it from the things outside."

"Oh, I know you will work up all the casuistical excuses," said the other; "perhaps he was rather snappy with his wife; but he's got the right on his side. Look here, you seem to me to be rather a deep dog. I believe you know more about this than you say. What the devil is going on in this infernal place? Why are you sitting up all night to see it through?"

"Well," said Father Brown patiently, "I rather thought my bedroom might be wanted."

"Wanted by whom?"

"As a matter of fact, Mrs. Potter wanted another room," explained Father Brown with limpid clearness. "I gave her mine, because I could open the window. Go and see, if you like."

"I'll see to something else first," said Rock grinding his teeth. "You can play your monkey tricks in this Spanish monkey-house, but I'm still in touch with civilisation." He strode into the telephone-booth and rang up his paper; pouring out the whole tale of the wicked priest who helped the wicked poet. Then he ran upstairs into the priest's room, in which the priest had just lit a short candle, showing the windows beyond wide open.

He was just in time to see a sort of rude ladder unhooked from the window-sill and rolled up by a laughing gentleman on the lawn below. The laughing gentleman was a tall and swarthy gentleman, and was accompanied by a blonde but equally laughing lady. This time, Mr. Rock could not even comfort himself by calling her laughter hysterical. It was too horribly genuine; and rang down the rambling garden-paths as she and her troubadour disappeared into the dark thickets.

Agar Rock turned on his companion a face of final and awful justice; like the Day of Judgement.

"Well, all America is going to hear of this," he said. "In plain words, you helped her to bolt with that curly-haired lover."

"Yes," said Father Brown, "I helped her to bolt with that curly-haired lover."

"You call yourself a minister of Jesus Christ," cried Rock, "and you boast of a crime."

"I have been mixed up with several crimes," said the priest gently. "Happily for once this is a story without a crime. This is a simple fire-side idyll; that ends with a glow of domesticity."

"And ends with a rope-ladder instead of a rope," said Rock. "Isn't she a married woman?"

"Oh, yes," said Father Brown.

"Well, oughtn't she to be with her husband?" demanded Rock.

"She is with her husband," said Father Brown.

The other was startled into anger. "You lie," he said. "The poor little man is still snoring in bed."

"You seem to know a lot about his private affairs," said Father Brown plaintively. "You could almost write a life of the Man with a Beard. The only thing you don't seem ever to have found out about him is his name."

"Nonsense," said Rock. "His name is in the hotel book."

"I know it is," answered the priest, nodding gravely, "in very large letters; the name of Rudel Romanes. Hypatia Potter, who met him here, put her name boldly under his, when she meant to elope with him; and her husband put his name under that, when he pursued them to this place. He put it very close under hers, by way of protest. Then Romanes (who has pots of money, as a popular misanthrope despising men) bribed the brutes in this hotel to bar and bolt it and keep the lawful husband out. And I, as you truly say, helped him to get in."

When a man is told something that turns things upside-down; that the tail wags the dog; that the fish has caught the fisherman; that the earth goes round the moon; he takes some little time before he even asks seriously if it is true. He is still content with the consciousness that it is the opposite of the obvious truth. Rock said at last: "You don't mean that little fellow is the romantic Rudel we're always reading about; and that curly haired fellow is Mr. Potter of Pittsburgh."

"Yes," said Father Brown. "I knew it the moment I clapped eyes on both of them. But I verified it afterwards."

Rock ruminated for a time and said at last: "I suppose it's barely possible you're right. But how did you come to have such a notion, in the face of the facts?"

Father Brown looked rather abashed; subsided into a chair, and stared into vacancy, until a faint smile began to dawn on his round and rather foolish face.

"Well," he said, "you see—the truth is, I'm not romantic."

"I don't know what the devil you are," said Rock roughly.

"Now you are romantic," said Father Brown helpfully. "For instance, you see somebody looking poetical, and you assume he is a poet. Do you know what the majority of poets look like? What a wild confusion was created by that coincidence of three good-looking aristocrats at the beginning of the nineteenth century: Byron and Goethe and Shelley! Believe me, in the common way, a man may write: 'Beauty has laid her flaming lips on mine,' or whatever that chap wrote, without being himself particularly beautiful. Besides, do you realise how old a man generally is by the time his fame has filled the world? Watts painted Swinburne with a halo of hair; but Swinburne was bald before most of his last American or Australian admirers had heard of his hyacinthine locks. So was D'Annunzio. As a fact, Romanes still has rather a fine head, as you will see if you look at it closely; he looks like an intellectual man; and he is. Unfortunately, like a good many other intellectual men, he's a fool. He's let himself go to seed with selfishness and fussing about his digestion. So that the ambitious American lady, who thought it would be like soaring to Olympus with the Nine Muses to elope with a poet, found that a day or so of it was about enough for her."

So that when her husband came after her, and stormed the place, she was delighted to go back to him."

"But her husband?" queried Rock. "I am still rather puzzled about her husband."

"Ah, you've been reading too many of your erotic modern novels," said Father Brown; and partly closed his eyes in answer to the protesting glare of the other. "I know a lot of stories start with a wildly beautiful woman wedded to some elderly swine in the stock market. But why? In that, as in most things, modern novels are the very reverse of modern. I don't say it never happens; but it hardly ever happens now except by her own fault. Girls nowadays marry whom they like; especially spoilt girls like Hypatia. And whom do they marry? A beautiful wealthy girl like that would have a ring of admirers; and whom would she choose? The chances are a hundred to one that she'd marry very young and choose the handsomest man she met at a dance or a tennis-party. Well, ordinary business men are sometimes handsome. A young god appeared (called Potter) and she wouldn't care if he was a broker or a burglar. But, given the environment, you will admit it's more likely he would be a broker; also, it's quite likely that he'd be called Potter. You see, you are so incurably romantic that your whole case was founded on the idea that a man looking like a young god couldn't be called Potter. Believe me, names are not so appropriately distributed."

"Well," said the other, after a short pause, "and what do you suppose happened after that?"

Father Brown got up rather abruptly from the seat in which he had collapsed; the candlelight threw the shadow of his short figure across the wall and ceiling, giving an odd impression that the balance of the room had been altered.

"Ah," he muttered, "that's the devil of it. That's the real devil. Much worse than the old Indian demons in this jungle. You thought I was only making out a case for the loose ways of these Latin Americans—well, the queer thing about you"—and he blinked owlishly at the other through his spectacles—"the queerest thing about you is that in a way you're right.

"You say down with romance. I say I'd take my chance in fighting the genuine romances—all the more because they are precious few, outside the first fiery days of youth. I say—take away the Intellectual Friendships; take away the Platonic Unions; take away the Higher Laws of Self-Fulfilment and the rest, and I'll risk the normal dangers of the job. Take away the love that isn't love, but only pride and vainglory and publicity and making a splash; and we'll take our chance of fighting the love that is love, when it has to be fought, as well as the love that is lust and lechery. Priests know young people will have passions, as doctors know they will have measles. But Hypatia Potter is forty if she is a day, and she cares no more for that little poet than if he were her publisher or her publicity man. That's just the point—he was her publicity man. It's your newspapers that have ruined her; it's living in the limelight; it's wanting to see herself in the headlines, even in a scandal if it were only sufficiently psychic and superior. It's wanting to be George Sand, her name immortally linked with Alfred de Musset. When her real romance of youth was over, it was the sin of middle age that got hold of her; the sin of intellectual ambition. She hasn't got any intellect to speak of; but you don't need any intellect to be an intellectual."

"I should say she was pretty brainy in one sense," observed Rock reflectively.

"Yes, in one sense," said Father Brown. "In only one sense. In a business sense. Not in any sense that has anything to do with these poor lounging Dagos down here. You curse the Film Stars and tell me you hate romance. Do you suppose the Film Star, who is married for the fifth time, is misled by any romance? Such people are very practical; more practical than you are. You say you admire the simple solid Business Man. Do you suppose that Rudel Romanes isn't a Business Man? Can't you see he knew, quite as well as she did, the advertising advantages of this grand affair with a famous beauty. He also knew very well that his hold on it was pretty insecure; hence his fussing about and bribing servants to lock doors. But what I mean to say, first and last, is that there'd be a lot less scandal if people didn't idealise sin and pose as sinners. These poor Mexicans may seem sometimes to live like beasts, or rather sin like men; but they don't go in for Ideals. You must at least give them credit for that."

He sat down again, as abruptly as he had risen, and laughed apologetically. "Well, Mr. Rock," he said, "that is my complete confession; the whole horrible story of how I helped a romantic elopement. You can do what you like with it."

"In that case," said Rock, rising, "I will go to my room and make a few alterations in my report. But, first of all, I must ring up my paper and tell them I've been telling them a pack of lies."

Not much more than half an hour had passed, between the time when Rock had telephoned to say the priest was helping the poet to run away with the lady, and the time when he telephoned to say that the priest had prevented the poet from doing precisely the same thing. But in that short interval of time was born and enlarged and scattered upon the winds the Scandal of Father Brown. The truth is still half an hour behind the slander; and nobody can be certain when or where it will catch up with it. The garrulity of pressmen and the eagerness of enemies had spread the first story through the city, even before it appeared in the first printed version. It was instantly corrected and contradicted by Rock himself, in a second message stating how the story had really ended; but it was by no means certain that the first story was killed. A positively incredible number of people seemed to have read the first issue of the paper and not the second. Again and again, in every corner of the world, like a flame bursting from blackened ashes, there would appear the old tale of the Brown Scandal, or Priest Ruins Potter Home. Tireless apologists of the priest's party watched for it, and patiently tagged after it with contradictions and exposures and letters of protest. Sometimes the letters were published in the papers; and sometimes they were not. But still nobody knew how many people had heard the story without hearing the contradiction. It was possible to find whole blocks of blameless and innocent people who thought the Mexican Scandal was an ordinary recorded historical incident like the Gunpowder Plot. Then somebody would enlighten these simple people, only to discover that the old story had started afresh among a few quite educated people, who would seem the last people on earth to be duped by it. And so the two Father Browns chase each other round the world for ever; the first a shameless criminal fleeing from justice; the second a martyr broken by slander, in a halo of rehabilitation. But neither of them is very like the real Father Brown, who is not broken at all; but goes stumping with his stout umbrella through life, liking most of the people in it; accepting the world as his companion, but never as his judge.

"You shall not covet your neighbor's wife."

The Strange Crime of John Boulnois

Mr. Calhoun Kidd was a very young gentleman with a very old face, a face dried up with its own eagerness, framed in blue-black hair and a black butterfly tie. He was the emissary in England of the colossal American daily called the *Western Sun*—also humorously described as the "Rising Sunset". This was in allusion to a great journalistic declaration (attributed to Mr. Kidd himself) that "he guessed the sun would rise in the west yet, if American citizens did a bit more hustling." Those, however, who mock American journalism from the standpoint of somewhat mellower traditions forget a certain paradox which partly redeems it. For while the journalism of the States permits a panto-mimic vulgarity long past anything English, it also shows a real excitement about the most earnest mental problems, of which English papers are innocent, or rather incapable. The *Sun* was full of the most solemn matters treated in the most farcical way. William James figured there as well as "Weary Willie,"[1] and pragmatists alternated with pugilists in the long procession of its portraits.

Thus, when a very unobtrusive Oxford man named John Boulnois wrote in a very unreadable review called

---

"The Strange Crime of John Boulnois" was first published in the February 1913 issue of *McClure's Magazine*.

[1] Weary Willy was a hobo character in an American comic magazine of the day.

the *Natural Philosophy Quarterly* a series of articles on alleged weak points in Darwinian evolution, it fluttered no corner of the English papers; though Boulnois's theory (which was that of a comparatively stationary universe visited occasionally by convulsions of change) had some rather faddy fashionableness at Oxford, and got so far as to be named "Catastrophism." But many American papers seized on the challenge as a great event; and the *Sun* threw the shadow of Mr. Boulnois quite gigantically across its pages. By the paradox already noted, articles of valuable intelligence and enthusiasm were presented with headlines apparently written by an illiterate maniac, headlines such as "Darwin Chews Dirt; Critic Boulnois says He Jumps the Shocks"—or "Keep Catastrophic, says Thinker Boulnois." And Mr. Calhoun Kidd, of the *Western Sun*, was bidden to take his butterfly tie and lugubrious visage down to the little house outside Oxford where Thinker Boulnois lived in happy ignorance of such a title.

That fated philosopher had consented, in a somewhat dazed manner, to receive the interviewer, and had named the hour of nine that evening. The last of a summer sunset clung about Cumnor and the low wooded hills; the romantic Yankee was both doubtful of his road and inquisitive about his surroundings; and seeing the door of a genuine feudal old-country inn, The Champion Arms, standing open, he went in to make inquiries.

In the bar parlour he rang the bell, and had to wait some little time for a reply to it. The only other person present was a lean man with close red hair and loose, horsey-looking clothes, who was drinking very bad whisky, but smoking a very good cigar. The whisky, of course, was the choice brand of The Champion Arms; the cigar he had probably brought with him from London. Nothing could be more different than his cynical negligence from the dapper dryness of the young American; but something in his pencil and open notebook, and perhaps in the expression of his alert blue eye, caused Kidd to guess, correctly, that he was a brother journalist.

"Could you do me the favour," asked Kidd, with the courtesy of his nation, "of directing me to the Grey Cottage, where Mr. Boulnois lives, as I understand?"

"It's a few yards down the road," said the red-haired man, removing his cigar; "I shall be passing it myself in a minute, but I'm going on to Pendragon Park to try and see the fun."

"What is Pendragon Park?" asked Calhoun Kidd.

"Sir Claude Champion's place—haven't you come down for that, too?" asked the other pressman, looking up. "You're a journalist, aren't you?"

"I have come to see Mr. Boulnois," said Kidd.

"I've come to see Mrs. Boulnois," replied the other. "But I shan't catch her at home." And he laughed rather unpleasantly.

"Are you interested in Catastrophism?" asked the wondering Yankee.

"I'm interested in catastrophes; and there are going to be some," replied his companion gloomily. "Mine's a filthy trade, and I never pretend it isn't."

With that he spat on the floor; yet somehow in the very act and instant one could realise that the man had been brought up as a gentleman.

The American pressman considered him with more attention. His face was pale and dissipated, with the promise of formidable passions yet to be loosed; but it was a clever and sensitive face; his clothes were coarse and careless, but he had a good seal ring on one of his long, thin fingers. His name, which came out in the course of talk, was James Dalroy; he was the son of a bankrupt Irish landlord, and attached to a pink paper which he heartily despised, called *Smart Society*, in the capacity of reporter and of something painfully like a spy.

Smart Society, I regret to say, felt none of that interest in Boulnois on Darwin which was such a credit to the head and hearts of the *Western Sun*. Dalroy had come down, it seemed, to snuff up the scent of a scandal which might very well end in the Divorce Court, but which was at present hovering between Grey Cottage and Pendragon Park.

Sir Claude Champion was known to the readers of the *Western Sun* as well as Mr. Boulnois. So were the Pope and the Derby Winner; but the idea of their intimate acquaintanceship would have struck Kidd as equally incongruous. He had heard of (and written about, nay, falsely pretended to know) Sir Claude Champion, as "one of the brightest and wealthiest of England's Upper Ten"; as the great sportsman who raced yachts round the world; as the great traveller who wrote books about the Himalayas, as the politician who swept constituencies with a startling sort of Tory Democracy, and as the great dabbler in art, music, literature, and, above all, acting. Sir Claude was really rather magnificent in other than American eyes. There was something of the Renascence Prince about his omnivorous culture and restless publicity—he was not only a great amateur, but an ardent one. There was in him none of that antiquarian frivolity that we convey by the word "dilettante."

That faultless falcon profile with purple-black Italian eye, which had been snap-shotted so often both for *Smart Society* and the *Western Sun*, gave everyone the impression of a man eaten by ambition as by a fire, or even a disease. But though Kidd knew a great deal about Sir Claude—a great deal more, in fact, than there was to know—it would never have crossed his wildest dreams to connect so showy

an aristocrat with the newly-unearthed founder of Catastrophism, or to guess that Sir Claude Champion and John
Boulnois could be intimate friends. Such, according to
Dalroy's account, was nevertheless the fact. The two had
hunted in couples at school and college, and, though their
social destinies had been very different (for Champion was
a great landlord and almost a millionaire, while Boulnois
was a poor scholar and, until just lately, an unknown
one), they still kept in very close touch with each other.
Indeed, Boulnois's cottage stood just outside the gates of
Pendragon Park.

But whether the two men could be friends much longer
was becoming a dark and ugly question. A year or two
before, Boulnois had married a beautiful and not unsuc-
cessful actress, to whom he was devoted in his own shy
and ponderous style; and the proximity of the household
to Champion's had given that flighty celebrity opportuni-
ties for behaving in a way that could not but cause painful
and rather base excitement. Sir Claude had carried the arts
of publicity to perfection; and he seemed to take a crazy
pleasure in being equally ostentatious in an intrigue that
could do him no sort of honour. Footmen from Pendragon
were perpetually leaving bouquets for Mrs. Boulnois;
carriages and motor-cars were perpetually calling at the
cottage for Mrs. Boulnois; balls and masquerades perpetually filled the grounds in which the baronet paraded
Mrs. Boulnois, like the Queen of Love and Beauty at a
tournament. That very evening, marked by Mr. Kidd for
the exposition of Catastrophism, had been marked by Sir
Claude Champion for an open-air rendering of *Romeo and
Juliet*, in which he was to play Romeo to a Juliet it was
needless to name.

"I don't think it can go on without a smash," said the
young man with red hair, getting up and shaking himself.

"Old Boulnois may be squared—or he may be square. But if he's square he's thick—what you might call cubic. But I don't believe it's possible."

"He is a man of grand intellectual powers," said Calhoun Kidd in a deep voice.

"Yes," answered Dalroy; "but even a man of grand intellectual powers can't be such a blighted fool as all that. Must you be going on? I shall be following myself in a minute or two."

But Calhoun Kidd, having finished a milk and soda, betook himself smartly up the road towards the Grey Cottage, leaving his cynical informant to his whisky and tobacco. The last of the daylight had faded; the skies were of a dark, green-grey, like slate, studded here and there with a star, but lighter on the left side of the sky, with the promise of a rising moon.

The Grey Cottage, which stood entrenched, as it were, in a square of stiff, high thorn-hedges, was so close under the pines and palisades of the Park that Kidd at first mistook it for the Park Lodge. Finding the name on the narrow wooden gate, however, and seeing by his watch that the hour of the "Thinker's" appointment had just struck, he went in and knocked at the front door. Inside the garden hedge, he could see that the house, though unpretentious enough, was larger and more luxurious than it looked at first, and was quite a different kind of place from a porter's lodge. A dog-kennel and a beehive stood outside, like symbols of old English country-life; the moon was rising behind a plantation of prosperous pear trees, the dog that came out of the kennel was reverend-looking and reluctant to bark; and the plain, elderly man-servant who opened the door was brief but dignified.

"Mr. Boulnois asked me to offer his apologies, sir," he said, "but he has been obliged to go out suddenly."

"But see here, I had an appointment," said the interviewer, with a rising voice. "Do you know where he went to?"

"To Pendragon Park, sir," said the servant, rather sombrely, and began to close the door.

Kidd started a little.

"Did he go with Mrs.—with the rest of the party?" he asked rather vaguely.

"No, sir," said the man shortly; "he stayed behind, and then went out alone." And he shut the door, brutally, but with an air of duty not done.

The American, that curious compound of impudence and sensitiveness, was annoyed. He felt a strong desire to hustle them all along a bit and teach them business habits; the hoary old dog and the grizzled, heavy-faced old butler with his prehistoric shirt-front, and the drowsy old moon, and above all the scatter-brained old philosopher who couldn't keep an appointment.

"If that's the way he goes on he deserves to lose his wife's purest devotion," said Mr. Calhoun Kidd. "But perhaps he's gone over to make a row. In that case I reckon a man from the *Western Sun* will be on the spot."

And turning the corner by the open lodge-gates, he set off, stumping up the long avenue of black pine-woods that pointed in abrupt perspective towards the inner gardens of Pendragon Park. The trees were as black and orderly as plumes upon a hearse; there were still a few stars. He was a man with more literary than direct natural associations; the word "Ravenswood" came into his head repeatedly.[2] It was partly the raven colour of the pine-woods; but partly also an indescribable atmosphere almost described in

[2] Mr. Kidd is brooding over Sir Walter Scott's novel *The Bride of Lammermoor* (1819).

Scott's great tragedy; the smell of something that died in the eighteenth century; the smell of dank gardens and broken urns, of wrongs that will never now be righted; of something that is none the less incurably sad because it is strangely unreal.

More than once, as he went up that strange, black road of tragic artifice, he stopped, startled, thinking he heard steps in front of him. He could see nothing in front but the twin sombre walls of pine and the wedge of starlit sky above them. At first he thought he must have fancied it or been mocked by a mere echo of his own tramp. But as he went on he was more and more inclined to conclude, with the remains of his reason, that there really were other feet upon the road. He thought hazily of ghosts; and was surprised how swiftly he could see the image of an appropriate and local ghost, one with a face as white as Pierrot's, but patched with black. The apex of the triangle of dark-blue sky was growing brighter and bluer, but he did not realise as yet that this was because he was coming nearer to the lights of the great house and garden. He only felt that the atmosphere was growing more intense, there was in the sadness more violence and secrecy—more—he hesitated for the word, and then said it with a jerk of laughter—Catastrophism.

More pines, more pathway slid past him, and then he stood rooted as by a blast of magic. It is vain to say that he felt as if he had got into a dream; but this time he felt quite certain that he had got into a book. For we human beings are used to inappropriate things; we are accustomed to the clatter of the incongruous; it is a tune to which we can go to sleep. If one appropriate thing happens, it wakes us up like the pang of a perfect chord. Something happened such as would have happened in such a place in a forgotten tale.

Over the black pine-wood came flying and flashing in the moon a naked sword—such a slender and sparkling rapier as may have fought many an unjust duel in that ancient park. It fell on the pathway far in front of him and lay there glistening like a large needle. He ran like a hare and bent to look at it. Seen at close quarters it had rather a showy look: the big red jewels in the hilt and guard were a little dubious. But there were other red drops upon the blade which were not dubious.

He looked round wildly in the direction from which the dazzling missile had come, and saw that at this point the sable façade of fir and pine was interrupted by a smaller road at right angles; which, when he turned it, brought him in full view of the long, lighted house, with a lake and fountains in front of it. Nevertheless, he did not look at this, having something more interesting to look at.

Above him, at the angle of the steep green bank of the terraced garden, was one of those small picturesque surprises common in the old landscape gardening; a kind of small round hill or dome of grass, like a giant mole-hill, ringed and crowned with three concentric fences of roses, and having a sundial in the highest point in the centre. Kidd could see the finger of the dial stand up dark against the sky like the dorsal fin of a shark and the vain moonlight clinging to that idle clock. But he saw something else clinging to it also, for one wild moment—the figure of a man.

Though he saw it there only for a moment, though it was outlandish and incredible in costume, being clad from neck to heel in tight crimson, with glints of gold, yet he knew in one flash of moonlight who it was. That white face flung up to heaven, clean-shaven and so unnaturally young, like Byron with a Roman nose, those black curls already grizzled—he had seen the thousand public

portraits of Sir Claude Champion. The wild red figure
reeled an instant against the sundial; the next it had rolled
down the steep bank and lay at the American's feet, faintly
moving one arm. A gaudy, unnatural gold ornament on
the arm suddenly reminded Kidd of *Romeo and Juliet*; of
course the tight crimson suit was part of the play. But there
was a long red stain down the bank from which the man
had rolled—that was no part of the play. He had been run
through the body.

Mr. Calhoun Kidd shouted and shouted again. Once
more he seemed to hear phantasmal footsteps, and started
to find another figure already near him. He knew the
figure, and yet it terrified him. The dissipated youth who
had called himself Dalroy had a horribly quiet way with
him; if Boulnois failed to keep appointments that had
been made, Dalroy had a sinister air of keeping appointments that hadn't. The moonlight discoloured everything,
against Dalroy's red hair his wan face looked not so much
white as pale green.

All this morbid impressionism must be Kidd's excuse for
having cried out, brutally and beyond all reason: "Did you
do this, you devil?"

James Dalroy smiled his unpleasing smile; but before he
could speak, the fallen figure made another movement of
the arm, waving vaguely towards the place where the sword
fell; then came a moan, and then it managed to speak.

"Boulnois ... Boulnois, I say ... Boulnois did it ...
jealous of me ... he was jealous, he was, he was ..."

Kidd bent his head down to hear more, and just managed
to catch the words:

"Boulnois ... with my own sword ... he threw it ..."

Again the failing hand waved towards the sword, and
then fell rigid with a thud. In Kidd rose from its depth all
that acrid humour that is the strange salt of the seriousness
of his race.

"See here," he said sharply and with command, "you must fetch a doctor. This man's dead."

"And a priest, too, I suppose," said Dalroy in an undecipherable manner. "All these Champions are papists."

The American knelt down by the body, felt the heart, propped up the head and used some last efforts at restoration; but before the other journalist reappeared, followed by a doctor and a priest, he was already prepared to assert they were too late.

"Were you too late also?" asked the doctor, a solid prosperous-looking man, with conventional moustache and whiskers, but a lively eye, which darted over Kidd dubiously.

"In one sense," drawled the representative of the *Sun*. "I was too late to save the man, but I guess I was in time to hear something of importance. I heard the dead man denounce his assassin."

"And who was the assassin?" asked the doctor, drawing his eyebrows together.

"Boulnois," said Calhoun Kidd, and whistled softly.

The doctor stared at him gloomily with a reddening brow—but he did not contradict. Then the priest, a shorter figure in the background, said mildly: "I understood that Mr. Boulnois was not coming to Pendragon Park this evening."

"There again," said the Yankee grimly, "I may be in a position to give the old country a fact or two. Yes, *sir*, John Boulnois was going to stay in all this evening; he fixed up a real good appointment there with me. But John Boulnois changed his mind; John Boulnois left his home abruptly and all alone, and came over to this darned Park an hour or so ago. His butler told me so. I think we hold what the all-wise police call a clue—have you sent for them?"

"Yes," said the doctor, "but we haven't alarmed anyone else yet."

"Does Mrs. Boulnois know?" asked James Dalroy, and again Kidd was conscious of an irrational desire to hit him on his curling mouth.

"I have not told her," said the doctor gruffly—"but here come the police."

The little priest had stepped out into the main avenue, and now returned with the fallen sword, which looked ludicrously large and theatrical when attached to his dumpy figure, at once clerical and commonplace. "Just before the police come," he said apologetically, "has anyone got a light?"

The Yankee journalist took an electric torch from his pocket, and the priest held it close to the middle part of the blade, which he examined with blinking care. Then, without glancing at the point or pommel, he handed the long weapon to the doctor.

"I fear I'm no use here," he said, with a brief sigh. "I'll say good night to you, gentlemen." And he walked away up the dark avenue towards the house, his hands clasped behind him and his big head bent in cogitation.

The rest of the group made increased haste towards the lodge-gates, where an inspector and two constables could already be seen in consultation with the lodge-keeper. But the little priest only walked slower and slower in the dim cloister of pine, and at last stopped dead, on the steps of the house. It was his silent way of acknowledging an equally silent approach; for there came towards him a presence that might have satisfied even Calhoun Kidd's demands for a lovely and aristocratic ghost. It was a young woman in silvery satins of a Renascence design; she had golden hair in two long shining ropes, and a face so startlingly pale between them that she might have been chryselephantine—made, that is, like some old Greek statues, out of ivory and gold. But her eyes were very bright, and her voice, though low, was confident.

"Father Brown?" she said.

"Mrs. Boulnois?" he replied gravely. Then he looked at her and immediately said: "I see you know about Sir Claude."

"How do you know I know?" she asked steadily.

He did not answer the question, but asked another: "Have you seen your husband?"

"My husband is at home," she said. "He has nothing to do with this."

Again he did not answer; and the woman drew nearer to him, with a curiously intense expression on her face.

"Shall I tell you something more?" she said, with a rather fearful smile. "I don't think he did it, and you don't either." Father Brown returned her gaze with a long, grave stare, and then nodded, yet more gravely.

"Father Brown," said the lady, "I am going to tell you all I know, but I want you to do me a favour first. Will you tell me *why* you haven't jumped to the conclusion of poor John's guilt, as all the rest have done? Don't mind what you say: I—I know about the gossip and the appearances that are against me."

Father Brown looked honestly embarrassed, and passed his hand across his forehead. "Two very little things," he said. "At least, one's very trivial and the other very vague. But such as they are, they don't fit in with Mr. Boulnois being the murderer."

He turned his blank, round face up to the stars and continued absentmindedly: "To take the vague idea first. I attach a good deal of importance to vague ideas. All those things that 'aren't evidence' are what convince me. I think a moral impossibility the biggest of all impossibilities. I know your husband only slightly, but I think this crime of his, as generally conceived, something very like a moral impossibility. Please do not think I mean that Boulnois could not be so wicked. Anybody can be wicked—as wicked as he chooses. We can direct our moral wills; but we can't generally change our instinctive tastes and ways of doing things. Boulnois might commit a murder, but not this murder. He would not snatch Romeo's sword from its romantic scabbard; or slay his foe on the sundial as on a kind of altar; or leave his body among the roses, or fling the sword away among the pines. If Boulnois killed anyone he'd do it quietly and heavily, as he'd do any other doubtful thing—take a tenth glass of port, or read a loose Greek poet. No, the romantic setting is not like Boulnois. It's more like Champion."

"Ah!" she said, and looked at him with eyes like diamonds.

"And the trivial thing was this," said Brown. "There were finger-prints on that sword; finger-prints can be detected quite a time after they are made if they're on some polished surface like glass or steel. These were on a polished surface. They were half-way down the blade of the sword. Whose prints they were I have no earthly clue; but why should anybody hold a sword half-way down? It was a long sword, but length is an advantage in lunging at an enemy. At least, at most enemies. At all enemies except one."

"Except one," she repeated.

"There is only one enemy," said Father Brown, "whom it is easier to kill with a dagger than a sword."

"I know," said the woman. "Oneself."

There was a long silence, and then the priest said quietly but abruptly: "Am I right, then? Did Sir Claude kill himself?"

"Yes" she said, with a face like marble. "I saw him do it."

"He died," said Father Brown, "for love of you?"

An extraordinary expression flashed across her face, very different from pity, modesty, remorse, or anything her companion had expected: her voice became suddenly strong and full. "I don't believe," she said, "he ever cared about me a rap. He hated my husband."

"Why?" asked the other, and turned his round face from the sky to the lady.

"He hated my husband because ... it is so strange I hardly know how to say it ... because ..."

"Yes?" said Brown patiently.

"Because my husband wouldn't hate him."

Father Brown only nodded, and seemed still to be listening; he differed from most detectives in fact and fiction in a small point—he never pretended not to understand when he understood perfectly well.

Mrs. Boulnois drew near once more with the same contained glow of certainty. "My husband," she said, "is a great man. Sir Claude Champion was not a great man: he was a celebrated and successful man. My husband has never been celebrated or successful; and it is the solemn truth that he has never dreamed of being so. He no more expects to be famous for thinking than for smoking cigars. On all that side he has a sort of splendid stupidity. He has never grown up. He still liked Champion exactly as he liked him at school; he admired him as he would admire a conjuring trick done at the dinner-table. But he couldn't be got to conceive the notion of *envying* Champion. *And Champion wanted to be envied.* He went mad and killed himself for that."

"Yes," said Father Brown; "I think I begin to understand."

"Oh, don't you see?" she cried; "the whole picture is made for that—the place is planned for it. Champion put John in a little house at his very door, like a dependant—to make him *feel* a failure. He never felt it. He thinks no more about such things than—than an absent-minded lion. Champion would burst in on John's shabbiest hours or

homeliest meals with some dazzling present or announce-
ment or expedition that made it like the visit of Haroun
Alraschid, and John would accept or refuse amiably with
one eye off, so to speak, like one lazy schoolboy agreeing
or disagreeing with another. After five years of it John
had not turned a hair; and Sir Claude Champion was
a monomaniac."

"And Haman began to tell them," said Father Brown,
"of all the things wherein the king had honoured him;
and he said: 'All these things profit me nothing while I see
Mordecai the Jew sitting in the gate.' "[3]

"The crisis came," Mrs. Boulnois continued, "when I
persuaded John to let me take down some of his specula-
tions and send them to a magazine. They began to attract
attention, especially in America, and one paper wanted to
interview him. When Champion (who was interviewed
nearly every day) heard of this late little crumb of success
falling to his unconscious rival, the last link snapped that
held back his devilish hatred. Then he began to lay that
insane siege to my own love and honour which has been
the talk of the shire. You will ask me why I allowed such
atrocious attentions. I answer that I could not have declined
them except by explaining to my husband, and there are
some things the soul cannot do, as the body cannot fly.
Nobody could have explained to my husband. Nobody
could do it now. If you said to him in so many words,
'Champion is stealing your wife,' he would think the
joke a little vulgar: that it could be anything but a joke—
that notion could find no crack in his great skull to get in
by. Well, John was to come and see us act this evening,
but just as we were starting he said he wouldn't; he had

---

[3] In the biblical Book of Esther, the King's favorite, Haman, becomes
obsessed when Mordecai refuses to bow to him.

got an interesting book and a cigar. I told this to Sir Claude, and it was his death-blow. The monomaniac suddenly saw despair. He stabbed himself, crying out like a devil that Boulnois was slaying him; he lies there in the garden dead of his own jealousy to produce jealousy, and John is sitting in the dining-room reading a book."

There was another silence, and then the little priest said: "There is only one weak point, Mrs. Boulnois, in all your very vivid account. Your husband is not sitting in the dining-room reading a book. That American reporter told me he had been to your house, and your butler told him Mr. Boulnois had gone to Pendragon Park after all."

Her bright eyes widened to an almost electric glare; and yet it seemed rather bewilderment than confusion or fear. "Why, what *can* you mean?" she cried. "All the servants were out of the house, seeing the theatricals. And we don't keep a butler, thank goodness!"

Father Brown started and spun half round like an absurd teetotum. "What, what?" he cried seeming galvanised into sudden life. "Look here—I say—can I make your husband hear if I go to the house?"

"Oh, the servants will be back by now," she said, wondering.

"Right, right!" rejoined the cleric energetically, and set off scuttling up the path towards the Park gates. He turned once to say: "Better get hold of that Yankee, or 'Crime of John Boulnois' will be all over the Republic in large letters."

"You don't understand," said Mrs. Boulnois. "He wouldn't mind. I don't think he imagines that America really is a place."

When Father Brown reached the house with the beehive and the drowsy dog, a small and neat maid-servant showed him into the dining-room, where Boulnois sat reading by a shaded lamp, exactly as his wife described him. A decanter of port and a wineglass were at his elbow; and the instant the priest entered he noted the long ash stand out unbroken on his cigar.

"He has been here for half an hour at least," thought Father Brown. In fact, he had the air of sitting where he had sat when his dinner was cleared away.

"Don't get up, Mr. Boulnois," said the priest in his pleasant, prosaic way. "I shan't interrupt you a moment. I fear I break in on some of your scientific studies."

"No," said Boulnois; "I was reading 'The Bloody Thumb.'" He said it with neither frown nor smile, and his visitor was conscious of a certain deep and virile indifference in the man which his wife had called greatness. He laid down a gory yellow "shocker" without even feeling its incongruity enough to comment on it humorously. John Boulnois was a big, slow-moving man with a massive head, partly grey and partly bald, and blunt, burly features. He was in shabby and very old-fashioned evening-dress, with a narrow triangular opening of shirt-front: he had assumed it that evening in his original purpose of going to see his wife act Juliet.

"I won't keep you long from 'The Bloody Thumb' or any other catastrophic affairs," said Father Brown, smiling. "I only came to ask you about the crime you committed this evening."

Boulnois looked at him steadily, but a red bar began to show across his broad brow; and he seemed like one discovering embarrassment for the first time.

"I know it was a strange crime," assented Brown in a low voice. "Stranger than murder perhaps—to you. The little sins are sometimes harder to confess than the big ones—but that's why it's so important to confess them. Your crime is committed by every fashionable hostess six times a week: and yet you find it sticks to your tongue like a nameless atrocity."

"It makes one feel," said the philosopher slowly, "such a damned fool."

"I know," assented the other, "but one often has to choose between feeling a damned fool and being one."

"I can't analyse myself well," went on Boulnois; "but sitting in that chair with that story I was as happy as a schoolboy on a half-holiday. It was security, eternity—I can't convey it ... the cigars were within reach ... the matches were within reach ... the *Thumb* had four more appearances to ... it was not only a peace, but a plenitude. Then that bell rang, and I thought for one long, mortal minute that I couldn't get out of that chair—literally, physically, muscularly couldn't. Then I did it like a man lifting the world, because I knew all the servants were out. I opened the front door, and there was a little man with his mouth open to speak and his notebook open to write in. I remembered the Yankee interviewer I had forgotten. His hair was parted in the middle, and I tell you that murder—"

"I understand," said Father Brown. "I've seen him."

"I didn't commit murder," continued the Catastrophist mildly, "but only perjury. I said I had gone across to Pendragon Park and shut the door in his face. That is my crime, Father Brown, and I don't know what penance you would inflict for it."

"I shan't inflict any penance," said the clerical gentleman, collecting his heavy hat and umbrella with an air of some amusement; "quite the contrary. I came here specially to let you off the little penance which would otherwise have followed your little offence."

"And what," asked Boulnois, smiling, "is the little penance I have so luckily been let off?"

"Being hanged," said Father Brown.

"You shall not covet ... anything that is your neighbor's."

The Green Man

A young man in knickerbockers, with an eager sanguine
profile, was playing golf against himself on the links that
lay parallel to the sand and sea, which were all growing
grey with twilight. He was not carelessly knocking a ball
about, but rather practising particular strokes with a sort of
microscopic fury; like a neat and tidy whirlwind. He had
learned many games quickly, but he had a disposition to
learn them a little more quickly than they can be learnt.
He was rather prone to be a victim of those remarkable
invitations by which a man may learn the Violin in Six
Lessons—or acquire a perfect French accent by a Correspondence Course. He lived in the breezy atmosphere
of such hopeful advertisement and adventure. He was at
present the private secretary of Admiral Sir Michael Craven,
who owned the big house behind the park abutting on the
links. He was ambitious, and had no intention of continuing indefinitely to be private secretary to anybody. But
he was also reasonable; and he knew that the best way
of ceasing to be a secretary was to be a good secretary.
Consequently he was a very good secretary; dealing with
the ever-accumulating arrears of the Admiral's correspondence with the same swift centripetal concentration with

"The Green Man" was first published in America in the November 1930
issue of *The Ladies' Home Journal.*

which he addressed the golf-ball. He had to struggle with the correspondence alone and at his own discretion at present; for the Admiral had been with his ship for the last six months, and, though now returning, was not expected for hours, or possibly days.

With an athletic stride, the young man, whose name was Harold Harker, crested the rise of turf that was the rampart of the links and, looking out across the sands to the sea, saw a strange sight. He did not see it very clearly; for the dusk was darkening every minute under stormy clouds; but it seemed to him, by a sort of momentary illusion, like a dream of days long past or a drama played by ghosts, out of another age in history.

The last of the sunset lay in long bars of copper and gold above the last dark strip of sea that seemed rather black than blue. But blacker still against this gleam in the west, there passed in sharp outline, like figures in a shadow pantomime, two men with three-cornered cocked hats and swords; as if they had just landed from one of the wooden ships of Nelson. It was not at all the sort of hallucination that would have come natural to Mr. Harker, had he been prone to hallucinations. He was of the type that is at once sanguine and scientific; and would be more likely to fancy the flying-ships of the future than the fighting ships of the past. He therefore very sensibly came to the conclusion that even a futurist can believe his eyes.

His illusion did not last more than a moment. On the second glance, what he saw was unusual but not incredible. The two men who were striding in single file across the sands, one some fifteen yards behind the other, were ordinary modern naval officers; but naval officers wearing that almost extravagant full-dress uniform which naval officers never do wear if they can possibly help it; only on great ceremonial occasions such as the visits of Royalty.

In the man walking in front, who seemed more or less unconscious of the man walking behind, Harker recognised at once the high-bridged nose and spike-shaped beard of his own employer the Admiral. The other man following in his tracks he did not know. But he did know something about the circumstances connected with the ceremonial occasion. He knew that when the Admiral's ship put in at the adjacent port, it was to be formally visited by a Great Personage; which was enough, in that sense, to explain the officers being in full dress. But he did also know the officers; or at any rate the Admiral. And what could have possessed the Admiral to come on shore in that rig-out, when one could swear he would seize five minutes to change into mufti or at least into undress uniform, was more than his secretary could conceive. It seemed somehow to be the very last thing he would do. It was indeed to remain for many weeks one of the chief mysteries of this mysterious business. As it was, the outline of these fantastic court uniforms against the empty scenery, striped with dark sea and sand, had something suggestive of comic opera; and reminded the spectator of *Pinafore*.[1]

The second figure was much more singular; somewhat singular in appearance, despite his correct lieutenant's uniform, and still more extraordinary in behaviour. He walked in a strangely irregular and uneasy manner; sometimes quickly and sometimes slowly; as if he could not make up his mind whether to overtake the Admiral or not. The Admiral was rather deaf and certainly heard no footsteps behind him on the yielding sand; but the footsteps behind him, if traced in the detective manner, would have given rise to twenty conjectures from a limp

---

[1] *H.M.S. Pinafore* or *The Lass That Loved a Sailor* (1878) was a comic opera in two acts, with music by Arthur Sullivan and a libretto by W. S. Gilbert.

to a dance. The man's face was swarthy as well as darkened with shadow, and every now and then the eyes in it shifted and shone, as if to accent his agitation. Once he began to run and then abruptly relapsed into a swaggering slowness and carelessness. Then he did something which Mr. Harker could never have conceived any normal naval officer in His Britannic Majesty's Service doing, even in a lunatic asylum. He drew his sword.

It was at this bursting-point of the prodigy that the two passing figures disappeared behind a headland on the shore. The staring secretary had just time to notice the swarthy stranger, with a resumption of carelessness, knock off a head of sea-holly with his glittering blade. He seemed then to have abandoned all idea of catching the other man up. But Mr. Harold Harker's face became very thoughtful indeed; and he stood there ruminating for some time before he gravely took himself inland, towards the road that ran past the gates of the great house and so by a long curve down to the sea.

It was up this curving road from the coast that the Admiral might be expected to come, considering the direction in which he had been walking, and making the natural assumption that he was bound for his own door. The path along the sands, under the links, turned inland just beyond the headland and solidifying itself into a road, returned towards Craven House. It was down this road, therefore, that the secretary darted, with characteristic impetuosity, to meet his patron returning home. But the patron was apparently not returning home. What was still more peculiar, the secretary was not returning home either; at least until many hours later; a delay quite long enough to arouse alarm and mystification at Craven House.

Behind the pillars and palms of that rather too palatial country house, indeed, there was expectancy gradually changing to uneasiness. Gryce the butler, a big bilious man abnormally silent below as well as above stairs, showed a certain restlessness as he moved about the main front-hall and occasionally looked out of the side windows of the porch, on the white road that swept towards the sea. The Admiral's sister Marion, who kept house for him, had her brother's high nose with a more sniffy expression; she was voluble, rather rambling, not without humour, and capable of sudden emphasis as shrill as a cockatoo. The Admiral's daughter Olive was dark, dreamy, and as a rule abstractedly silent, perhaps melancholy; so that her aunt generally conducted most of the conversation, and that without reluctance. But the girl also had a gift of sudden laughter that was very engaging.

"I can't think why they're not here already," said the elder lady. "The postman distinctly told me he'd seen the Admiral coming along the beach; along with that dreadful creature Rook. Why in the world they call him Lieutenant Rook—"

"Perhaps," suggested the melancholy young lady, with a momentary brightness, "perhaps they call him Lieutenant because he is a Lieutenant."

"I can't think why the Admiral keeps him," snorted her aunt, as if she were talking of a housemaid. She was very proud of her brother and always called him the Admiral; but her notions of a commission in the Senior Service were inexact.

"Well, Roger Rook is sulky and unsociable and all that," replied Olive, "but of course that wouldn't prevent him being a capable sailor."

"Sailor!" cried her aunt with one of her rather startling cockatoo notes, "he isn't my notion of a sailor. The Lass that Loved a Sailor, as they used to sing when I was young ... Just think of it! He's not gay and free and whats-its-name. He doesn't sing chanties or dance a hornpipe."

"Well," observed her niece with gravity. "The Admiral doesn't very often dance a hornpipe."

"Oh, you know what I mean—he isn't bright or breezy or anything," replied the old lady. "Why, that secretary fellow could do better than that."

Olive's rather tragic face was transfigured by one of her good and rejuvenating waves of laughter.

"I'm sure Mr. Harker would dance a hornpipe for you," she said, "and say he had learnt it in half an hour from the book of instructions. He's always learning things of that sort."

She stopped laughing suddenly and looked at her aunt's rather strained face.

"I can't think why Mr. Harker doesn't come," she added.

"I don't care about Mr. Harker," replied the aunt, and rose and looked out of the window.

The evening light had long turned from yellow to grey and was now turning almost to white under the widening moonlight, over the large flat landscape by the coast; unbroken by any features save a clump of sea-twisted trees round a pool and beyond, rather gaunt and dark against the horizon, the shabby fishermen's tavern on the shore that bore the name of the Green Man. And all that road and landscape was empty of any living thing. Nobody had seen the figure in the cocked hat that had been observed, earlier in the evening, walking by the sea; or the other and stranger figure that had been seen trailing after him. Nobody had even seen the secretary who saw them.

It was after midnight when the secretary at last burst in and aroused the household; and his face, white as a ghost, looked all the paler against the background of the stolid face and figure of a big Inspector of Police. Somehow that red, heavy, indifferent face looked, even more than the white and harassed one, like a mask of doom. The news was broken to the two women with such consideration or concealments as were possible. But the news was that the body of Admiral Craven had been eventually fished out of the foul weeds and scum of the pool under the trees; and that he was drowned and dead.

Anybody acquainted with Mr. Harold Harker, secretary, will realise that, whatever his agitation, he was by morning in a mood to be tremendously on the spot. He hustled the Inspector, whom he had met the night before on the road down by the Green Man, into another room for private and practical consultation. He questioned the Inspector rather as the Inspector might have questioned a yokel. But Inspector Burns was a stolid character; and was either too stupid or too clever to resent such trifles. It soon began to look as if he were by no means so stupid as he looked; for he disposed of Harker's eager questions in a manner that was slow but methodical and rational.

"Well," said Harker (his head full of many manuals with titles like "Be a Detective in Ten Days"). "Well, it's the old triangle, I suppose. Accident, Suicide, or Murder."

"I don't see how it could be accident," answered the policeman. "It wasn't even dark yet and the pool's fifty yards from the straight road that he knew like his own doorstep. He'd no more have got into that pond than he'd go and carefully lie down in a puddle in the street. As for suicide, it's rather a responsibility to suggest it, and rather improbable too. The Admiral was a pretty spry and successful man and frightfully rich, nearly a millionaire in fact; though of course that doesn't prove anything. He seemed to be pretty normal and comfortable in his private life too; he's the last man I should suspect of drowning himself."

"So that we come," said the secretary, lowering his voice with the thrill, "I suppose we come to the third possibility."

"We won't be in too much of a hurry about that," said the Inspector to the annoyance of Harker, who was in a hurry about everything. "But naturally there are one or two things one would like to know. One would like to know—about his property, for instance. Do you know who's likely to come in for it? You're his private secretary; do you know anything about his will?"

"I'm not so private a secretary as all that," answered the young man. "His solicitors are Messrs. Willis, Hardman and Dyke, over in Suttford High Street; and I believe the will is in their custody."

"Well, I'd better get round and see them pretty soon," said the Inspector.

"Let's get round and see them at once," said the impatient secretary.

He took a turn or two restlessly up and down the room and then exploded in a fresh place.

"What have you done about the body, Inspector?" he asked.

"Dr. Straker is examining it now at the Police Station. His report ought to be ready in an hour or so."

"It can't be ready too soon," said Harker. "It would save time if we could meet him at the lawyer's." Then he stopped and his impetuous tone changed abruptly to one of some embarrassment.

"Look here," he said, "I want ... we want to consider the young lady, the poor Admiral's daughter, as much as possible just now. She's got a notion that may be all nonsense; but I wouldn't like to disappoint her. There's some friend of hers she wants to consult, staying in the town at present. Man of the name of Brown; priest or parson of some sort—she's given me his address. I don't take much stock in priests or parsons, but—"

The Inspector nodded. "I don't take any stock in priests or parsons; but I take a lot of stock in Father Brown," he said. "I happened to have to do with him in a queer sort of society jewel case. He ought to have been a policeman instead of parson."

"Oh, all right," said the breathless secretary as he vanished from the room. "Let him come to the lawyer's too."

Thus it happened that, when they hurried across to the neighbouring town to meet Dr. Straker at the solicitor's office, they found Father Brown already seated there, with his hands folded on his heavy umbrella, chatting pleasantly to the only available member of the firm. Dr. Straker also had arrived, but apparently only at that moment, as he was carefully placing his gloves in his top-hat and his top-hat on a side-table. And the mild and beaming expression of the priest's moonlike face and spectacles, together with the silent chuckles of the jolly old grizzled lawyer, to whom he was talking, were enough to show that the doctor had not yet opened his mouth to bring the news of death.

"A beautiful morning after all," Father Brown was saying. "That storm seems to have passed over us. There were some big black clouds, but I notice that not a drop of rain fell."

"Not a drop," agreed the solicitor toying with a pen; he was the third partner, Mr. Dyke; "there's not a cloud in the sky now. It's the sort of day for a holiday." Then he realised the newcomers and looked up, laying down the pen and rising. "Ah, Mr. Harker, how are you? I hear the Admiral is expected home soon." Then Harker spoke, and his voice rang hollow in the room.

"I am sorry to say we are the bearers of bad news. Admiral Craven was drowned before reaching home."

There was a change in the very air of the still office, though not in the attitudes of the motionless figures; both were staring at the speaker as if a joke had been frozen on their lips. Both repeated the word "drowned" and looked at each other, and then again at their informant. Then there was a small hubbub of questions.

"When did this happen?" asked the priest.

"Where was he found?" asked the lawyer.

"He was found," said the Inspector, "in that pool by the coast, not far from the Green Man, and dragged out all covered with green scum and weeds so as to be almost unrecognisable. But Dr. Straker here has—What is the matter, Father Brown? Are you ill?"

"The Green Man," said Father Brown with a shudder. "I'm so sorry ... I beg your pardon for being upset."

"Upset by what?" asked the staring officer.

"By his being covered with green scum, I suppose," said the priest, with a rather shaky laugh. Then he added rather more firmly, "I thought it might have been seaweed."

By this time everybody was looking at the priest, with a not unnatural suspicion that he was mad; and yet the next crucial surprise was not to come from him. After a dead silence, it was the doctor who spoke.

Dr. Straker was a remarkable man, even to look at. He was very tall and angular, formal and professional in his dress; yet retaining a fashion that has hardly been known since Mid-Victorian times. Though comparatively young, he wore his brown beard very long and spreading over his waistcoat; in contrast with it, his features, which were both harsh and handsome, looked singularly pale. His good looks were also diminished by something in his deep eyes that was not squinting, but like the shadow of a squint. Everybody noticed these things about him, because the moment he spoke, he gave forth an indescribable air of authority. But all he said was:

"There is one more thing to be said, if you come to details, about Admiral Craven being drowned." Then he added reflectively, "Admiral Craven was not drowned."

The Inspector turned with quite a new promptitude and shot a question at him.

"I have just examined the body," said Dr. Straker, "the cause of death was a stab through the heart with some pointed blade like a stiletto. It was after death, and even some little time after, that the body was hidden in the pool."

Father Brown was regarding Dr. Straker with a very lively eye, such as he seldom turned upon anybody; and when the group in the office began to break up, he managed to attach himself to the medical man for a little further conversation, as they went back down the street. There had not been very much else to detain them except the rather formal question of the will. The impatience of the young secretary had been somewhat tried by the professional etiquette of the old lawyer. But the latter was ultimately induced, rather by the tact of the priest than the authority of the policeman, to refrain from making a mystery where there was no mystery at all. Mr. Dyke admitted, with a smile, that the Admiral's will was a very normal and ordinary document, leaving everything to his only child Olive; and that there really was no particular reason for concealing the fact.

The doctor and the priest walked slowly down the street that struck out of the town in the direction of Craven House. Harker had plunged on ahead of him with all his native eagerness to get somewhere; but the two behind seemed more interested in their discussion than their direction. It was in rather an enigmatic tone that the tall doctor said to the short cleric beside him:

"Well, Father Brown, what do you think of a thing like this?"

Father Brown looked at him rather intently for an instant, and then said:

"Well, I've begun to think of one or two things; but my chief difficulty is that I only knew the Admiral slightly; though I've seen something of his daughter."

"The Admiral," said the doctor with a grim immobility of feature, "was the sort of man of whom it is said that he had not an enemy in the world."

"I suppose you mean," answered the priest, "that there's something else that will not be said."

"Oh, it's no affair of mine," said Straker hastily but rather harshly. "He had his moods, I suppose. He once threatened me with a legal action about an operation; but I think he thought better of it. I can imagine his being rather rough with a subordinate."

Father Brown's eyes were fixed on the figure of the secretary striding far ahead; and as he gazed he realised the special cause of his hurry. Some fifty yards farther ahead the Admiral's daughter was dawdling along the road towards the Admiral's house. The secretary soon came abreast of her; and for the remainder of the time Father Brown watched the silent drama of two human backs as they diminished into the distance. The secretary was evidently very much excited about something; but if the priest guessed what it was, he kept it to himself. When he came to the corner leading to the doctor's house, he only said briefly: "I don't know if you have anything more to tell us."

"Why should I?" answered the doctor very abruptly; and striding off, left it uncertain whether he was asking why he should have anything to tell, or why he should tell it.

Father Brown went stumping on alone, in the track of the two young people; but when he came to the entrance and avenues of the Admiral's park, he was arrested by the action of the girl, who turned suddenly and came straight

towards him; her face unusually pale and her eyes bright
with some new and as yet nameless emotion.

"Father Brown," she said in a low voice, "I must talk to
you as soon as possible. You must listen to me, I can't see
any other way out."

"Why certainly," he replied, as coolly as if a gutter-boy
had asked him the time. "Where shall we go and talk?"

The girl led him at random to one of the rather tumble-
down arbours in the grounds; and they sat down behind a
screen of large ragged leaves. She began instantly, as if she
must relieve her feelings or faint.

"Harold Harker," she said, "has been talking to me
about things. Terrible things."

The priest nodded and the girl went on hastily. "About
Roger Rook. Do you know about Roger?"

"I've been told," he answered, "that his fellow-seamen
call him The Jolly Roger, because he is never jolly; and
looks like the pirate's skull and crossbones."

"He was not always like that," said Olive in a low voice.
"Something very queer must have happened to him. I
knew him well when we were children; we used to play
over there on the sands. He was harum-scarum and always
talking about being a pirate; I dare say he was the sort
they say might take to crime through reading shockers;
but there was something poetical in his way of being
piratical. He really was a Jolly Roger then. I suppose he
was the last boy who kept up the old legend of really
running away to sea; and at last his family had to agree to
his joining the Navy. Well ..."

"Yes," said Father Brown patiently.

"Well," she admitted, caught in one of her rare moments
of mirth, "I suppose poor Roger found it disappointing.
Naval officers so seldom carry knives in their teeth or wave
bloody cutlasses and black flags. But that doesn't explain

the change in him. He just stiffened; grew dull and dumb, like a dead man walking about. He always avoids me; but that doesn't matter. I supposed some great grief that's no business of mine had broken him up. And now—well, if what Harold says is true, the grief is neither more nor less than going mad; or being possessed of a devil."

"And what does Harold say?" asked the priest.

"It's so awful I can hardly say it," she answered. "He swears he saw Roger creeping behind my father that night; hesitating and then drawing his sword ... and the doctor says father was stabbed with a steel point ... I *can't* believe Roger Rook had anything to do with it. His sulks and my father's temper sometimes led to quarrels; but what are quarrels? I can't exactly say I'm standing up for an old friend; because he isn't even friendly. But you can't help feeling sure of some things, even about an old acquaintance. And yet Harold swears that he—"

"Harold seems to swear a great deal," said Father Brown.

There was a sudden silence; after which she said in a different tone: "Well, he does swear other things too. Harold Harker proposed to me just now."

"Am I to congratulate you, or rather him?" inquired her companion.

"I told him he must wait. He isn't good at waiting." She was caught again in a ripple of her incongruous sense of the comic: "He said I was his ideal and his ambition and so on. He has lived in the States; but somehow I never remember it when he is talking about dollars; only when he is talking about ideals."

"And I suppose," said Father Brown very softly, "that it is because you have to decide about Harold that you want to know the truth about Roger."

She stiffened and frowned, and then equally abruptly smiled, saying: "Oh, you know too much."

"I know very little, especially in this affair," said the priest gravely. "I only know who murdered your father." She started up and stood staring down at him stricken white. Father Brown made a wry face as he went on: "I made a fool of myself when I first realised it; when they'd just been asking where he was found, and went on talking about green scum and the Green Man."

Then he also rose; clutching his clumsy umbrella with a new resolution, he addressed the girl with a new gravity.

"There is something else that I know, which is the key to all these riddles of yours; but I won't tell you yet. I suppose it's bad news; but it's nothing like so bad as the things you have been fancying." He buttoned up his coat and turned towards the gate. "I'm going to see this Mr. Rook of yours. In a shed by the shore, near where Mr. Harker saw him walking. I rather think he lives there." And he went bustling off in the direction of the beach.

Olive was an imaginative person; perhaps too imaginative to be safely left to brood over such hints as her friend had thrown out; but he was in rather a hurry to find the best relief for her broodings. The mysterious connection between Father Brown's first shock of enlightenment and the chance language about the pool and the inn, hag-rode her fancy in a hundred forms of ugly symbolism. The Green Man became a ghost trailing loathsome weeds and walking the countryside under the moon; the sign of the Green Man became a human figure hanging as from a gibbet; and the tarn itself became a tavern, a dark subaqueous tavern for the dead sailors. And yet he had taken the most rapid method to overthrow all such nightmares, with a burst of blinding daylight which seemed more mysterious than the night.

For before the sun had set, something had come back into her life that turned her whole world topsy-turvy once more; something she had hardly known that she desired until it was abruptly granted; something that was, like a dream, old and familiar, and yet remained incomprehensible and incredible. For Roger Rook had come striding across the sands, and even when he was a dot in the distance, she knew he was transfigured; and as he came nearer and nearer, she saw that his dark face was alive with laughter and exultation. He came straight towards her, as if they had never parted, and seized her shoulders saying: "Now I can look after you, thank God."

She hardly knew what she answered; but she heard herself questioning rather wildly why he seemed so changed and so happy.

"Because I am happy," he answered. "I have heard the bad news."

All parties concerned, including some who seemed rather unconcerned, found themselves assembled on the garden-path leading to Craven House, to hear the formality, now truly formal, of the lawyer's reading of the will; and the probable, and more practical sequel of the lawyer's advice upon the crisis. Besides the grey-haired solicitor himself, armed with the testamentary document, there was the Inspector armed with more direct authority touching the crime, and Lieutenant Rook in undisguised attendance on the lady; some were rather mystified on seeing the tall figure of the doctor, some smiled a little on seeing the dumpy figure of the priest. Mr. Harker, that Flying Mercury, had shot down to the lodge-gates to meet them, led them back on to the lawn, and then dashed ahead of them again to prepare their reception. He said he would be back in a jiffy; and anyone observing his piston-rod of energy could well believe it; but, for the moment, they were left rather stranded on the lawn outside the house.

"Reminds me of somebody making runs at cricket," said the Lieutenant.

"That young man," said the lawyer, "is rather annoyed that the law cannot move quite so quickly as he does. Fortunately Miss Craven understands our professional difficulties and delays. She has kindly assured me that she still has confidence in my slowness."

"I wish," said the doctor, suddenly, "that I had as much confidence in his quickness."

"Why, what do you mean?" asked Rook, knitting his brows; "do you mean that Harker is too quick?"

"Too quick and too slow," said Dr. Straker, in his rather cryptic fashion. "I know one occasion at least when he was not so very quick. Why was he hanging about half the night by the pond and the Green Man, before the Inspector came down and found the body? Why did he meet the Inspector? Why should he expect to meet the Inspector outside the Green Man?"

"I don't understand you," said Rook. "Do you mean that Harker wasn't telling the truth?"

Dr. Straker was silent. The grizzled lawyer laughed with grim good humour. "I have nothing more serious to say against the young man," he said, "than that he made a prompt and praiseworthy attempt to teach me my own business."

"For that matter, he made an attempt to teach me mine," said the Inspector, who had just joined the group in front. "But that doesn't matter. If Dr. Straker means anything by his hints, they do matter. I must ask you to speak plainly, doctor. It may be my duty to question him at once."

"Well, here he comes," said Rook, as the alert figure of the secretary appeared once more in the doorway.

At this point Father Brown, who had remained silent and inconspicuous at the tail of the procession, astonished everybody very much; perhaps especially those who knew him. He not only walked rapidly to the front, but turned facing the whole group with an arresting and almost threatening expression, like a sergeant bringing soldiers to the halt.

"Stop!" he said almost sternly. "I apologise to everybody; but it's absolutely necessary that I should see Mr. Harker first. I've got to tell him something I know; and I don't think anybody else knows; something he's got to hear. It may save a very tragic misunderstanding with somebody later on."

"What on earth do you mean?" asked old Dyke the lawyer.

"I mean the bad news," said Father Brown.

"Here, I say," began the Inspector indignantly; and then suddenly caught the priest's eye and remembered strange things he had seen in other days. "Well, if it were anyone in the world but you I should say of all the infernal cheek—"

But Father Brown was already out of hearing, and a moment afterwards was plunged in talk with Harker in the porch. They walked to and fro together for a few paces and then disappeared into the dark interior. It was about twelve minutes afterwards that Father Brown came out alone.

To their surprise he showed no disposition to re-enter the house, now that the whole company were at last about to enter it. He threw himself down on the rather rickety seat in the leafy arbour, and as the procession disappeared through the doorway, lit a pipe and proceeded to stare vacantly at the long ragged leaves about his head and to listen to the birds. There was no man who had a more hearty and enduring appetite for doing nothing.

He was, apparently, in a cloud of smoke and a dream of abstraction, when the front doors were once more flung open and two or three figures came out helter-skelter, running towards him, the daughter of the house and her young admirer Mr. Rook being easily winners in the race. Their faces were alight with astonishment; and the face of Inspector Burns, who advanced more heavily behind them, like an elephant shaking the garden, was inflamed with some indignation as well.

"What *can* all this mean?" cried Olive, as she came panting to a halt. "He's gone!"

"Bolted!" said the Lieutenant explosively. "Harker's just managed to pack a suitcase and bolted! Gone clean out of the back door and over the garden-wall to God knows where. What *did* you say to him?"

"Don't be silly!" said Olive, with a more worried expression. "Of course you told him you'd found him out, and now he's gone. I never could have believed he was wicked like that!"

"Well!" gasped the Inspector, bursting into their midst. "What have you done now? What have you let me down like this for?"

"Well," repeated Father Brown, "what have I done?"

"You have let a murderer escape," cried Burns, with a decision that was like a thunderclap in the quiet garden; "you have helped a murderer to escape. Like a fool I let you warn him; and now he is miles away."

"I have helped a few murderers in my time, it is true," said Father Brown; then he added, in careful distinction, "not, you will understand, helped them to commit the murder."

"But you knew all the time," insisted Olive. "You guessed from the first that it must be he. That's what you meant about being upset by the business of finding the body. That's what the doctor meant by saying my father might be disliked by a subordinate."

"That's what I complain of," said the official indignantly. "You knew even then that he was the—"

"You knew even then," insisted Olive, "that the murderer was—"

Father Brown nodded gravely. "Yes," he said. "I knew even then that the murderer was old Dyke."

"Was *who*?" repeated the Inspector and stopped amid a dead silence; punctuated only by the occasional pipe of birds.

"I mean Mr. Dyke, the solicitor," explained Father Brown, like one explaining something elementary to an infant class. "That gentleman with grey hair who's supposed to be going to read the will."

They all stood like statues staring at him, as he carefully filled his pipe again and struck a match. At last Burns rallied his vocal powers to break the strangling silence with an effort resembling violence.

"But, in the name of heaven, why?"

"Ah, why?" said the priest and rose thoughtfully, puffing at his pipe. "As to why he did it.... Well, I suppose the time has come to tell you, or those of you who don't know, the fact that is the key of all this business. It's a great calamity; and it's a great crime; but it's not the murder of Admiral Craven."

He looked Olive full in the face and said very seriously: "I tell you the bad news bluntly and in few words; because I think you are brave enough, and perhaps happy enough, to take it well. You have the chance, and I think the power, to be something like a great woman. You are not a great heiress."

Amid the silence that followed it was he who resumed his explanation.

"Most of your father's money, I am sorry to say, has gone. It went by the financial dexterity of the grey-haired gentleman named Dyke, who is (I grieve to say) a swindler. Admiral Craven was murdered to silence him about the way in which he was swindled. The fact that he was ruined and you were disinherited is the single simple clue, not only to the murder, but to all the other mysteries in this business." He took a puff or two and then continued.

"I told Mr. Rook you were disinherited and he rushed back to help you. Mr. Rook is a rather remarkable person."

"Oh, chuck it," said Mr. Rook with a hostile air.

"Mr. Rook is a monster," said Father Brown with scientific calm. "He is an anachronism, an atavism, a brute survival of the Stone Age. If there was one barbarous superstition we all supposed to be utterly extinct and dead in these days, it was that notion about honour and independence. But then I get mixed up with so many dead superstitions. Mr. Rook is an extinct animal. He is a plesiosaurus. He did not want to live on his wife or have a wife who could call him a fortune-hunter. Therefore he sulked in a grotesque manner and only came to life again when I brought him the good news that you were ruined. He wanted to work for his wife and not be kept by her. Disgusting, isn't it? Let us turn to the brighter topic of Mr. Harker.

"I told Mr. Harker you were disinherited and he rushed away in a sort of panic. Do not be too hard on Mr. Harker. He really had better as well as worse enthusiasms; but he had them all mixed up. There is no harm in having ambitions; but he had ambitions and called them ideals. The old sense of honour taught men to suspect success; to say, 'This is a benefit; it may be a bribe.' The new nine-times-accursed nonsense about Making Good teaches men to identify being good with making money. That was all that was the matter with him; in every other way he was a thoroughly good fellow, and there are thousands like him. Gazing at the stars and rising in the world were all Uplift. Marrying a good wife and marrying a rich wife were all Making Good. But he was not a cynical scoundrel; or he would simply have come back and jilted or cut you as the case might be. He could not face you; while you were there, half of his broken ideal was left.

"I did not tell the Admiral; but somebody did. Word came to him somehow, during the last grand parade on board, that his friend the family lawyer had betrayed him. He was in such a towering passion that he did what he could never have done in his sense; came straight on shore in his cocked hat and gold lace to catch the criminal; he wired to the police station, and that was why the Inspector was wandering round the Green Man. Lieutenant Rook followed him on shore because he suspected some family trouble and had half a hope he might help and put himself right. Hence his hesitating behaviour. As for his drawing his sword when he dropped behind and thought he was alone, well that's a matter of imagination. He was a romantic person who had dreamed of swords and run away to sea; and found himself in a service where he wasn't even allowed to wear a sword except about once in three years. He thought he was quite alone on the sands where he played as a boy. If you don't understand what he did, I can only say, like Stevenson, 'you will never be a pirate.' Also you will never be a poet; and you have never been a boy."

"I never have," answered Olive gravely, "and yet I think I understand."

"Almost every man," continued the priest musing, "will play with anything shaped like a sword or dagger, even if it is a paper knife. That is why I thought it so odd when the lawyer didn't."

"What do you mean?" asked Burns, "didn't what?"

"Why, didn't you notice," answered Brown, "at that first meeting in the office, the lawyer played with a pen and not with a paper-knife; though he had a beautiful bright steel paper-knife in the pattern of a stiletto? The pens were dusty and splashed with ink; but the knife had just been cleaned. But he did not play with it. There are limits to the irony of assassins."

After a silence the Inspector said, like one waking from a dream: "Look here ... I don't know whether I'm on my head or my heels; I don't know whether you think you've got to the end; but I haven't got to the beginning. Where do you get all this lawyer stuff from? What started you out on that trail?"

Father Brown laughed curtly and without mirth.

"The murderer made a slip at the start," he said, "and I can't think why nobody else noticed it. When you brought the first news of the death to the solicitor's office, nobody was supposed to know anything there, except that the Admiral was expected home. When you said he was drowned, I asked when it happened and Mr. Dyke asked where the corpse was found."

He paused a moment to knock out his pipe and resumed reflectively: "Now when you are simply told of a seaman, returning from the sea, that he had drowned, it is natural to assume that he had been drowned at sea. At any rate, to allow that he may have been drowned at sea. If he had been washed overboard, or gone down with his ship, or had his body 'committed to the deep', there would be no reason to expect his body to be found at all. The moment that man asked where it was found, I was sure he knew where it was found. Because he had put it there. Nobody but the murderer need have thought of anything so unlikely as a seaman being drowned in a land-locked pool a few hundred yards from the sea. That is why

I suddenly felt sick and turned green, I dare say; as green as the Green Man. I never can get used to finding myself suddenly sitting beside a murderer. So I had to turn it off by talking in parables; but the parable meant something, after all. I said that the body was covered with green scum, but it might just as well have been seaweed."

It is fortunate that tragedy can never kill comedy and that the two can run side by side; and that while the only acting partner of the business of Messrs. Willis, Hardman and Dyke blew his brains out when the Inspector entered the house to arrest him, Olive and Roger were calling to each other across the sands at evening, as they did when they were children together.

A NOTE ON FOOTNOTES

The footnotes in this volume need a word of explanation. The Father Brown stories are liberally sprinkled with literary and historical allusions that may be unfamiliar to today's readers.

Chesterton's allusions are not merely decorative, but add much to the atmosphere and meaning of the stories. From time to time, the allusions even provide a clue to the mystery at hand. Our references and citations, therefore, have been provided to help the reader enjoy the stories more. The information in the notes is limited to that purpose.

Readers who do not need or want the information will find these footnotes unobtrusive and easy to ignore.